"Wilderness of the Heart"
The story of Jacob Fahlstrom / Oza Windib

By Jason Bergeron

Foreword

This is a work of fiction, based on the incredible story of real-life trapper and frontiersman Jacob Fahlstrom. I spent two years researching historical records, documents, and written memoires for what is factual. For the gaps in the historical record, and there are many, I have used imagination to create a picture of what might have been. What they experienced, the conversations they had, and the emotions they might have felt.

Jacob Fahlstrom is widely known as the first Swedish settler in the state of Minnesota. How he got there is an incredible story of struggle and perseverance. He was orphaned at the age of nine in Stockholm, Sweden. A shipwreck off the coast of England left him homeless on the streets of London. Eventually travelling to America with the Hudson's Bay Company, he was lost in the vast wilderness in what is today Manitoba, Canada. Luckily, he was rescued by an Ojibwe hunting party. A woman in the tribe raised Jacob as her own. He lived a life of adventure and heartache, trying to find home, family and love in a place splintered by fur trade disputes, ancient tribal hostilities, and skin color.

In writing this novel, I have tried to be as true as possible to historical events, locations, and dates. Some characters have been created for the purpose of storytelling. I hope that I have succeeded with accurate tribe names and cultural references. I have made a determined effort to get it right. If I have failed anywhere in my story, I apologize.

I hope you enjoy this action packed, complex and heartbreaking story. It's a vivid portrait of pain, loss, and the conflicted struggle of the wild human animal within us all.

-Jason Bergeron

Dedication

This book is dedicated to a man who embodied the character and strength that Jacob Fahlstrom possessed. In fact, he was the source for much of the personality I ascribed to Jacob. He was a dedicated member of the White Earth Nation in Minnesota and took great pride in his Anishinaabe, Ojibwe culture. My favorite expression of that pride was a t-shirt he wore frequently. It said, "Fighting illegal immigration since 1492." His sense of humor and love of all things wild would certainly have made Jacob very proud of his great, great, Grandson, Gerald Folstrom. The father of my beautiful and amazing wife.

Chapter 1.
Endless Wild

10 miles east of Lake Winnipeg, Manitoba
June 14, 1812. Neither the city of Winnipeg nor the province of
Manitoba exists at the time.

He was just a boy. A twelve-year-old boy with spindly arms and a tuft of blond hair sticking out from under his wolf-skin cap. An untamed wilderness surrounded him. Trees, each identical to the next, in never ending repetition. A sea of spruce, like waves on the ocean, rolling off into the distance. An unimaginable acreage of uninhabited land stretching on for what seemed like uncountable miles. The damp musky smell of wet moss wafted, and a churning river echoed in the distance. Columns of light blast through a complex weave of branches. This was a valley of giants. Swaying and creaking in the wind, these colossal creatures of lumber reached skyward and sucked up everything the sun had to offer, leaving grass to suffocate in darkness below. It's the way of the wild. Death comes often and often it's unintentional, just a matter of circumstance. No malice. Just the way things are.

Branches cracked as a bull moose pushed its way out of thick underbrush. Without a care in the world, the massive beast walked further out into the clearing to enjoy the sun's warmth. Twelve hundred pounds of fury with a rack six feet across. Enough meat to feed twenty men for days.

Slowly the boy slid the strap of his Barnett musket off his shoulder. His hands shook nervously as he struggled to pour a full charge of 150 grains of gunpowder into the muzzle. Then, for good measure, he added a few grains more. He pulled a greased patch from his caribou hide bag and wrapped it around a 50-caliber ball. He jammed the ball down hard with the ramrod, setting it in the breach. For luck, he pulled a caramel-colored agate stone from his pocket and rubbed it against the bronze plate on the side of his gun. Embossed into the bronze was an ornate dragon with long fangs and a slithering tongue. The markings of the Hudson's Bay Company. The largest fur trade operation in the world. On the top of the boy's right hand was a ghastly scar between his thumb and forefinger. The scar was bright pink against his pale white skin. A badge of struggle manifest in physical form. It extended from the base of his thumb to his wrist. Forever emblazoned on his flesh. Was it a badge of courage or incompetence?

Sweltering humidity and nerves caused a bead of sweat to form on his brow. His heart raced. *This is the one,* the boy thought to himself. *If I take down this monster, maybe they'll quit thinking I'm just a dumb kid.* To steady himself, he leaned his shoulder against a tree. Slowly he poured a bit of powder into the pan, wiped a drip of sweat out of his left eye, then pulled the hammer to full cock. He took aim, breathed in deeply, and pulled the trigger. The flintlock hammer struck the frizzen and, with a spark, the gunpowder ignited. Less than an eyes-blink later a hot ball of lead exploded from the barrel. Trailed by a puff of smoke, the ball hurtled at 1000 feet per second toward the moose. Just slightly slower than the speed of sound. Meaning you might hear the shot, but you'd never be able to do anything about it. Birds flew from branches as the sound echoed through the forest. The moose stumbled.

"Got him," the boy whispered to himself while looking through a cloud of smoke with the taste of gunpowder on his lips. The moose staggered once again then quickly bolted into the forest.

Far away, amid tall grass and cattails, an Ojibwe hunter heard the shot and looked up from the duck he was gutting with a large trade knife. The hunter wore a hat made of elk hide with two eagle feathers sticking out the top. He picked up his rifle and gestured for the other 6 Indians to follow. They headed on foot in the direction of the gunshot.

Back at the clearing the boy rubbed the side of his face, now stinging with pain. "Damn it," he yelled with no one but a couple of jackrabbits to hear. He had held the gun too loose. It kicked back and clocked him in the jaw when he fired the shot. His ear was ringing and there was a deep cut dripping blood down the side of his neck. He rubbed his ear hoping the ringing would stop. No such luck.

The boy scanned the wilderness hoping to catch a glimpse of the fleeing moose. As he looked down into the valley he saw an endless expanse of pine trees, spruce swamps, and rivers that stretched on forever. Perhaps even a bit further. He looked back, wondering how far away the rest of the Hudson's Bay Company hunting crew might be. For a moment he pondered what to do, then pushed his way through the heavy brush in pursuit of the moose.

To a hawk flying overhead the boy was just a tiny dot amongst this vast natural enormity. Fallen branches crunched underfoot as he struggled to climb a rocky hill covered with bright green moss. The boy grabbed a low-hanging spruce branch and pulled himself to the top of a plateau. On the plateau, the trees seemed to grow directly out of the rocky ground. No dirt. Just rock, moss, and trees. The sheer magnitude of the forest took his breath and, honestly, scared the shit out of him. This was no place for a young boy to be alone. This forest had grandeur and beauty, but make no mistake, death lurked quietly in nature's shadow.

With his ear ringing and all sounds a bit muffled, the boy walked along a riverbank. He located a fresh set of moose tracks and followed them for more than a mile. Crouching down to a pile of olive-sized droppings, he gave them a soft touch. Still warm. All is not lost. *Getting closer now,* the boy thought. *How far can an injured moose run, anyway? ...I feel dizzy. I think I'm going to barf.* The boy continued following the moose tracks up through the trees, then a flash of movement blurred past in his peripheral vision. It was the moose. The boy followed the tracks and blood trail for a long time. Then a raindrop splashed on his arm. He continued searching for another several minutes until the rain became so heavy the trail of blood was entirely washed away. Suddenly, *ka-boom!* A clap of thunder reverberated through the forest, like Thor's hammer smashing the clouds. As the rain increased in intensity the boy scrambled for cover. *Oh man, not thunder. Anything but thunder.* For the boy, thunder was forever linked to a shipwreck off the coast of London. If it weren't for a lucky piece of wood floating his way, he most certainly would have drowned. Into the distant trees the sun sank, shrouding the forest in darkness. The boy was growing up, but he had not outgrown a strong fear of the dark. Does anyone really? As he jogged at a medium pace, looking for shelter, he experienced a feeling that something was sneaking up behind him. *Does everyone feel like that,* wondered the boy? *Or is it just me? Does it mean I'm a coward?*

Now wet, cold and in near complete darkness, the boy sat shivering at the base of a large rock overhang. An ominous feeling began to sink in. The boy was becoming aware of his situation. He had no idea where he was. No idea where the rest of the Hudson's Bay Company hunters were. No idea what to do next. Nothing was recognizable, yet everything seemed the same. Every stream and pond looked just like all the others. This place, which in the light of day was awe-inspiring, now inspired only one thing. Fear.

Echoing through the woods there were sounds of howling wolves, shrieking owls, and horrible unexplained noises. The boy tried to compose himself and act brave. After all, he had come to America to become a fur trader and frontiersman. How would it look to the men of the Hudson's Bay Company if he sat here fretting like a big baby? *They'd laugh and say, "See, we told you that you didn't belong. Stupid kid."*

Then, when it seemed impossible, the rain poured down even heavier. The boy clutched his H.B.C. trade gun with soaking wet hands and white knuckles. His head occasionally darted from side to side, scanning what little he could see of the forest. This went on for about twenty minutes then complete exhaustion weighed too heavy on his eyelids and he submerged into sleep.

Chapter 2.
Lost and Alone

A ray of sunlight pushed its way into the boy's eye, causing it to blink and flutter. He forced himself to a seated position and listened to the sound of the morning forest. Birds chirping, wind whistling through the trees, and a faint rush of a stream flowing. *Stream flowing?* The boy thought to himself as he popped to his feet and ran toward the sound. There, through some birch trees and on the other side of a large hill, was the stream. He stumbled along as fast as his weakened body would take him down to the rocky shore. He crouched beside the water. It was cold and clear. Thankful for his good fortune, the boy scooped water up in his hands and began dumping it into his mouth. It felt good to wash the cool water over his hair and face. He closed his eyes as he scooped another couple handfuls, again pouring the cool water over his face.

When he opened his eyes, there it was. Across the stream stood the injured moose, blood dripping noticeably from its shoulder down its front leg and into the water. A ripple effect followed the red splash. The stream was narrow. In fact, so narrow, the moose was less than twenty feet away. Close enough that the boy could smell the beast's wet, musty fur. It looked up calmly and snorted. The boy froze, hoping the moose would wander off. But it just stood there, eyes locked on him. The boy was surprised at how long the moose's eyelashes were and a bit terrified that he was close enough to observe that detail. As the moose raised its head higher, the enormity of the beast became more apparent and more real. The boy slowly rose from his crouched position then began stepping backward, not daring to turn his back. He walked this way for about 5 steps. Then suddenly he could see the moose's front shoulder muscles tense and it darted after him. He turned and ran as fast as he could, but it was useless. The moose was too fast and gained rapidly. The boy could feel the ground shake with every forceful stride of the moose. The sound of air rapidly blasting from the creature's nostrils was terrifying. Then it happened. Just as the boy turned to look back, the moose pivoted its head and drove its antler into his ribcage. A sickening sound of ripping flesh and cracking bone echoed in the boy's ears as he flew through the air. He landed near the base of a large tree. Rising to his feet on wobbly legs the boy held up his hand as the moose approached slowly. The sound of the creature's hooves sinking into the mud could be heard with every slurping step. The beast's antlers made contact with the boy's chest, pushing him against the tree. The moose snorted loudly then pushed harder. The boy was entirely helpless, pinned between the moose's antlers and the tree. The moose continued pushing with so much force the boy's feet came up off the ground. This went on until all the air was expelled from his lungs and his body went limp. As the moose pulled back the boy fell to the ground. No sign of life remained. The boy's face was as pale as his whitish blond hair. The moose sniffed him, tilted its head as if assessing a threat, turned, and walked off into the woods.

The boy remained there in a crumpled pile for several hours then he awoke to the sound of birds cawing. He struggled to hold his head up while he watched two crows rip the guts out of a dead gopher. He chuckled to himself, not able to avoid seeing the parallel. Nature can have a really messed up sense of humor sometimes. The boy's side pulsed with pain, and it was wet to the touch. Blood had soaked through his shirt. He pulled his shirt up then delicately touched his ribcage to inspect the damage. It was very tender, and he winced noticeably as he felt the exposed bone. He knew finding a secure location was the only way to survive the night. So, ignoring the pain, he struggled to his feet, slung his trade gun over his shoulder, and gingerly climbed his way up into a tree. About 10 feet up, he found a secure spot where two branches grew close together. A good spot to prop himself up. The boy pulled a hunting knife from its sheath at his waist and cut the leather strap from his shoulder bag. He wrapped the strap around the tree and then around his waist. He tied a double knot to make sure it wouldn't come loose. For the moment, he was secure.

The moon's cold glow bathed the forest in blue. Cicadas buzzed in the trees and the shrill howl of a wolf broke the night's calm. The boy's eyes popped open. *That wolf is close,* he thought as he pulled his Barnett rifle over his shoulder, then turned his head to scan the surroundings. His hands trembled on the gun as a tear dripped down his cheek.

Under the shroud of fear and in the heavy fog of bodily trauma the boy's mind wandered back to his home in Stockholm, Sweden. He heard his mom calling from the back porch, "Jacob! Jacob come in for dinner. You've played out there all day." What the boy wouldn't give to be back in that safe place. To feel the comfort of his mother's love. Her soft kisses on his forehead. The warmth of her hugs.

Slumped over, up in the tree, the boy said to himself, "Mom." He seemed to say it for no other reason than to feel the word move across his lips. In a choked-up voice he continued, "I'm scared, Mom. I don't know what to do."

Sinking into a dream-like state, he could feel the presence of his mother as if she were right there with him. As if he were transported back in time, it was so real, a memory came to him. It was the time he fell from the rafters of the boathouse when he was 5 years old. A large gash on his forehead was dripping blood. His mother placed a cloth over the wound and pressed on it to stop the bleeding.

"Is it bleeding?" asked Jacob.

His mother lowered her face to look Jacob directly in the eye and said, "You don't have to worry, captain, I'm fixing it. You're gonna to be just fine."

Jacob looked into her blue eyes, absorbing all the love they projected. She pulled him close and squeezed.

Up in the tree, Jacob fell asleep. He dozed for several hours until, once again, he awoke, and the visions continued. There on a steep hill laid Jacob and his mother. They looked up at beautiful stars against a sky of dark black.

"See those up there?" asked his mother. Then she turned her head toward Jacob. Their faces were only inches apart.

"You mean the stars?"

She chuckled a bit then said, "No, those aren't stars, Jacob. Those are mirrors."

"What do you mean? Those are..."

"Shush. Let me finish. Those are mirrors. They're reflecting all the light that comes from your beautiful heart."

Jacob smiled as a tear of love dripped down his mother's cheek. Jacob turned on his side and reached over to wipe the tear as the delusion world merged with the real.

Now, back in reality, Jacob reached out with his hand trying to feel his mother's soft face. He could almost feel the warmth and he didn't want the vision to fade away. He remembered the way she would tickle him and laugh. He laughed with her. Jacob reached out with both hands. As if in a trance, he moved his hands and he was comforted. Then, once again, the howl of a wolf cut the night sky. It was closer now. Other howls and yelps could be heard coming from different directions. The wolves were organizing, converging on the scent of blood. Jacob's blood.

Instinct drove the pack. Individually they seemed nothing more than dogs, but together their synchronous actions were ominous and lethal. High-pitched yelps echoed through the forest as the wolves gathered at the base of the tree. Jacob could spot at least 6 of them, maybe more. They circled below sniffing, yelping, and looking up. They licked the blood at the base of the tree as they barked and grunted to each other in their predatory code. Suddenly, the alpha charged the tree, leaping up as high as he could. His fangs were exposed in a menacing snarl. Jacob was shocked at how close the wolf came to getting a grip on his foot. The other wolves joined in. They pushed off the tree as they leaped up. The moist noises as their jaws opened and the sound of their teeth snapping together stirred a primal fear in Jacob. He could smell the sour odor of their breath and saliva flew as they continued their attack. Then, as quickly as it began, the alpha decided there were better options for dinner. He stopped growling and headed into the forest. The rest of the pack dutifully followed. The last wolf, a younger pup, gave Jacob one last look before he too also turned and ran off. Jacob was now in shock. Thankful to be alive, he took the opportunity to inspect his injury once again. He tried to pull up his shirt but stopped. It was stuck. The blood had dried and adhered to his skin. Slowly he pulled the shirt with enough force to peel it away from the open wound at the side of his body. He felt the tip of a rib that had pierced his flesh. Jacob's eyes rolled back, then his head fell forward as he lost consciousness. His body fell sideways off the tree branch and turned 180 degrees. His musket dropped to the ground. Now hanging upside down, only the leather strap kept him in the tree.

It was morning when the Ojibwe hunting party arrived. They followed the sound of the gunshot and had been tracking Jacob for days. The Indians had long braided hair, black like campfire embers. Eagle feathers were woven into the braids. They wore deerskin leggings and boots topped with ornate beadwork. Their shirts were colorful. The Indian wearing an elk hide hat with eagle feathers sticking out the top was Oseeka. The leader of the hunting party. He noticed the musket lying at the base of a tree. He picked up the musket and closely inspected the dragon embossed in the bronze side plate.

"Hudson's Bay Company," he said to the others. He crouched down and touched the bloodstain on the grass. He looked around, then up. A loud gasp of shock followed by random curse words in Ojibwe. The sight of Jacob hanging upside down in the tree startled them. The most shocking feature was Jacob's blond hair. It was long, so it dangled down a good 8 inches from the top of his head. The morning light shimmered off it with dramatic effect. Jacob's arms hung down and apart positioning his body in a position that resembled an upside-down crucifixion. The Indians chattered amongst themselves. They were fearful of what this freakish sight meant. Was the creator angry with them? Was this boy a bad omen? What special forces made his hair the color of dry prairie grass? One of the Indians reached up and touched Jacob's hair, studying it. Oseeka examined Jacob closely. Then he turned to the others.

"This boy is trouble. We leave him here?" Two of the Indians climbed the tree and cut the leather strap around Jacob's waist. As his body fell limp, a large warrior supported his weight then slowly lowered him to the ground. He knelt and put a hand on Jacob's forehead.

"Hot," the large warrior said.

"Leave him," said Oseeka. "Let's go." The group joined Oseeka and walked about thirty feet. It was then that the large warrior stopped. The others walked a few paces more until they noticed. Then they all turned back to look at him.

"It's not right," the large warrior said.

"Forget it. He could be a curse. It's not our problem," Oseeka said. The group then turned and began walking.

"I won't," yelled the large warrior.

Now angrier, Oseeka said, "Why do you make trouble? This could anger the creator. We must go!"

"You go. I will stay. I won't leave a boy to die in the woods alone."

Oseeka made a frustrated grunting sound as he threw down the musket. He then walked up to the large warrior and yelled, "Okay. You take him. You carry him. He is yours to feed. Your problem. I won't allow him to be a burden or a curse on the tribe."

The group watched as the large warrior walked back to the tree, scooped up Jacob and draped him over his shoulder. He caught up to the group then walked past them, not saying a word. They continued walking up a winding rocky trail until disappearing into the towering spruce trees.

Chapter 3.
The Ojibwe Village

The hunting party shuffled through long prairie grass as they approached the Ojibwe village. The encampment sat next to a large lake. So large, in fact, you couldn't see across. Wind blew the water's surface pushing the waves up into whitecaps. There were more than 30 wigwams scattered about, cloaked in birch bark. Dogs, a mix of huskies and mixed breed mutts, barked wildly. Women abandoned their work and children stopped playing to get a good look. They ran toward the approaching group. Their whooping was very loud. The large Indian carrying Jacob walked through the gauntlet of villagers. His arms dangled down from his unconscious body and swayed as the large Indian walked. Occasional droplets of blood dripped from Jacob's fingertips. With his blond hair and blood-soaked shirt, he was quite a site. Villagers inspected Jacob as if he were a strange animal. Once beyond the throng of villagers, the large Indian arrived at a wigwam near the lake shore. He laid Jacob down on the ground, pulled back the buffalo hide door flap, and poked his head inside. The wigwam, made of animal hide and tree bark draped over sturdy wooden branches, smelled of days-old smoke and armpits. In the corner of the wigwam, sitting on a stump, was Nimkii Makwa (Thunder Bear). He was shirtless and wore doeskin leggings. His dark black hair was wet from a recent swim. He was a powerful man of somewhere around 19 years. That's an approximate age because the Ojibwe don't pay much attention to white man calendars. Tall and lean, Thunder Bear's chest and arms were cut with deep grooves of wiry muscle owed to a life carrying fur bundles and portaging canoes. A prominent scar cut across the side of his neck, a permanent memorial of a narrow escape from certain death. He wore two long eagle feathers at the back of his head. His eyes had the power to either burn through you or warm your heart, depending on which side of his demeanor you resided. Men ten years his elder admired him.

"Where do I put him?" the large Indian asked in Ojibwe. Thunder Bear simply shrugged. Then a female voice, in Ojibwe, could be heard from outside the wigwam. "Lay him on the buffalo hide by the fire," she said.

Thunder Bear bristled at the suggestion by his mother, Diindiisi (Blue Jay), who now came inside the wigwam following the large Indian.

"Why do you do this? He is not our concern," said Thunder Bear. "I don't want him here!"

"Nimkii Makwa, he is a boy. If we don't help him, who will?" said Blue Jay, pleading for sympathy.

"He won't replace Giwedin Ziibi (North River). I won't help him. He's not our responsibility. He should be a slave."

"This has nothing to do with Giwedin Ziibi."

"Come on Mother, of course it does. You feel a need to replace my brother. I know you haven't gotten over his death."

Blue Jay stared into the fire for a moment then answered, "This boy has no one. He is my responsibility," said Blue Jay. "If you don't support me, I..." Blue Jay carefully considered her words, then continued, "...my heart will break." The comment hung in silence for a long time as Thunder Bear absorbed it.

"I won't call him brother," said Thunder Bear. He shook his head, grabbed his doeskin shirt, and walked out.

Blue Jay sighed, then turned to Jacob's unconscious body. Leaning forward she placed her ear next to his mouth to feel for breath. He seemed lifeless, but she could feel just a bit of warmth coming out. She examined the huge gash in his side and the severe bruising which extended up to his chest and around to the middle of his back. There was a loud crack as she set the broken ribs. She stitched Jacob's side with needle and deer intestine. Then, after gently wiping away blood, she applied a paste of spruce syrup and healing herbs to the wound. It was now quite red and inflamed from infection. As she examined Jacob's face, her lips moved from a concerned expression into a smile. He was so gentle looking, she thought. She felt his wavy blond hair and brushed it back off his forehead. "Poor boy," she said in Ojibwe. "Where did you come from? How did you get here?" Blue Jay pulled a blanket up over Jacob's chest, rose to her feet, and walked to the wigwam door. As she was leaving, she turned and looked back. "You're going to be just fine," she promised. In her heart, she knew it was unlikely he would ever wake again.

Two days went by, and Jacob was still unconscious. Blue Jay prepared herself to accept his death. With a towel, she wiped sweat from his brow. He was clearly fighting a high fever caused by the injury and its accompanying infection. Though it didn't look promising, she never gave up. She continued to give him water and tried to feed him soft mushed corn and soup. Daily she applied healing herbs and medicine to the wound.

One evening while sitting by the fire ring Blue Jay was approached by Oseeka, the Indian that led the hunting party. "Is the boy dead?" he asked.

"No. I think he is getting better," Blue Jay answered, knowing it was a lie.

"You're spending too much time helping him. You're not getting your work done."

"I will catch up. He needs me now."

"I promised you could help him if it didn't become a distraction. It has."

"Give me one more day. I will know by then. He will either live

... or not," she pleaded.

Curtly Oseeka demanded, "One day. No more." He then walked off, leaving Blue Jay sitting at the fire ring. She rubbed her lower lip nervously.

In the complete darkness of night, a scream shattered the quiet. Blue Jay popped up from a deep sleep. She ran outside the wigwam and lit a torch with the burning campfire then returned inside. Jacob groaned and gurgled with pain. He coughed and blood spilled from his open mouth. He rolled onto his side then struggled to sit up. Once upright he noticed Blue Jay coming over. "Where am I?" asked Jacob in English. "Who are you?"

Not understanding the language, Blue Jay said nothing. Jacob felt the stitches on his side. "Did you do this?" he asked. Blue Jay did not understand and just shook her head. Jacob continued, "Did you see any of the other hunters I was with? White men like me."

Not able to answer, Blue Jay spoke in Ojibwe. "You should rest. You need a couple days to get your strength back," suggested Blue Jay. Too exhausted to continue further Jacob laid down, covered himself, and fell asleep almost immediately.

The next morning, Jacob awoke to an empty wigwam. He noticed a kettle containing a heavy, dark, bubbling broth cooking over the fire. He was scared to touch it for fear he might be punished, but he was too hungry to resist. He grabbed a wooden spoon, scooped out a small piece of meat, then quickly shoved it into his mouth. The salty, smoky taste of the deer meat was good. It was tender and easy to chew and swallow. He ate another larger piece just as the wigwam's door flap flew open. An old man entered the tent with Oseeka. The old man had frizzy gray hair that stood up in all directions as if it were gray flames roaring off the top of his head. He was short and thin. Jacob chewed covertly, trying his best to conceal the piece of meat he had just shoved into his mouth. The old man knelt by Jacob, felt his face, and smelled his blond hair. The man was uncomfortably close. So close that Jacob could smell his bad breath. The old man turned toward Oseeka and asked in

Ojibwe, "Where did you find him?"

"South of the Manigotagan River. Near the big lake," answered Oseeka. For several minutes Oseeka and the old man had a discussion bordering on an argument about whether Jacob would become a slave or adopted as a member of the tribe. After the discussion, the old man studied Jacob's blue eyes intently. He peered so deeply Jacob felt as if the stare was reaching deep into his soul. The scene was unusual, but Jacob was not frightened. The old man had a friendly face and warm smile. Even with half his teeth missing.

He began to speak very slowly, "This boy is a riddle. A sign from the spirit of the woods." The old man blankly stared for a moment then turned toward Oseeka. "This boy is like the white elk. Hair the color of winter grass. Like the herd, we should protect him. This boy's presence might be a gift, but it could also be a warning. We must heed this warning and learn what the Great Spirit is telling us."

Oseeka walked over and knelt beside the old man. "I think we could trade him to the Sioux as a slave. He is almost a man and would bring a good price."

Suddenly Jacob blurted out in Ojibwe, "No. I can hunt. I can help the tribe."

Oseeka and the old man were shocked to hear this white child, with the gun of a fur trader, speak Ojibwe. They were very puzzled by it. Oseeka switched to sign language and signed to the old man.

"I know what that means too," said Jacob again in Ojibwe.

Now the old man was more impressed than shocked. He turned to Oseeka and said, "We keep this one around. See where it goes."

For the next several days, Jacob stayed in the wigwam alone, only leaving to relieve himself in the trees. To the villagers, Jacob was a freak, an oddity over which they were obsessed. They watched and studied his every move. They even inspected his excrement, poking at it with sticks as if it held some secret message. Jacob was surrounded by this large group of people but felt isolated and alone. One day he wandered across the village and down to the lake shore. He watched as the wind pushed waves up onto the coarse-grained sand and between his toes. From behind he heard a voice.

"Why are you here?" said the woman who was rapidly approaching. She held a large stick at her side.

In Ojibwe, Jacob answered, "Just watching the lake."

The woman raised the stick and hit Jacob across his shoulder, knocking him to the ground. She continued beating him as he sat in the sand on his knees. Jacob struggled to block the stick with his forearms and hands. Many of the blows landed on his injured ribs. This caused incredible pain and Jacob fell to a laying position on his side. Lying, curled up in a ball, trying to protect himself Jacob asked, "Why are you doing this?"

The woman threw down the stick and kicked sand into Jacob's face. Then she said, "You don't belong here. You are not a part of us." She left Jacob lying there as she walked back toward the village. Several feet away, she turned her head and said, "You need to leave here and go back where you belong."

Jacob thought to himself. *I would. But I don't have a place where I belong?*

After the beating, several other incidents of verbal abuse, and threats, Jacob was fearful for his safety. He did not venture out into the village anymore, so his only human contact was with Blue Jay who visited him a few times a day. Checking on him to make certain he was doing okay.

Early one morning, Jacob pushed open the flap of the wigwam and noticed an Indian sitting beside a burning fire. Startled, Jacob looked around, not knowing what to do. The Indian stood and turned toward Jacob. It was Thunder Bear, Blue Jay's son. He gestured toward the trees, indicating that Jacob was free to go. Jacob half ran, half stumbled into the woods. Calmly, Thunder Bear roasted meat over the fire. A few minutes later, sweaty and winded, Jacob returned from the trees and limped over to the fire. Thunder Bear scantly acknowledged Jacob's return. Casually he cocked his head toward a stump, indicating Jacob should sit. Thunder Bear spoke in English. His English was not good, but Jacob was able to follow. He explained that Jacob was free to stay or go. If he needed help to get back to his people, the tribe would assist.

Jacob wasn't certain why he didn't reveal to Thunder Bear that he could speak Ojibwe. Maybe it was because he didn't dare interrupt? Maybe he felt more comfortable keeping it a secret.

Thunder Bear extended a branch with a piece of roasted deer meat impaled on the end. Jacob reached out and accepted the steaming chunk of venison and ate it. He nodded his head and smiled at Thunder Bear. While chewing Jacob said in English, "Good."

"Good," retorted Thunder Bear. His tone was flat and abrupt. "It was not my decision to let you stay. I will help because I respect my mother. Nothing more." With that Thunder Bear rose to his feet and walked off.

The next morning Blue Jay approached Jacob and knelt beside him. Softly she touched his hair and smiled. She said in Ojibwe, "I'm Blue Jay." Jacob did not respond. Blue Jay smiled and pointed to her chest and repeated, "Blue Jay." Then she pointed at Jacob. He looked past her long eye lashes into her kind brown eyes and answered, "Jacob Fahlstrom." Jacob's lingering Swedish accent made Blue Jay giggle. She promised to take care of Jacob. Eventually, a tear dripped down her cheek. Jacob reached up and wiped the tear. Blue Jay hugged Jacob. The kind of hug you can feel from the surface of your skin all the way through your ribcage to your heart. Jacob, recalling his mother in Stockholm, sobbed. It had been four years since he had felt the caring touch of a mother. He wanted to accept the hug, but oddly, he felt the love as pain and pulled away. Blue Jay was disappointed by the rejection but patient and understanding. She held up her hand as if remembering something, then pulled an item out of her woven bag. It was a black leather book.

"Is it yours? They found it in the woods by your musket," she said in Ojibwe.

Jacob was frozen in a moment of stunned silence. A large tear clung to the edge of his eyelid. Then, with a blink, the little wet ball of emotion rolled across his cheek and dripped off his chin. Jacob shook his head up and down, yes. After wiping dry his eyes, he reached out for the small book. It was a bible. Jacob opened the dark black leather cover and touched the message inside that was scrawled in Swedish. It said, *"No matter what."*

"My mother gave me this. It was her promise of how she would always love me," Jacob explained.

"Where is your family, Jacob? Do you want to go to them?" Blue Jay said slowly, making certain Jacob would be able to understand.

Jacob reached down and touched the ground with his hand. He drew a rough map in the dirt depicting the ocean and the location of Sweden. Then in Ojibwe, he said, "My home is here. But I don't have a home there anymore."

Blue Jay asked in Ojibwe, "Do you have a family where you got lost Jacob?" Jacob shook his head no. The two sat together for several minutes. They had run out of things to say. For now, a caring smile said enough.

As the sun rose, Jacob awoke to the smell of cooking meat. He walked outside and Blue Jay offered him a wooden bowl containing roasted moose liver. Jacob took the bowl and said in English, "Thank you."

To which she answered, "Thank you."

"No, no, no," Jacob responded with a chuckle. You say, you're welcome."

Blue Jay simply laughed. They continued to laugh as they finished their early morning meal. Blue Jay reached out and touched Jacob's nose. Jacob reached out and touched Blue Jay's nose. Blue Jay extended an arm to hug Jacob, but he pulled away. Sitting close, they quietly watched the fire burn.

That night there was a particularly clear sky. Not a cloud to be seen. It was as if the chill of fall had squeezed out every bit of moisture. Jacob lay on his back looking up in complete awe at the uncountable stars and the bright moon. He exhaled, and a breath emerged from his mouth in the form of a wispy cloud. The abundant moonlight made it easy for Jacob to notice a tall Indian approaching from across the village. A single eagle feather was braided into his long hair. He wore full-length leggings, ornately stitched moccasins, and a deerskin shirt adorned with turquoise and red beading. Several necklaces that hung from his neck swayed and rattled as he walked. Dark angular brows gave him an appearance that was intense. On the left side of his face a single braid hung down over his shoulder. Silver hairs mixed in the braid revealed his age. In his hands he carried Jacob's Barnett Musket. Blue Jay, who was brushing leaves off the wigwam noticed his approach. The man spoke to her in Ojibwe, dismissing her. He pointed to himself and struggled for the words to speak in English. "I am Weshcubb. I need you tell me where from this." Weshcubb held out the weapon and nodded down toward it.

Trying to avoid trouble, Jacob began to speak slowly. "Uh, that's my musket."

Weshcubb tapped the gun and continued speaking in English. He continued to struggle with the language. "Where from?"

Pointing to the North, Jacob answered in Ojibwe, "York Factory, way North. Where the land meets Hudson's Bay. The gateway to the Atlantic. Many days travel by water." Jacob drew a map in the dirt. With a stick he traced the route then once again pointed north and added, "That way." Weshcubb, impressed by Jacob's ability to speak Ojibwe and his grasp of navigation, watched attentively. Jacob continued, "I was with the Hudson's Bay Company."

Weshcubb, recognizing the words, interrupted. "Hudson's Bay Company. Fur trade."

"Yes." Jacob answered, then continued, "They trade for furs. Trade Knives, kettles, beads, blankets ..."

Weshcubb abruptly stood up and waved for Jacob to follow. They walked past several wigwams until they reached a large one near the spruce forest with painted red circles. They entered the wigwam and Weshcubb opened a chest, pulled back a blanket and underneath the blanket were six muskets.

"We traded for these with North West Company. But they brought a death sickness. Devastating loss. No more trade for a very long time. So, with no powder, the guns no good." Weshcubb dropped the useless gun back into the chest and roughly pulled the blanket over top of them.

In Ojibwe, Jacob said, "I know the traders at York Factory." Weshcubb turned his head inquisitively. "I can talk to them. They'll trade guns, black powder, and lead balls for good pelts. We'll need lots of pelts," Jacob explained. A small smile came to Weshcubb then his face immediately reverted to its normal intense expression.

"In spring, you will go to York to trade. Get guns for hunt," Weshcubb said as he walked away. Just before exiting he turned back and added, "Thank you Oza Windib." Then, beads rattling, he walked off leaving Jacob standing alone in the wigwam by the chest.

Jacob wondered. *Did he just call me Oza Windib? Is that my name now?* Jacob pulled back the blanket and looked at the guns in the chest. They seemed old and in bad condition. Jacob took one last look at his Barnett musket. Tempted to keep the gun, Jacob's hand lingered close for a moment, but then he thought better of it, replaced the blanket, and turned away.

Chapter 4.
Rabbit Hunt

Jacob spent the late fall and early winter exploring and hunting with the boys of the village. His ability to speak Ojibwe had now progressed to a level of complete fluency. He joined in games of lacrosse and watched closely as the other boys interacted, trying to learn how to fit in. He pretended his white skin wasn't different, but it was often a barrier to friendship. Jacob let his hair grow long. He rubbed it with campfire soot attempting to make it dark like the other boys. Never quite fitting in, he was often left standing off to the side, alone.

Almost every day, the group would go out into the woods. They'd dance and paint their faces like the warriors. They studied the habits of animals. It was their goal in life to become great hunters, providers, and warriors. The boys allowed Jacob to come along, but they never fully accepted him as "one of them."

Blue Jay made leggings of deerskin and moccasins with intricate beads to show her love for Oza Windib. That name, which Weshcubb had given to Jacob, stuck. Now everyone in the village called him Oza Windib, which in English means "Yellow Head." Clearly a reference to his blond hair. Jacob liked that he was given an Indian name, but he didn't like the way it exposed and called attention to the trait that made him different from everyone else.

All day long, Blue Jay performed her tasks and chores to contribute to the tribe. Collecting firewood, making clothing, and skinning animal pelts for trade. She also spent a considerable amount of time cooking. Blue Jay was a great cook. Every day when Jacob returned from the forest, he looked forward to what was in the pot over the fire. His favorite was her venison and wild rice stew. Her food, like her love, was available in abundance. Jacob needed that love so much, but he struggled to accept it.

Blue Jay was totally dedicated to Jacob. She was a mother and a father to him. She stressed the importance of being alert. That, as a hunter, stealth was critical for success. Stealth was also important for safety in case of an attack by enemy tribes, most likely Sioux, who the Ojibwe were not on good terms with. The main reason for the conflict was that the Ojibwe had pushed the Sioux west to maintain dominance of the fur trade in the Great Lakes area. The Ojibwe also had historical grudges and disputes with the Assiniboine and Arikara, tribes which occupied lands to the west, and north of Sioux territory.

By February winter had sunk its icy teeth deep into the Lake of the Woods region. Several feet of billowy snow blanketed the forest. The boys trudged clumsily along in snowshoes as they hunted deep in the woods. With every step the loud crunching of snow could be heard. Suddenly, in the distance, a rabbit darted across the trail. An opportunity to hunt! Several of the boys took aim with their bows and fired. One arrow found its mark and impaled the rabbit to a tree that was located directly behind it. Jacob, noticing it was his arrow, celebrated. But all was not well. Big Bear, an overly large for his age13-year-old, pushed Jacob aside and declared, "That's my arrow."

Jacob contested. "Look, quail feathers with a red dot. I'm pretty sure that's my arrow."

"Not yours," Big Bear insisted. The group of boys looked on nervously.

"It is mine," blurted Jacob.

This was met with a swinging fist. Jacob's nose spurted blood as he fell to the ground. The others laughed and a couple of the boys kicked Jacob as he lay on the ground. They did a mock war dance around Jacob. The group was whooping and chanting.

Big Bear yelled, "Are you going to cry for mommy, white baby? Maybe you should swim back to your white people. White baby."

The remainder of the group joined in calling him "white baby" in a derogatory way, mocking him.

Jacob struggled to his knees, but Big Bear kicked him in the middle of his back, again knocking him down to the ground. The boys laughed and ran off. On the way past, one boy leaned forward and spit on Jacob's forehead. With a groan, Jacob sat up and wiped off the foamy white mess that was dripping down his cheek. Red Coyote, who was at times friendly to Jacob, paused momentarily and looked down with concern. He just stood there, as if about to speak, but then turned and ran off into the woods.

Jacob struggled to his feet and watched Red Coyote disappear into the trees. He listened to the crunching of snowshoes and felt emotional pain with every step. Jacob began to cry. The kind of cry where your legs won't work and crumple below you. Not sure why that happens. Maybe your body hopes curling up into a ball and making you smaller will make the pain smaller. It never does. Your body is delusional that way.

Jacob lay in the snow for several minutes. The inside of his chest felt like his heart had turned into molten iron and was burning its way through his body and out his back. Looking up at the clouds, Jacob became aware of blood running from his nose. It dripped slowly across his cheek and around to the back of his neck. He began creating a plan in his mind for leaving this place. He could walk north until he hit the Hayes River. From there he could make his way to Oxford House, the nearest H.B.C. trading post. As he began to form a plan for his departure, a figure emerged from the trees. It was Thunder Bear.

Jacob was surprised. To this point he had barely acknowledged Jacob's presence. Thunder Bear bent down on one knee and touched Jacob on the forehead. He looked Jacob in the eye, nodded, then scooped him up like a fur bundle.

They walked a few steps then Jacob asked, "Why are you doing this?"

There was a long pause before Thunder Bear answered. "I'm your brother."

Jacob let the words sink in as they continued down the narrow, snow-covered path. Thunder Bear carried Jacob over his shoulder for miles through the deep snow, all the way back to the village. He set Jacob down by Blue Jay's wigwam. Pausing for a moment he looked closely at Jacob, studying this unusual boy.

"I still don't think you should be here," Thunder Bear said.

Jacob was about to say something when Thunder Bear turned and walked away.

Chapter 5.
Trade

It was May 1813. Morning brought a pre-dawn glow to the Ojibwe village on Lake of the Woods. Inside a wigwam Jacob lay curled up in a buffalo blanket. The gathering heat from the morning sun woke Jacob and he sat upright, rubbed his eyes, and wandered sleepily outside. Loud chirping of birds signaled spring's renewed territorial struggles. With the spring bloom, it smelled like a cartload of flowers were dropped from the sky. He walked down to the lake, scooped up a handful of the fresh, cold water and drank. He then splashed water onto his face causing goose bumps on his arms and a chill up the back of his neck. Lake of the Woods is a very large body of water in the northern part of what is today Minnesota. The water doesn't warm to a comfortable temperature until deep into summer.

Suddenly a loud, deep timbered voice yelled, "Oza Windib! Come." It was Weshcubb who was standing at the edge of the woods with two men.

Jacob ran across the open meadow, stopping by Weshcubb.

"This is Ma-jijuan and Matunaagd Machk," said Weshcubb. Ma-jijuan, which in English meant Flowing Creek, was a short man with a young-looking face. He seemed self-conscious of his left hand, which was absent three fingers, claimed by a Sioux tomahawk. Noticing Jacob's gaze Flowing Creek casually slid his hand into the pocket of his capote. True to his name he was a skilled navigator of waterways from Lake of the Woods all the way to Montreal. Matunaagd Machk, which in English translates to Fights Bear, was a large barrel-chested man. His high forehead and intense eyes were unsettling. He was the kind of man you don't mess with. Fights Bear, who towered over the others, wore three eagle feathers in his long black hair each with several notches signifying enemies killed in battle. Weshcubb explained these two men, along with Jacob, were to build a canoe large enough to hold the load of furs to be taken to York Factory. Jacob was to guide them and serve as translator.

Weshcubb said directly to Jacob, "You've traveled these waters and know these men of the Hudson's Bay Company. You speak good English and can do trade. You will go with Flowing Creek and Fights Bear. Stay out of their way and do what they say. Your job is to speak English and do trade. That's it. Understood?"

Jacob answered simply. "Got it." He longed for respect. Why was it so difficult to earn? Why did everyone assume that he was worthless, just because he was young? Weshcubb slapped Fights Bear on the shoulder in a sign of affection and without a word the three Indians walked away, leaving Jacob alone.

The tribe had worked for weeks gathering the necessary supplies to build the canoe. Large strips of bark were cut from silver birch trees; cedar wood was harvested and chiseled into shape. Hundreds of feet of spruce root had been collected, boiled, and split for lacing together critical joints. With a precision only decades of experience could foster, the group went about the task of crafting the canoe. For several long days they worked. They told stories, sang Ojibwe songs, and poked fun at one another. Hard work mixed with joking was the way of the village. Jacob loved the clever back and forth. Every day had its share of stunts pulled and clever tricks played. Though amused by the banter, Jacob never felt a part of the fun. He felt like an outsider. *I guess it's because I'm different.* He thought.

One day, as Fights Bear diligently worked away lacing the top of the canoe with spruce root one of the women snuck some spruce gum onto his stool. Spruce gum is a mix of spruce pitch, powdered charcoal, and animal fat. It is very sticky and dries hard. Fights Bear stretched his back, walked over to his stool, and sat. The woman who snuck the spruce gum onto Fights Bear's seat snickered, as did several others. Then Fights Bear attempted to stand up. He stumbled and almost fell. The stool was now stuck to his butt. He spun around wondering what animal had attacked him from behind. The group roared with laughter and whooping. Fights Bear yanked and pulled on the stool, but it wouldn't come loose. To assist, another Indian brave pulled on the stool causing the entire back of Fights Bear's trousers to be torn off with a loud ripping sound. This ignited the group with uproarious laughter as Fights Bear tried helplessly to cover his bare behind while simultaneously trying to get ahold of the Indian brave.

The brave dodged, laughed, and pleaded in Ojibwe, "I didn't do it. It wasn't me."

The group laughed as Fights Bear chased the brave all the way to the lake where he picked him up and threw him into the water.

A few days later, on a chilly and windless morning, Fights Bear, Flowing Creek, and Jacob placed large rocks inside the canoe to test its seams. Once they felt confident the vessel would hold water, they grabbed paddles and ventured out onto the lake, staying close to the shoreline in case their inspection wasn't thorough. The birch bark canoe skimmed like a dream through the glass smooth water. It was a work of fine craftsmanship. They all nodded with pride in what they had built. Jacob, however, knew the journey would be long and difficult. To get to York Factory they would have to cross Lake Winnipeg, an enormous body of water. With paddles alone the long journey from southern edge to norther tip would be punishing.

...

On the day they headed north, the sun shined, and a strong wind blew. The twenty-six-foot canoe was loaded with supplies. Six large ninety-pound fur bundles, pemmican, corn, and wild rice. Also, three muskets including Jacob's Barnett were carefully hidden on board. Each man carried a hunting knife, a bow, and a quiver full of arrows for hunting and protection against any river travelers with nefarious intentions. The village was abuzz with excitement. It had been a long time since there was a journey to trade furs. Weshcubb nodded with approval to Fights Bear and Flowing Creek. Jacob who sat in the middle of the canoe felt pretty much as worthless as the rest of the cargo sitting there in a pile, doing nothing. He wanted to help but was not trusted to do so.

Blue Jay approached and wished Jacob luck. She attempted to put on a happy face, but her pouting lip gave her away. Recognizing her concern, Jacob gave a small smile and said, "I'll be fine." Blue Jay put an arm around Jacob, and he awkwardly slipped away from the hug.

Long days were spent on the Winnipeg River. Sometimes floating with the current and sometimes paddling around large rocks. These waters flow generally northwest to Lake Winnipeg, more than 140 miles from Lake of the Woods. During a heavy rainstorm Fights Bear retrieved a canvas tarp from the pile of cargo in the middle of the canoe. He and Flowing Creek huddled underneath to get out of the soaking rain. In the back of the canoe Jacob sat shivering with water dripping from his chin. Finding some empathy for this pitiful sight, Fights Bear reluctantly waved for Jacob to join them under the tarp. For hours Flowing Creek and Fights Bear told stories and joked as if Jacob were not even there.

Late the next afternoon they reached their first significant marker of the journey. Five days of hand blisters, mosquitos and springtime rapids were endured. They paddled from the fresh water of the Winnipeg River into the cloudy and muddy waters of Lake Winnipeg. Jacob, seated amongst the cargo, began to explain, "This lake is massive. Much larger than Lake of the Woods and not broken up with islands."

Fights Bear, who paddled up front, asked without turning

around, "How do you know this?"

Jacob waited for the two Indians to stop paddling then explained, "I've been on this lake before. Not too far away is where I got lost in the woods. I came all the way down from Lake Winnipeg's northern tip with a Hudson's Bay Company crew. To travel from the north to the south of Lake Winnipeg required ten-hour days of paddling for more than fifteen days.

Fights Bear's eyes widened, and his body cringed in anticipation of, soon to be coming his way, pain. Flowing Creek contemplated the distance across and said, "That's a lot of paddling with no river current."

"Awe shit," added Fights Bear.

The Indians paddled the canoe over to a sandy portion of shoreline. Flowing Creek sat in the sand, lit his pipe, and had a smoke. He said, "Let's rest we've got a lot of work waiting for us tomorrow."

"Too bad we don't have another warrior with us to share the load," noted Fights Bear.

Jacob said, "I can help. Just because I'm a kid doesn't mean I can't do my share of the work."

Flowing Creek exhaled a large smoke ring then said, "The only reason you're here is to speak English to the traders. Just stay out of our way." Jacob, with all the strength he could muster, threw a stone into the lake and walked into the woods.

"Sure, go off and cry. We're not coming in there to find you," yelled Fights Bear. Hearing no reply from the trees, Fights Bear and Flowing Creek laughed and began to prep for dinner.

Meanwhile, off in the woods, Jacob searched for a small tree. He found a birch that seemed the perfect size then used his hatchet to chop it down. He worked diligently on the tree for a long time. Back at the camp, Fights Bear and Flowing Creek had finished dinner and were enjoying the warmth of a campfire as the sky darkened. Jacob emerged from the woods carrying the birch tree which was now cut into two pieces and assembled in the shape of a cross. The longer part of the birch was about seven feet tall. Jacob laid it on the beach next to Fights Bear.

"This is going to save us a lot of work," said Jacob.

"A cross? What are you going to pray to your Jesus god?" questioned Flowing Creek. Fights Bear laughed then said,

"You're not getting food. If you're not here to help cook, you don't eat."

"Come on, there's some left," urged Flowing Creek.

"No. No work, no food," said Fights Bear. Then he threw the last few pieces of meat out

into the muddy lake water. "Maybe Oza Windib can use his cross to pray for some dinner?"

Jacob's head hung down. He fought hard to stop the tears that were trying to push their

way out. He asked, "Why do you have to be so cruel? All I want to do is help. I just want to be your friend."

Fights Bear answered, "I'm cruel because I don't like people like you. White men have raped women in our village. White men have stolen from us. They cheat us when we trade, and they bring sickness." He spat on the ground then asked, "Why would I be your friend?"

"I didn't do those things. I can't change the color of my skin or my hair. It's just the way I am," said Jacob. "Just because my skin looks like theirs doesn't make me one of the people that did those horrible things."

There was a long quiet pause. Only the crackle of the fire and waves pushing up onto the shore could be heard.

Then Jacob broke the silence. He said, "It's not a cross."

"Doesn't matter what it is," scoffed Fights Bear.

"Don't you see? It's a sail!"

There was no response from the other two. Jacob ran over to the canoe and grabbed some rope and the canvas tarp they used to shelter themselves from the rain. He walked back carrying the tarp over his shoulder. Fights Bear and Flowing Creek watched him curiously. Jacob worked for several minutes then stood up his creation. He motioned toward it and said, "It's a sail! It catches the wind and will push us across still water."

"It's a sail," said Flowing Creek. He continued to think, remembering the European ships he had seen before on Lake Superior when they traded with the North West Company. Slowly the realization of how helpful this will be sunk in. "Oza Windib, this is a good thing you have done. We will save many days of rowing ... many blisters."

"Probably won't work. Another broken white promise," huffed Fights Bear.

Jacob couldn't help but smile a bit when he saw Flowing Creek nod his head with approval.

Early the next morning they loaded the canoe and paddled a short distance away from shore. Flowing Creek helped Jacob set up the sail. The boat floated for a while, then there was a strong gust of wind and the birch tree mast nearly pulled Jacob into the water. Fights Bear shook his head. After a moment of struggle the sail was secured in place. Jacob moved to the back of the canoe. Working two ropes that were tied to the bottom sides of the sail, Jacob kept control as a gust of wind caught it and began pushing the canoe across the water. Flowing Creek cheered loudly as they continued to pick up speed. He yelled, "Yes! Jacob, we are flying!" The canoe, under the power of Jacob's sail, moved swiftly across the glistening surface of Lake Winnipeg. Grudgingly, Fights Bear had to smile about how easy it was to ride the wind instead of paddling all day.

Later that night, on the shore of Lake Winnipeg the three pulled the canoe from the water. It was windy with a chill in the air. Cold enough to see your breath.

"You did good Oza Windib," said Flowing Creek as he scraped his flint against his knife sending a spark into a pile of finely shredded cedar bark. He then added several wood shavings whittled from a branch to get the flame going. "You've saved us many days of paddling."

"Thank you," Jacob responded. He then walked over and added wood to another fire that was burning nearby. They had built five campfires along the shore and a short distance into the trees. Multiple fires made it seem like a larger group was camped. This kept passersby from getting funny ideas. Jacob dropped a tree branch onto a fire and sparks flew up and floated off into the inky black sky.

They would spend nine nights at various points along the shore of Lake Winnipeg before reaching its northern tip. They then traversed Playgreen Lake and entered the Jack River where, on the left bank, stood a small timber structure. A flag hung from a simple tree branch mounted next to the front door. It gently slapped back and forth. The flag was mostly red with the English Union Jack in the upper left corner and large white letters in the lower right. The letters were H.B.C.

Jacob immediately recognized the Hudson's Bay Company flag from his time at York Factory. They paddled to a small wooden dock that was in a bad state of disrepair. They tied up the canoe and wobbled their way across dock to the water's edge. As they approached, the door of the trading post creaked open and a thin man with gray hair cautiously emerged. Suspenders held up his sagging pair of doeskin leggings. He held a musket at the ready. The approach of these unfamiliar Indians surprised him. He typically traded with Cree people and these men had a distinctly different look. The thin man questioned, "What's your business? Better speak up or I'll put a hole in ya'." There was a pause as Jacob and the others froze. "You speak English?" asked the trader as he now shouldered his weapon.

"No, no. no," Jacob urged raising his hands clearly showing they were unarmed. "I mean yes ... yes, I do speak English. We're on our way to York Factory. We've got furs we intend to trade."

The trader inquired, "Why not just trade your furs here with me?"

"I have friends up there and some business to take care of,"

Jacob answered. He knew that this man would try to cheat them and quickly decided they had a much better chance up at York Factory. The trader lowered his musket, cocked his head, and surveyed the three with a squinted, skeptical eye.

"You hungry?"

"Yes, sir. We could use a hot meal," replied Jacob. The trader walked sideways back to the door, still not giving his full trust.

"All right, come on in," he said hesitantly. "I'll get you some dinner and you can spend the night. But then you've got to move on."

"Yes, sir. Thank you," said Jacob, then he turned and relayed the message in Ojibwe to Fights Bear and Flowing Creek.

The sweet smell of burning cedar wood and musty animal furs filled the room. The trader gestured to Jacob and the two Indians to sit. In the hearth a small flame flickered.

"What's your name?" Jacob asked the trader who was standing by the wood stove heating a pot.

"Frederick Taylor."

Jacob was hoping for a bit more conversation. "How long you been here, Frederick?"

"Been on the Jack River three years now. Was at Oxford House another fourteen before that."

"Don't you have a family?" Jacob continued his questioning. Frederick walked over carrying three steaming bowls on a tray. He carefully set down a bowl in front of Jacob, Fights Bear and Flowing Creek.

A bit annoyed, Frederick responded, "Listen, kid. I just don't like people much. I'd prefer we just sit here and enjoy our soup in quiet." He then walked across the room, sat at his desk, and proceeded to do paperwork. Without even looking up, he said, "Best route to York Factory is the Hayes River. There's less portages than the Nelson and you'll find wild game more plentiful. If you need provisions, I can't help ya', but you'll come across the Oxford post in about seventy miles. They can set you up more adequately."

"Thank you, sir," answered Jacob, trying to be as polite and respectful as he could.

"A man by the name McGregor there will help as long as you have a couple pelts in exchange." Now turning to look at Jacob, Frederick added, "With McGregor you'd best handle all the tradin'. McGregor won't deal directly with no Indians. Thinks it's below him to talk to savages."

The comment stung Jacob and he didn't conceal his feelings very well. There was a momentary pause, then Frederick turned back to his paperwork not speaking another word.

The next morning, only a few minutes after sunrise, Jacob and the others were leaving the post. As they paddled away Frederick yelled, "Good luck. Don't get eaten by a god damned polar bear!" Proud of his humor, he laughed a raspy and screechy laugh. Then turned and walked back to the cabin.

It took another three weeks to make it across the 400-miles of interconnected waterways from the Jack River post to York Factory. Along their journey every water condition was encountered. Hairy Lake had long grass sticking out above the water. It was so thick, at times the canoe could barely make it through. Portions of the river were very wide and white caps were common. Some of the rivers were so shallow the men had to get out of the canoe and walk it along the water's edge. Currents also varied. Sometimes almost nothing. Other times raging rapids. One consistent feature for nearly the entire distance was the light green underbrush on shore backed by towering black spruce. In some areas the shore had almost no soil; the spruce seemed to grow right out of rock. Not great for sleeping. A frequent dinner was Northern Pike which were abundant in the Hayes River. Black bear, moose and caribou were frequently seen wandering the shoreline. The musical voice of loons could be heard most evenings. And bugs, lots of bugs. Mosquitos, dark flies, and massive biting horse flies. At times the mosquitos were such a nuisance that Jacob, Fights Bear and Flowing Creek had to break camp in the middle of the night and get back on the water.

It was the only way to escape the buzzing bloodthirsty devils.

One morning on the Hayes River, just past Swampy Lake, Jacob dove into the water to bathe. He emerged from the water covered with leeches. Upon closer inspection the water looked almost black it was so completely infested. Flowing Creek helped Jacob clear himself of the slithering creatures by pouring whiskey over them.

It was a warm June morning shortly after dawn when the birch bark canoe arrived at Fishing Island, signaling York Factory was near. Fishing Island was the first in a series of islands as the Hayes River nears Hudson Bay. Giving away its distant past as ocean bottom, there were sandy hills and cliffs running forty feet high on the islands. With York Factory less than seven miles away, Jacob alerted the others. Shortly after, the buildings of York Factory came into view on the left bank of the river. Many temporary shelters, teepees, and wigwams stood outside York Factory, a short distance from the trading post. Dozens of canoes lined the shore. Jacob, Fights Bear, and Flowing Creek steered the birch bark canoe to the water's edge being careful not to bump into the others. Jacob and Fights Bear each grabbed a bundle of pelts. To make the awkward and heavy bundle easier to carry, the men attached a leather strap around their forehead for leverage as the bundle rested on their back. This way, most of the carrying was done by the core of the body and legs. Flowing Creek remained with the canoe to keep watch on the remaining four bundles. Jacob and Fights Bear made their way up the grassy hill. The ground was very wet and mushy. Boardwalks connected all the major buildings of the fort. At the top of the hill was a large rectangular timber structure made of stacked logs with a cedar shingle roof. It was the trading post. They joined a long line of traders and Indians waiting to get inside. The man next to them, a short Englishman with a scruffy beard and an almost entirely toothless smile, leaned over toward Jacob and Fights Bear.

He asked, "Speak English?" They turned and looked at the man blankly. Jacob nodded in the affirmative. "I'll trade for your pelts right here and you won't have to wait in line." Again, the man's comment was met with little response.

Eventually Jacob answered, "We're okay to wait. We came a long way to get here..." Jacob paused, then continued his comment with emphasis, "...to see the trader."

Insulted, the scruffy Englishman blurted, "Oh, you think you're a better trader than me? Think you can get a better deal in there? I think not. They're low-life cheats. And besides, they may not even trade with savages directly. They prefer to work with just the traders. Especially if the In-yans are drunk. You ain't drunk are ya?" That's how the man pronounced the word. In-yans. Maybe because of the lack of teeth. Maybe he was simply as ignorant as he looked.

Jacob replied, "We're not savages. We keep the pelts coming to this place. We're good at what we do."

Insulted by the snub, the Englishman snapped back by sniffing the air. "You sure smell like savages."

"Please stop, we don't want any trouble. We're just here to trade," said Jacob trying to diffuse the situation.

The man was having none of it. Refusing to let the matter go, he continued, now getting closer to Jacob's face. It was apparent that Jacob was a good foot taller than the Englishman who looked him up and down. An inspection of sorts. "You're kind'a pale for an In-yan ain't ya? And ... you talk weird. Are you a white man?" The Englishman reached over and pushed Jacob's bangs up and off his face.

Instantly, Fights Bear's powerful hand snapped out like a rattlesnake and clamped onto the Englishman's wrist. The grip was so strong the his hand instantly turned a blueish white.

"All right, let's not go getting out of control. You don't want to end up in the brig do ya'?" squeaked the Englishman.

Jacob turned to Fights Bear and said quietly in Ojibwe, "Let his hand free. It's okay." Fights Bear let the wrist free and spoke to Jacob in Ojibwe.

The Englishman asked, "What's he saying?"

"He said if you leave now you might live." The man laughed, but quickly the laugh faded into a subtle cough. He backed up, turned away, and walked toward the fort. He looked back and Fights Bear took a step toward him, faking he was about to give chase. The man shifted from a casual walk to a full-on run. Jacob laughed and Fights Bear chuckled along.

Inside the trading post a wooden carved counter dominated the room. Against one wall was a huge pile of furs. The daily take of the Hudson's Bay Company. Behind the counter were all the trade goods. Blankets, gunpowder kegs, fishing nets, decorative beads, fabric, knives, kettles, barrels of whiskey, and more. It took another half hour before Jacob and Fights Bear reached the counter and it was finally their turn. In an unmistakable Scottish accent, the trader working the counter asked, "What ya' got der?"

"Six bundles of pelts. Ninety pounds each," Jacob said, attempting to project authority with his squeaky pre-adolescent voice.

The Scot adjusted the tam o' shanter bonnet on his head then slid a leather-bound ledger close. He grabbed the edge of the page and flipped to the next. The Scot rose higher in order to see over the counter and looked down at the bundles at Jacob's feet. "I only see two bundles."

"The others are at the canoe," answered Jacob tilting his head in the direction of the river.

"You don't look native. Are you Ojibwe?" asked the Scot.

Jacob became a bit flustered by the question. He hesitated for an instant, then answered, "Yes. Lake of the Woods band."

"That's a long trip to York from way down there." Now getting a closer look at Jacob's face, the Scot was struck with a feeling of recognition. He dropped his pen onto the counter. It was somewhat the appearance, but mostly the voice. That little remnant of Swedish accent.

"Swede boy? That you?" There was a pause and the Scot continued, "I'm fair puckled, but I think I'm seein' a ghost. Is ya' little Jacob Fahlstrom?"

Jacob stood wide-eyed like a rabbit caught in a snare. He had hoped that he wouldn't encounter anyone he knew at the factory, much less be recognized. The Scot continued, "That is you. Thought for sure you was a gonner."

Fights Bear was beginning to get agitated by the exchange. Jacob turned to him and explained in Ojibwe. He assured Fights Bear it would be okay. Then Jacob turned back to the Scot and said, "Yes, I'm Jacob Fahlstrom."

"Did they kidnap ya'? You weren't tortured was ya'? I'll arrest that backwoods savage right now."

Jacob swallowed hard, then calmly began, "You shouldn't talk about people like that. Hunters from the tribe found me in the woods. They saved my life."

The Scot continued, "Keep yer heid. No reason to get upset." The Scot pushed up Jacob's chin to get a better look at his face. "Well, I'm glad ya' didn't meet yer' maker out der in those woods. I'm William Louttit from the Orkneys. I was on the Eddystone wit' ya'. We came across togetter. Don't ya' member?"

"You taught me to load a musket," acknowledged Jacob.

"That's right and ya' did pure dead brilliant Swede Boy." The Scot paused and decided it was time to dispense with the idle chitchat and get down to business. "Okay now we can trade, and I'll give you a good, fair price for yer pelts." He examined the furs in the bundle. "These are pure barry. Real good. Deep winter fur?"

Jacob responded, "We only trap in late winter. It's mostly beaver. Some lynx and otter mixed in but not many. We also have four buffalo hide blankets."

Becoming a bit more serious, the Scot noted, "Now, like I said, I'll make a trade. But ya' know I'll have to tell Captain Macdonell that you're here at the factory. You're under contract."

"William, can't we just do the trade then I'll leave right away. No one will know," pleaded Jacob.

Rubbing his forehead and eyes the Scot was torn. "I want to help you, you know I do, Jacob. But I just bloody can't." There was a pause then the Scot continued, "The Captain is a fair man. He knows you're just a boy. But you do owe some years of service to the H.B.C. fer your passage."

Hearing their discussion, an English soldier who was patrolling the trading post approached the counter and addressed Jacob, "I'll escort you to the captain. Your..." The soldier paused looking at Fights Bear trying to guess their connection.

Jacob chimed in, "...friend."

The soldier continued, "Your, uh, friend can stay with the pelts."

In Ojibwe Jacob explained to Fights Bear what was happening and tried his best to reassure him that it was okay.

Fights Bear squinted at Jacob not feeling good about this. "I will come too," insisted Fights Bear.

"No, you have to stay here with the pelts," Jacob said sliding one of the bundles toward Fights Bear with his foot as the soldier grabbed Jacob's upper arm.

Bright shafts of light beamed through multiple windows in a long, high-ceilinged hallway. As Jacob and the English soldier approached a closed door, loud yelling could be heard coming from inside Captain Macdonell's office. The door opened and a short Irishman carrying a stack of papers scurried out like a bug fleeing a swatting hand. The soldier stepped inside the doorway with Jacob. The captain gestured for them to enter. The room was large and almost entirely empty except for a small wooden desk and chair in the middle of the room. On the wall behind Captain Macdonell hung a large H.B.C. flag. Jacob and the soldier approached the front side of the small desk. The soldier spoke, "We've found a deserter, Captain."

"I'm not a deserter. I was lost in the woods," protested Jacob.

"Silence!" the captain yelled, his deep baritone voice echoing around the cavernous room. "You will speak only when spoken to and I, only I, will determine who is, or is not, a deserter." He stood, adjusted the front of his wool britches, and walked around the desk.

He looked down at Jacob, rubbing his five o'clock shadow. The whiskers were so coarse the scrunching sound of his fingers rubbing against the whiskers filled the room. His head tilted to the side. "You're Swede Boy," the captain said. Half statement Half question. "I'll be bloody god damned. We lost you over by Lake Winnipeg. How did you make it? That's the deep-ass woods. Swamp, wolves, bear, thick underbrush for hundreds of miles..."

Wondering if it was now okay to speak, Jacob's questioning eyes rose to meet Captain Macdonell's. "Go ahead," urged the captain.

"I was in the woods. Drank lake water. I ate cattail roots. Then I got trampled by a moose. I thought I was gonna' die, but an Ojibwe hunting party found me. They took me back to their village and I've stayed among them. A woman at the village helped me recover from my injuries and takes care of me. You have to let me go back."

Banging his fist on his desk Macdonell shouted, "I don't *have to* do anything." He reached back toward his desk and grabbed a document. He displayed the paper right in front of Jacob's face. "See that. That's your signature. You have two years left until the termination date of your contract and that doesn't even cover the time you've been absent. What would you suggest I do? Just let every man who signs a binding contract with the H.B.C. go ahead and wander off into the woods to play Indian?" There was a long pause. "I'm askin' you a question Swede Boy," yelled Macdonell.

"I'm not playing Indian, sir."

Macdonell surveyed Jacob from head to toe and added, "You sure as hell look like it."

Jacob urged, "I live with these people now. I'm not playing anything. I want to go back."

"I admire your guts Swede Boy. You come in here lookin' like an uncivilized savage..."

Jacob interrupted, "Please don't call us that."

"What did you say?" screamed Macdonell, loud enough to make the windows rattle.

Jacob went on, "I just don't like it. It's not fair, sir. The tribe isn't uncivilized. We just look at the world differently ... care about different things."

The captain sat on the corner of the desk, thought for a moment, then pushed further, "You're really one of them?" Jacob nodded his head. "And they trust you?"

Jacob answered, "Yes, sir."

A bit of a smile found its way onto the captain's face. "Not the worst thing in the world to have one of my men on the inside, closely connected to Ojibwe fur trading partners right in the heart of North West Company territory. How big is this tribe? How many pelts do you think you could get us next year?"

Jacob answered, "About eighty in the tribe. Thirty warriors. With a full season of trapping, I bet we could bring in at least twenty bundles. There are some nearby tribes we're on good terms with as well. I might be able to get even more furs from them."

The captain put his hat on and walked across the room toward the door. Puzzled, the English soldier spoke up. "Sir? What do I do with him?"

The captain stopped and turned his head. "Get him a musket, provisions and as many traps as we can spare. Schedule an Orkney boat to rendezvous at Jack River post next spring."

"Sir?" The soldier was now entirely confused.

The captain continued, "I've just promoted Swede Boy ... I mean Mister Fahlstrom from laborer to H.B.C. fur trading agent for the Rainy River district. I'll get you the paperwork in the morning." Macdonell continued walking toward the door.

Completely stunned and not knowing what to say, Jacob mumbled, "Thank you sir."

"I'm not doin' you no favors Swede Boy. I see an opportunity to bring in a nice pile of furs and I'm takin' it." The captain walked through the door then abruptly stopped and turned back to Jacob. "Now Mr. Fahlstrom, if you run off or don't come in with my twenty bundles of pelts next spring, I'll track you down and you'll hang." Jacob's eyes widened as the weight of the captain's words sank in.

Ka-thud, ka-thud, ka-thud. Macdonell's boot steps echoed as he walked down the hall.

With the few hours that remained of the day Jacob negotiated the trade of their six fur bundles. In return they received six powder horns and four kegs of gunpowder, five trade guns, beans, salt pork, hard biscuit, metal pots, blankets, flint & steel, and other goods. Jacob, in his new position as trading agent was also provisioned with new doeskin breeches, a capot for winter, and an English military "Brown Bess" flintlock rifle. This Brown Bess was a cavalry issue short barrel. Just twenty-six inches in length, the barrel was lightweight and maneuverable, easy to carry and load. A good marksman could get off four shots in sixty seconds. The barrel opening, designed to accommodate the .75 caliber ball, was large and intimidating. Not many get shot by a ball that size and live to talk about it. No one is certain how the gun got its name. The English soldiers claimed the name was in honor of Queen Elizabeth. Jacob thought the gun was impressive with its dark wooden stock, silver flintlock mechanism and gold butt plate.

Trading was done for the day and Jacob, Fights Bear and Flowing Creek set up camp for the night. Fights Bear and Flowing Creek were sitting next to a roaring fire. Flowing Creek grabbed a pinch of tobacco out of his side pouch and stuffed it into the wooden tip of a long pipe. Flowing Creek said, "Oza Windib, sit and have a smoke with us."

Jacob finished storing some of his gear then answered, "I have to walk a bit. Trying to find an old friend."

"Want me to come with? Shouldn't be wandering around by yourself," said Fights Bear.

"It's okay. I'll be back soon." Jacob turned and walked off. For the next hour he wandered about the York Factory grounds scanning for the familiar lodge of his friend Akami, an old Cree man who befriended him when he first arrived at York Factory. Akami was the one who taught Jacob how to speak Cree, Ojibwe, and so many other things. Jacob worried that he couldn't find Akami or even his lodge. After all, Akami was at York Factory in the winter because he was too sick to travel. Jacob checked the cemetery but didn't see anything. He hoped that was good news but wasn't sure. There wouldn't typically be a grave marker for a Cree trapper. Would he even be buried in the cemetery at all?

As he walked back toward the fort, some huskies ran past, and Jacob called out, "Two-Eye? Is that you?"

Then Jacob whistled in a manner that resembled the song of a golden-winged warbler. Suddenly one of the dogs froze in his tracks, turned, and sat at attention. The huskie tilted its head curiously. Jacob yelled, "Two-Eye!" The dog ran full speed and jumped up at Jacob's chest almost knocking him over. Jacob stumbled backward and went down on one knee. He rubbed the dogs head and looked into his eyes, which were two different colors. One blue and one brown. Jacob laughed out loud as the two fell over sideways. Spruce trees swayed in the gusting wind. In the distance storm clouds rumbled and flickered with light.

It was July by the time Jacob, Flowing Creek and Fights Bear were back on Lake of the Woods. Jacob sat atop the heap of cargo in the middle of the birch bark canoe. A swirling gust of wind blew his long blond hair in all directions. First forward across his face, then whipping back and upward on his head. For the first time since being rescued by the hunting party, Jacob was not self-conscious of his hair color. In fact, on this day he wore it proudly. The canoe bounced up and down in the deep white capped waves. One wave, which seemed to have a mind of its own, pushed the canoe sideways causing Jacob to fall backward. Fights Bear roared with a laugh. A bit angry Jacob yelled in English, "Oh yeah, real funny."

Fights Bear replied flatly, also in English, "Oh yeah. Real funny." To this Jacob cracked up and all three men laughed together. By sundown, with loons singing their whimsical night song in the distance, they arrived back at the village. They were home.

Chapter 6. Ojibwe Ways

Over the passing months Jacob became more assimilated into the tribe. In every way, except for his white skin, Jacob was Ojibwe. Though only thirteen, his trading connections with the H.B.C. and his ability to speak multiple languages elevated his status. The problem was that he was not of pure Ojibwe blood. This made the tribal leadership skeptical and made him a continued target of bullying. Most everyone in the tribe kept Jacob at arm's length. They remained uncertain about the strange blond-haired boy.

Thunder Bear, feeling it was his responsibility to his mother, took on the role of mentor to Jacob. They'd spend hours wandering the woods and navigating rivers. Thunder Bear taught Jacob how to track large prey like deer, moose, and elk. He showed him how to set and bait traps. After months of work, Jacob was able to survive for days without a weapon or food. Jacob loved exploring and wanted to be a great woodsman and fur trapper. He listened intently to everything Thunder Bear said and mimicked everything he did. Others in the tribe often joked that Jacob was Thunder Bear's blond shadow.

On a walk through the woods, Thunder Bear reached over and put a hand on Jacob's shoulder.

"You need to slow down, Oza. Think more, do less. Listen more, learn more. The woods will teach you if you observe her closely. Slow down, breathe, and think. That's how you live long enough to be a cranky old man with no hair like Mitsqualli." The two began to laugh. Jacob wondered if maybe Thunder Bear's resentment was diminishing a little bit.

Thunder Bear pulled a long strip of buffalo fur from his bag and tied it around Jacob's head, covering his eyes. "I'm going to go off into the woods and you need to find me with your ears. You'll hear sounds of the woods, and you'll hear sounds kind of like the woods, but not quite right. That will be me."

"But how will..." Jacob began.

He was interrupted by Thunder Bear. "Shhh, no talking, just listen Oza. Listen and think." Thunder Bear then ran off at full speed leaving Jacob standing alone, his eyes covered with the strip of buffalo fur. Jacob stepped carefully trying not to trip and fall. He noticed how the fur blindfold smelled like the smoke of burning pine logs.

Okay, stop being distracted, he thought to himself and began listening ... really listening to the woods. He could hear the tweet of sparrows, robins chatting to one another, the tapping of a distant black-backed woodpecker and the scurrying of some small creature, most likely a rabbit off to the right, about thirty feet away in the underbrush. Creaking spruce limbs could be heard above as a faint whistle of wind pushed them into a slow sway. Then, there it was, tapping on a distant tree. But too off-cadence to be the woodpecker. It was Thunder Bear. Jacob walked cautiously in the direction of the tapping. He reached out in front of him, swimming his way through the forest trying to avoid whacking his face on a tree. He walked and listened.

Suddenly, to his left, the whistle of the wind took a melodic turn that just wasn't normal. Jacob turned and headed that direction. Jacob walked another forty feet. Now, what was the forest telling him? He heard the howl of a wolf. Laughing out loud Jacob yelled, "A little obvious don't you think? A wolf howling this early in the day?" He headed in the direction of the wolf howl. *Hmmm, that's strange*, Jacob thought as he could now smell burning sweetgrass in the complete opposite direction of the wolf howl. *Could Thunder Bear have moved that quickly? Doesn't seem possible.* Regardless, Jacob turned and headed toward the sweet smoky aroma as that was certainly a clue. *Is Thunder Bear playing a trick of some kind?*

Jacob stumbled his way awkwardly through the trees and down a sloping ravine. He could now hear running steps coming from the same direction as the burning sweetgrass. The steps made a loud *swoosh, swoosh, swoosh* as the powerful strides ripped through tall grass. Then Jacob heard Thunder Bear yell, "Oza, lay down on the ground. Now."

Why was he ruining the game, Jacob wondered, but he did what his brother instructed because he trusted him. Falling to his belly he could hear the *woo-whish* of feathers as an arrow flew just overhead. He then heard the arrow hitting its fleshy target and the thud of something heavy hitting the ground and sliding across the dirt not more than twenty feet away. Jacob sat up, pushed the buffalo fur blindfold up onto his forehead and turned. There lying on the ground was a gray wolf. There was foam around its mouth and an arrow through its heart. It was a large wolf, must have been at least 120 pounds, but its coat looked mangy and the froth at the mouth indicated disease.

"It must have the drooling sickness," said Thunder Bear, crouching down to examine, but careful to keep his distance. He used a stick to push the animal's lip up to get a closer look at the teeth and gums. "See how wet the fur around his mouth is? They become confused, lost, and scared." After a contemplative pause, Thunder Bear continued, "Which makes them dangerous. It's sad I had to kill him. But he would have died soon anyway."

"You're starting to care about me," Jacob said. Thunder Bear did not reply, so Jacob continued, "Just a little bit. You might even like me."

Thunder Bear looked over at Jacob.

Jacob looked intently at Thunder Bear, then noted, "Well. At least you didn't say no."

Somewhat annoyed, but knowing Jacob was right, Thunder Bear simply turned away and began walking down a well-worn trail. Jacob rose to his feet and followed. On the way back to the village Thunder Bear taught Jacob how to throw people off his trail with what he called "footstep tricks." He explained how you could walk on your toes to make it seem you are tracking game quietly. Walking backward for a great distance to mask your direction. Carrying a heavy object to make deeper footprints. This makes the tracker think you're carrying a large animal after a hunt or carrying furs. Obscuring footprints by sweeping with a branch, then throwing a few leaves and stones over the area to make it appear natural and undisturbed. Using water to erase your path. Climbing up into trees and across trees to throw off your trail. And creating multiple paths by walking a distance, matching your footsteps walking backward then going off in multiple directions repeating this. This technique could make your tracker think you are an entire group of men, not just one. Thunder Bear stressed that knowing how to throw someone off your trail simultaneously teaches you how to trail others.

"Isn't that a lot of extra work and time?" asked Jacob.

Thunder Bear walked a few steps, walked backward in his footprints then jumped up into a tree. He looked down at Jacob. "You can never be certain which time it will be wasted time or which time it will keep you from getting your throat cut."

Wind howled through the pines on a dark and cloudy night. Leaves swirled beside the water's edge. The river churned with whitecaps and a birch bark canoe bobbed up and down. Jacob, who sat on the canoe's floor, scraped a flint against steel and a spark fell to the tinder he had gathered. He turned his back, shielding the growing flame from the wind that seemed to be trying everything it could to extinguish the flame. Water splashed up over the side of the canoe into Jacob's face. The cold sting of the water made him shiver. Thunder Bear laughed at Jacob's unfortunate dousing. He held out a torch and Jacob lit it ablaze with the flame. Thunder Bear held the torch out over the water to attract fish. Jacob stood next to him with his elbow bent and a spear held next to his ear poised to strike.

"The water bends the light to trick you, so don't be fooled. Strike to the side of the fish. That's where he really is," said Thunder Bear in a low whisper. In the water, just below the surface Jacob could see several fish. Must have been six or more. He focused on the largest one and lunged down hard with the spear. The spear sunk into the mucky bottom of the river. This continued for a long time. Jacob repeatedly attempted to spear the fish. Many times, Thunder Bear pleaded with him to stop, complaining that it was cold, and they could try again another day. But Jacob refused to give up. They stayed out on the river for more than two hours, as Jacob would not stop until he speared two fish in a row. By the time he accomplished this Thunder Bear was frustrated, cold and tired. He was ready to lose his temper with Jacob just about the time he speared two fish on consecutive lunges with the spear. At this Thunder Bear and Jacob both cheered loudly. An owl near the river hooted its disgust with the noise.

In the distance, a man's voice erupted from a wigwam, "Shut up! It's almost morning." Jacob and Thunder Bear looked at each other and began to laugh. They tried hard to control the volume, so the laugh came out more like a choking cough mixed with yodeling.

In the north, winter never knocks at the door. It kicks it in and throws stuff at you. In fact, of all the seasons, winter is by far the orneriest. Summer heat can be uncomfortable, sweaty, and sometimes stinky, but winter will kill you. On Lake of the Woods in January a burning fire is the only thing between you and winter's icy fangs. Your joints cramp up and skin cells can meet an icy death in minutes. Yep, winter literally hurts, so it's a quiet time in the Ojibwe village, a time of huddling around the fire in the lodge, telling stories and sharing laughter. Other than daily checking and setting of beaver traps, it's time to stay inside.

One particularly cold night, Blue Jay's wigwam glowed with a sliver of pre-dawn sunlight. She sat up and looked over at the pile of blankets where Jacob should have been sleeping. Noticing the fire had burned down to embers she added another couple logs then walked out into the brisk wind. Her dark black hair waved and fluttered. She scanned the horizon and there, by a leafless maple tree, sat Jacob poking the snow with a stick. Funny how a benign act as simple as poking the snow with a stick can communicate so much about a boy's state of mind to an observer. Blue Jay knew Jacob was upset. She walked over and gently caressed his blond curls.

Blue Jay knelt beside him and asked, "Where's your mother?" She leaned forward, attempting to look him in the eye. "Jacob, I will take you to her. I want you to be happy. Do you know where she is?"

Jacob tilted his head up, now facing Blue Jay. With trembling emotion in his throat, he began, "I was supposed to be a big brother." Jacob stopped talking for a long time. His back moved upward with a quick breath, the way it does when people try to hold back tears. "Something was wrong. Everyone started yelling, crying and they pushed me out of the room." With tears welling up in his eyes, Jacob continued, "They should've let me stay."

Blue Jay, with her bulky, but soft, doeskin mitten, wiped a tear off Jacob's cheek, "Oh, Jacob ..."

"She didn't hug me back," said Jacob.

"Oh, Jacob."

"When they let me in the room, she didn't hug me back." Jacob paused with a sniffle. "She didn't ..." Jacob's voice trailed off into a high-pitched sob. After a long pause he continued, "I always told her how bad I wanted a brother. Maybe it's my fault? She shouldn't have had more kids..."

Blue Jay placed her hands on Jacob's cheeks, "Oh, Jacob, no. It's not your fault." Jacob turned away from her and wept quiet. She gently grabbed his chin and turned his face toward her. She moved in close and said, "Jacob. It's not your fault."

There was a long moment of silence, then Jacob answered, "I know. But it feels like it is."

Blue Jay hugged Jacob. She rubbed the top of his head and asked, "What about your father? Where is he?" Jacob stared off into the distance as if he didn't hear her. "Jacob?" questioned Blue Jay.

Jacob rubbed his eyes and shook his head. "My father was always hard on me. He thought it would make me strong. He didn't beat me. So, I should be thankful for that, I guess. But, so many times, I wished that he would've. A good slap would've let me know that, at least, he was paying attention to me." After a long pause Jacob continued, "Ya' know that man never once told me he loved me." Blue Jay pulled on Jacob's arm coaxing him up. The two walked over to the wigwam, entered, and sat down next to the fire. After several minutes of staring into the burning flames Jacob continued as if he had never stopped. "After Mom died it got worse. I think looking at me made him think of her. It made him sad ... and angry. Can you imagine your father being angry with you ... just for existing? I wasn't much better, I acted bad and disobeyed him all the time. I wouldn't eat, ran off for hours, I broke things around the house on purpose. I think I just missed being loved." Jacob walked over to the woodpile, grabbed a piece of split pine, and threw it on the fire. "My mother was so gentle and patient. I always knew she was there for me ... no matter what. That's what she wrote in the bible she gave me." Jacob pulled the small black book out of the pocket of his leather pack. He opened the book and there on the inside cover was text, beautifully handwritten. That handwritten note was all Jacob had left of his mother or, for that matter, his entire family. He touched the words his mother had written as he read in Swedish, *"Oavsett vad."* Then he repeated the words in Ojibwe. "No matter what." Blue Jay looked closely at the words on the inside cover of the book. She touched them softly. Jacob looked at her and continued, "At bedtime she would come into my room to tuck me in. Before she left, she always asked, *'How do I love you?'* Then I would always answer ... *'No matter what.'* And she would say, *'That's right.'* Then tickle me, make a funny face, or kiss me all over the top of my head. I missed that when she was gone."

Jacob stood and walked across the wigwam. "My father was a merchant sailor. He was always gone, mostly traveling east to Russia and Lithuania carrying lumber and iron to trade for pottery, spices and other artifacts. Once Mom was gone, he would arrange for me to stay at the neighbor's house. But, if he was going to be gone only a short time, I would stay by myself at home. During one trip I was home by myself, and it had been longer than usual. The food in the cupboards was almost gone and I began to worry. Then I was excited to hear a knock on the door. My father was finally home. I ran to the door and flung it open. But standing there was not my father. It was my uncle Andrew. His eyes were red and watery as he took off his hat and crumpled it in his hands. I knew what he was going to say before he opened his mouth. He told me that my father's ship was attacked by raiders, and they stole everything. He said they must have been heavily armed. None of the crew survived the attack. Then, he said the words, *'Your father didn't survive.'* He said how sorry he was. I yelled, *'No! It's not true! You're lying.'* I ran up the stairs and locked myself in my room. I still have a hard time believing that my father is dead. I know it's true in my mind, but there was never a funeral. Never a burial. Never a goodbye. They said the ship wasn't discovered until many days after the attack. The bodies were in no condition to be transported, so they were all laid to rest in the Baltic Sea. They assured me that a preacher prayed for his soul, but that didn't mean a whole lot to me. My parents weren't the church going kind." Jacob was feeling exhausted. He sat down then sprawled out on the blanket. Looking up at the smoke leaving the small hole at the top of the wigwam he said, "I've been so alone ... for so long." Blue Jay leaned over and pulled Jacob close. Close enough for their hearts to feel the beating of the other's. Jacob pulled away a bit, not knowing how to handle the affection, but Blue Jay pulled him in even closer.

Chapter 7.
Sweden

March 1810. Gothenburg, Sweden.
Three years earlier.

It was a brisk, foggy morning. Seagulls squawked as they soared above the frigid water. A large merchant ship entered the Port. Carved into a wooden plaque on the rear of the schooner was the name Uppsala.

On deck a young boy ran toward the captain's quarters. The wavy blond hair is a dead give-away. It's Jacob, three years earlier. This was the time shortly after his father's death. Jacob was taken in by his uncle Andrew and served as a cabin boy on his uncle's vessel. His uncle taught him well in the ways of the sea and Jacob became a skilled navigator and sailor. But his uncle never treated him like family. Maybe he just didn't have it in him. Maybe, as the captain of the ship, he didn't want to show favoritism toward his nephew in front of the crew. Either way, Andrew expressed no love. He was a harsh man with a short temper and an unhealthy attachment to the bottle; most days drinking himself beyond shit faced. Andrew was abusive. On several occasions he hit Jacob hard enough to draw blood. With Andrew, Jacob had a source of food and shelter, but he certainly didn't have much more than that.

Jacob, now at the door of the captain's quarters, pounded loudly informing his uncle of their arrival in Gothenburg. Inside, Andrew crawled out from under the covers and staggered across the wood planked floor. His foot struck a bottle knocking it over and spilling the remaining drops of whiskey.

It took a few hours to load the Uppsala with iron, tar, and lumber. Once ready, the schooner and crew continued their journey to London. The sun was just beginning its ascent over a calm Baltic Sea. The merchant vessel was nothing more than a dot on the horizon as an orange band of light burst in every direction capped by billowy clouds of white and infinite shades of gray.

Days later, the Uppsala reached the North Sea, the shallow northeastern arm of the Atlantic. With the low-lying nature of much of its southern coast, the North Sea can experience storms with disastrous tides. That potential of danger stood in sharp contrast with the festivity that erupted every time the Uppsala would pass a fishing vessel. A waving of flags and sounding of horns would commence.

As the Uppsala neared England Jacob looked out over the churning water then up at the dark clouds. He didn't like what he saw. Having grown up on the sea, Jacob was familiar with indicators of an approaching storm. This one felt like a bad one. The cold breeze was foreboding. As lightning crackled its way across the clouds, Jacob ran to his uncle's cabin and pounded loudly on the door. No answer came, as Andrew had over-sampled the rum stock again. He was passed out on his cot. Jacob ran frantically from crewmember to crewmember trying to sound the warning, but with no captain on deck, the crew was unresponsive.

"We have to change course eastward! We're headed straight into a squall," Jacob yelled in an effort to be heard over the howling wind.

At the wheel of the ship, the first mate looked down at Jacob and answered, "We'll do no such thing. To change course now will make us late for our delivery."

Jacob approached the first mate and begged. "If you don't

change course now there'll be nothing to deliver." Waves splashed over the bow and soaked the deck. Jacob pleaded one last time. "We gotta' lower the sails." He pointed upward. "Look. They're ripping from the riggings."

"Quiet, damn it! Or, I'll have you confined to quarters," threatened the first mate. The storm hit with terrible ferocity. The ship bobbed up and down, frequently disappearing in the massive troughs. You could hear the wood groaning as the ship bent and twisted from the sheer force of the sea. Overhead thunder rumbled across the sky. Jacob scrambled for cover. Water was leaking between the wrenching timbers of the hull. Lightning crashed as massive waves washed across the deck. Jacob held onto the boom with all his strength. Cold, wet wind blew in his face and soaked his blond curls. Now he was terrified. The ship went sideways, and a massive wave pushed the starboard side with such force it turned the vessel over. Jacob was tossed into the frigid water and was narrowly missed by toppling masts and rigging. He clung to a floating piece of wooden decking that bobbed up and down amongst the waves. A large whitecap washed over Jacob's head submerging him under the surface. Once back above, Jacob was choking for air and spitting up the salty, gritty water. He clung to the floating piece of wood, kicked his feet, and paddled as hard as he could toward shore. As he bobbed up and down between the waves, he could see lanterns burning in the distance. A large wave pushed him with so much force he lost his grip on the piece of wood. He sank deep under water. The tossing waves made it difficult for Jacob to know which way was up. He reached his arms above his head and pulled against the water. Continuing this for several seconds, Jacob was losing breath. He kept pulling at the water. Just when he thought he might black out, his head cut the surface and he gasped for air. As his lungs were filling, another wave pushed water into his mouth. Jacob choked and coughed up water. He turned his head in all directions, then located the lantern lights and swam toward them.

"Hello! Is anyone out there? Hello," a man yelled with the raspy old voice of a seaman.

Jacob was elated. Someone was close. "I'm here. I need help," yelled Jacob with as much volume as he could muster. Jacob could now hear the sloshing of oars through the water. He yelled again, "I'm here."

"There! Over there. Look a boy is in the water," yelled a man in one of the boats with two others aboard. Both were soaked having been retrieved from the water. The men hoisted Jacob over the side of the boat. He continued to spit up water and choke. Lying down on the floor, Jacob said a silent prayer as the oars sloshed and pulled their way to shore.

The failure of the crew to make proper course corrections proved disastrous. The ship was shattered to pieces by protruding rocks and sank to the bottom near Herne Bay, England. Fourteen men were lost, never to be seen again. Another deposit into Davy Jones's Locker. Had the Uppsala been further out at sea it's doubtful there would have been any survivors. Good fortune was on their side. Men on shore had witnessed the toppling ship and rowed boats out to the debris, rescuing some before the tossing waves could pull them under.

The next several days were spent trying to salvage what remained of their cargo and any other items they managed to pull from the water. The iron hopelessly sank to the bottom and the tar made a horrible mess. The lumber was the only cargo the crew was able to recover. Andrew Fahlstrom secured a small freighter to haul the lumber up the Thames River to London. On the way, mass destruction from the storm was evident. Uprooted trees lay along the shoreline and numerous roof tiles floated in the water. Buildings had broken windows and chimney stacks were knocked over by the brute force of the wind. A foul odor filled the air as dead fish and birds littered the waterfront.

In London Andrew sold the lumber to raise money for passage back to Stockholm. Unfortunately, instead of finding transport, the surviving crew found the local pubs and gambling halls. A good portion of the money was gone. Back at the Inn, barely able to stand upright, Andrew hovered in the doorway to Jacob's room. He placed a hand on the doorframe to steady himself then belched loudly. Jacob feared his uncle in this condition.

"What are you looking at?" The words spilled out of Andrew's inebriated mouth like water splashing over the side of a glass. "Why did I get stuck with a motherless waste? You can't even navigate my ship." The words cut into Jacob's heart. He pulled the covers over his head to tune out the stammering drunkard, hoping he would just go away. But a fury raged inside of Jacob. It bubbled over and he was unable to restrain himself.

From beneath the covers Jacob fired words of defiance. "It's your fault!

"Whaaatt?" slurred Andrew.

Now popping up from under the covers Jacob yelled, "That's right. The Uppsala went down because of you. I tried to warn you, but you were too drunk. Too drunk and too stupid."

Andrew wobbled toward Jacob. "You worthless orphan." He picked up Jacob and threw him against the wall. Jacob crashed down on a table, turning it into a pile of kindling in the process. Andrew staggered forward, but with the advantage of not being a drunken asshole, Jacob was able to slip by him and head out the door. He ran full speed into the shadowy gas-lit streets of the East End. This was London's most destitute and crime-ridden neighborhood. Though, to call it a neighborhood was a bit of a stretch. Maybe a term like slum is a more appropriate description? Jacob ran past homeless old men curled up near buildings, sailors brawling, and prostitutes purveying their wares. He ran until the birds began to chirp and the sun showed itself on the horizon.

Never again would Jacob hear from his uncle. Never again would he return to Sweden. Whether Andrew went straight back to Stockholm or searched London to find Jacob it will never be known. Jacob had escaped, but to where and to what?

Chapter 8.
East End Wharf

On a night darkened inky black by storm clouds, Jacob walked down an alley that smelled like the inside of a goat's colon. London had recently experienced rapid population growth to almost one million sacks of pasty white flesh. This population swell and rapid industrialization were causing, to put it lightly, severe issues. There was choking, sooty fog. The Thames River was thick with human sewage, that would often catch fire. The streets were covered with mud, but upon a closer whiff, any nose could tell you it wasn't mud at all. Horses, being the primary method of transport, left behind thousands of pounds of plump and squishy brown apples every day. Street sweepers would clear the way for rich people to cross the road without "dirtying" their shoes. Coal powered the city and chimneys belched dark smoke all day, every day. Orphans roamed the streets because disease and factory life caused the death of many parents. Alcohol and opium addiction only made the problem worse. The children with parents didn't have it much better. Child labor was rampant with many working for little pay in extremely dangerous conditions. Often the children were "sold" as pauper apprentices. To call it anything other than slavery was simply a lie constructed of untrue words and terminology.

Jacob was weak with hunger. He had gone two days with very little food. He crossed the street and snuck into the pens at

Smithfield Market to steal feed from the sheep troughs. He grabbed as much slop as he could scoop up with both hands. It dripped between his fingers as he walked. He sat in the filthy street eating his prize. The slop looked twice as bad as it smelled and tasted even worse. After choking down the last bite Jacob was startled by the approach of a woman so large, she jiggled when she walked. She wielded a broken pitch-fork handle and gave chase, testing Jacob's ability to make a run for it. The woman with bloated ankles pursued Jacob across the many winding animal pens and into a narrow alley. She was gaining and about to grab Jacob's collar when, suddenly, a hay cart rolled out in front of them. Jacob slid on his side under the cart, leaving the woman and her bloated ankles behind. She yelled hysterically. Jacob was certain that the woman was yelling vile curse words, but he didn't speak English. He had no way of knowing for certain what spewed from her mouth.

Feeling the presence of another person in the alley behind him, Jacob slowly turned. It was dark, but the silhouette was clearly that of a young boy. The shadowy figure motioned for Jacob to follow. The two ran for several blocks, darting down alleys and cutting through shops until finally getting far enough away from the hefty woman to feel safe.

Now, under the flickering light of a gas lamp, Jacob got a closer look at the boy. He had a large scar that ran from the edge of his mouth to his ear on the left side of his face. His jacket was covered with soot and torn in several places. He wore a large, black-rimmed hat and a kerchief stuffed into his shirt. It appeared he was trying to dress like one of the city's high society types, but the smudges of dirt on his face, his bare feet and the ill-fitting nature of his ensemble revealed him as the street urchin he clearly was.

A language barrier stunted communication. Edmund began to speak, and Jacob raised his hand stopping him. Then in Swedish, explained that he did not speak English. They were able to exchange names and with hand gestures they got by. The boy's name was Edmund. He was very thin and short. Jacob thought his general demeanor simply didn't match his age. The look in his eyes seemed akin to that of an old man. Projecting a long life already filled with trials, devastations, and pain. Edmund's parents both died of cholera two years previous. He now worked as a climbing boy to a chimney sweep. Beaten, exploited, and abused, Edmund never knew what it was like to have a full belly or a good night's sleep. His childhood was over before it had begun. Often his master, with complete disregard for Edmund's safety, would light a fire under him to quicken Edmund's departure up the chimney. At times he was shackled with irons on his ankles to prevent his escape. Jacob felt a renewed appreciation for the life he had with a mother who loved him deeply, a home with everything he needed, and an impressive level of freedom for a young boy. He felt ashamed for under-appreciating what he had. Well, at least what he used to have.

Edmund led Jacob into an abandoned old building that looked like it had been taken apart then put back together with a bunch of pieces missing. The wooden floor was warped from years of rain leaking through the mostly shingle-less roof. At the end of the hall there was a large barrel blocking a doorway. Edmund moved the barrel aside and the two walked in. The room was large, but only a small corner of it seemed to be inhabited. Old cots and wooden boxes defined the space. There were piles of straw with blankets where people were sleeping.

Edmund announced, "I found another vagabond for our crew." The others, now struggling to wake, sat up and looked toward Edmund and Jacob.

"Who's that? We don't need nobody else in our crew. New kids is nothin' but trouble," blurted a tall, black-haired boy with dark brown eyes that seemed like bottomless pits beyond his frail and sunken sockets.

"Come on, Charlie. You were new once. He's a good chap. I can vouch for 'im," pleaded Edmund.

"No way. He'll probably steal everything we got," retorted Charlie.

Edmund chuckled as he approached Charlie. He put his hand on

Charlie's shoulder. "Like we have anything worth stealing?" Charlie and the others laughed along as Edmund did have a point. "We can always use someone who can run. You should see this blondie go. I tell ya what, he could help as a runner to create diversion or somethin'."

Charlie replied, "We got our crew. Don't need some blond oddity standing out and getting us caught." After much debate, no final decisions were made. But begrudgingly, they agreed to let Jacob stay the night. Maybe they thought he might be a good addition. More likely, they were just too tired to argue with Edmund anymore. They all went to sleep, so Jacob found a spot in the corner where he curled up. He was out cold in seconds. This was the first time he had slept in more than 40 hours.

The next morning, in the light of day with the loud chatter of seagulls coming through a very large hole in the roof, Jacob got a better look at the crew. They were a scraggly bunch. Their time living like a pack of wolves showed. There was Charlie. He never had a father and ran away from his mother, an opium addicted prostitute. Elizabeth, the only girl in the group, had long brown hair that she wore pulled back into a ponytail. She had a natural beauty that rose above her sorry situation and the drabness of her clothing. The other two boys, Henry and Otto, had been together the longest. It had been four years now surviving on the streets for them. They were both about eleven years old, but neither knew for sure when their birthday was. The group gathered to eat what was left of some stale bread and moldy fruit.

"We need to go down to the financial district and find some rich people to give us some ... uh, donations," said Otto. By donations, Otto, of course, meant that while one of them engaged the person, the others would pick their pockets.

Charlie tossed aside an apple that was just too disgusting to eat. "Yep! Time to fill our pockets."

Edmund chimed in, "Let's have Jacob help. Prove his worth, ya' know."

Charlie busted out laughing. "Yeah, right. What good would he be? He can't even speak English."

Edmund went silent and his right eyebrow went up as a brilliant idea struck him. Funny the way an eyebrow can be connected to brain activity like that.

On Lombard Street, in the heart of the financial district, carriages creaked and rattled past in a bustle of activity. Horses dumped their smelly cargo, splatting onto the road. The crew emerged from a garbage filled ally, Charlie leading the way. The upper crust of London society was out in full regalia. There were large crowds of people milling about. Many gentlemen in fine-tailored suits and ladies with ornate dresses walked toward their restaurant or coffeehouse of choice. Otto and Henry were collecting tips for placing their jackets over the piles of horse-poop so the socialites could cross the street without soiling their shoes. Edmund pushed Jacob toward a tall woman wearing a red dress with a fox stole draped across her shoulders. Jacob approached but said nothing.

The woman said, "What is it, boy?" There was a long pause as Jacob did not know what to do. "Spit it out, kid. Why are you delaying me?" insisted the woman.

Her date stepped up with a scowl on his face. He looked down at Jacob and said, "Come on. This street rat will just try to steal something from you. Let's go."

The man tugged on the woman's arm and was coaxing her away when Jacob spoke up in Swedish. "I am lost. I need help."

Having no idea what Jacob was saying the woman asked, "Do you speak English?" Jacob just stood there with a blank stare.

"Come on," her date urged, still pulling on her elbow.

Jacob continued speaking in Swedish.

The woman pleaded, "We have to help this poor boy. He doesn't even speak English. I think he is lost."

Now getting frustrated, her date pulled a shilling from his pant pocket and handed it to Jacob. As he did this, Charlie stealthily extracted a silver watch from the man's coat pocket.

Jacob stood there for a moment, then the man yelled, "Go on

now! Off with you." With this Jacob sprinted off toward the pre-arranged meet-up place. When Jacob arrived Otto, Edmund and Charlie were already counting their loot. Jacob was holding out his hand with the shilling. Charlie snatched it from his palm.

Otto said, "Jacob, you did good. Nice work." Jacob, not able to speak English, simply nodded, thinking their smiles must mean they said something positive.

Edmund walked over, shook his head up and down slowly, then smiled a huge smile at Jacob. He said, "Good! You ... did good."

Jacob picked up the meaning and smiled. He parroted, "You did good." Otto walked up and patted Jacob on the back. The crew had found their brilliant scheme to get rich. Of course, to them, getting rich meant they'd be able to eat for a couple days. It worked flawlessly. Jacob's innocent appearance combined with his blond hair and Swedish language was a gold mine. The ladies would always take pity on him, and the crew would do their thing. They worked this angle for many months. Along the way, Jacob acquired a pretty good grasp of the English language. Or at least the English spoken by his new crew. They spoke a crude street version of the Queen's English laced heavily with obscene expletives and slang. This foul-mouthed language was called "the water dialect," referring to the locale from which it was spawned. The East End.

Jacob earned friendship among the group with his knowledge of the sea, sailing, and how to navigate by the stars. He refined his ability to speak English through his storytelling. Almost nightly, he would tell stories of sailing voyages, monsters that live deep in the woods, and Viking tales. These were the stories his mother told him as a very young boy. As time went on, the other children grew attached to Jacob. They were amused by the clever endings of his stories and his sense of humor. They also found it hilarious when Jacob sang Swedish folk songs. The entire crew would laugh hysterically. Not because Jacob couldn't sing. He, in fact, had a good singing voice. They simply found his Swedish accent hilarious. So, never one to shy away from getting a reaction, Jacob sang frequently.

Chapter 9.
Best Friend

Thunder shook the clouds overhead. An East End cannery rooftop was cloaked in opaque darkness lit only for fleeting seconds by the flash of distant lightning. Two silhouetted figures sat under a tattered awning. The rain fell in that way that made it seem like the sky was leaking, maybe crying. Jacob and Edmund leaned back as close as they could to the brick wall, but the rain was relentless. It mocked them. The awning was an inadequate shield, its fabric streaked with large tears and gaping holes. Edmund turned toward Jacob with rainwater dripping off the side of his face. Through shivering lips, he asked, "What do you want Jacob?"

There was a pause as Jacob pondered what his friend was getting at, then Jacob asked, "What do you mean, Ed? I'm just sitting here. I don't want anything. Except maybe a roaring fire ... and an umbrella." Jacob laughed, proud of his joke.

"No, I mean what do you want for your life?" Ed pushed, wanting Jacob to be serious for once.

Feeling the demeanor of Ed's tone, Jacob looked up at the clouds, thought for a couple seconds then answered, "I guess I never thought about it much."

Ed continued, "You gotta' know what you want. Gotta' have a dream. Otherwise, how do you know when you get there?"

"You make a good point," confirmed Jacob somewhat flippant.

"I'm serious, Jacob. When a stupid dream's the only thing you got to live for, what else you got to do but dream." Ed threw a loose piece of brick. It skittered across the roof and bounced over to the next. "When your life is this bad, you gotta' think about the way it should be, Jacob."

"You're a deep thinker. That's what I like about you," said Jacob, then he asked, "What do you want Ed?"

Ed took a moment to gather up all the thoughts he had on this topic. For years they'd been banging around in the back of his head. Now he finally had someone to share them with. "I want to have people that care about me. I want to be self-sufficient ... and not that stealing crap that we do. I want to earn my own way, not taking it from someone else." There was a pause as Jacob soaked it in and Ed savored the sound of finally saying these words out loud. "You know what I want most of all?" asked Ed. "I don't want anyone to own me. No chimneysweep ordering me around. I don't want to be a chimneysweep's slave anymore. I want my life to be my life. No one else's."

Jacob nodded his head as Ed spoke. He smiled, then said, "I like what you want Ed. It's a nice dream."

Somewhat frustrated, Ed pressed his point. "It's not a dream. It's a plan. I'm gonna' make it happen one day." Ed walked over to the building's edge. He pointed to the dark silhouetted ships in the harbor and added, "I'm gonna' hop on one of those ships and get the heck out of this god damned place." After a pause Ed continued, "As long as I believe and keep trying, it'll happen."

Jacob interrupted, "Ed, I believe you. And I believe that someday we're gonna' make it happen." Jacob thrust out his right hand toward Ed and said, "Shake on it!" Ed reached out, firmly grabbed Jacob's hand, and shook.

The two thoroughly soaked East End gutter rats took one last lingering look at the ships on the wharf then decided to make a run for home. They'd already done all the lingering they could trying to wait this storm out. Lightning flashed through the clouds as they sprinted off into the night, splashing through ankle-deep puddles.

...

Ed had to work all day and often into the evening, as did Charlie and Elizabeth. Jacob, having grown up the son of a well-to-do merchant, was quite shocked by their work schedules. Henry and Otto, along with Jacob, spent their days scavenging or stealing food and trying to stay dry. They told each other stories, played jokes on people in the city, and on each other.

The crew was constantly on the lookout for the "buzzards." That's what Otto called the men who made their living capturing vagrant children and forcing them into "apprenticeships." In 1800s London, an apprenticeship was basically slavery in all but name. This practice was completely legal, so if you were caught, there was nothing to be done. The police supported it.

At night, Charlie, Elizabeth, and Edmund would return with porridge slops and black bread to share. Jacob always anxiously awaited Ed's return. Ed was Jacob's closest friend among the group and the two stayed up late at night counting stars, playing cards, and reminiscing about the loving mothers they both were missing so much. Were it not for Ed's job, or "slavery work" as they called it, they would have been together every minute of the day.

...

Jacob and Ed ran down the street at full speed. They darted behind a cluster of bushes. A police officer trailed behind blowing a whistle. Jacob and Ed watched quietly as he passed by. Once the officer was safely out of earshot, they burst out laughing. The boys walked to the street's edge and sat. Jacob reached into his pocket and retrieved a cigar they had just snatched from the humidor shop. He passed the cigar to Ed who lit it and began puffing. Smoke wafted above their heads.

"Jacob, tell me a Viking story," Ed begged.

Jacob thought for a moment, then began, "Okay, I'll tell you about Odin."

Ed questioned, "Who's Odin?"

Jacob smiled, entertained by the way Ed could never just let a story be told. He always had to interrupt with questions.

Jacob said, "If you'll keep your knickers on, I was about to get to that. Odin is the all-father of the Viking people. My people. He is the most powerful of all gods. He only has one eye because he gave one up to get supreme knowledge and wisdom. He has two ravens, Huginn and Muninn, that sit on his shoulders. Every morning Odin sends out Huginn and Muninn to oversee and gather information. They fly all over the world and bring important messages back to Odin. Imagine that; every day, they fly across the entire world."

Ed jumped in, "Wow, the whole world?"

"Yes, Ed. The whole world. That's what I just said. Right?" Jacob stood and picked up a long narrow tree limb from the ground. He broke off the remaining branches and held it like a spear. He continued the story. "Odin has a magical spear called Gungnir. When he throws it, the spear never misses its target. It's said that the Sons of Ivaldi made Odin's spear. The Sons of Ivaldi are tiny gnomes who live in the deep forest."

"Is that where Odin lives, Jacob? In the deep forest?" asked Ed.

Jacob rolled his eyes, then continued, "No, the forest is great, but not great enough for the likes of Odin. Odin lives in Asgard, the home of the gods located in the sky. Asgard has many realms. The greatest of all the realms is Valhalla. This realm is ruled by Odin. There is a great hall with walls made of solid gold."

Seeing that Ed was about to again interrupt, Jacob held up his hand gesturing for him to keep quiet. He chuckled a bit, then continued, "This great hall is called 'the hall of the slain.' Warriors who bravely die in battle on earth arrive at Valhalla where they spend all day fighting and killing each other then they're brought back to life and spend the night feasting on an endless supply of pork."

Ed, not able to restrain himself, interrupted. "Pork? Why pork? Have you ever seen pigs? They eat their own poop."

"I don't know, Ed, that's how the story goes. They feast on pork. Poop eating pork."

Ed crushed out the cigar, flicked it away, and asked, "Well, why not beef? Seems more of a rewarding meat. Higher class, ya' know."

Jacob scratched his forehead in frustration and answered, "Okay, Ed, for you, we'll change a story that's been around for a thousand years. I'm sure the most powerful god in all the universe won't mind. The meat in the story is now beef." Jacob cupped his hand as if whispering to an unseen person. "Sorry, Odin, we had to change your thousand-year-old story because my friend Ed has a problem with pork. I hope you don't mind."

Ed laughed, then punched Jacob in the arm and took off running. Jacob chased him down and put him in a headlock.

"Say I'm the smartest person in the world and I'll let you go," said Jacob.

With a strained voice, Ed answered, "No way. I'll never say it."

"Come on, say Jacob's the smartest."

"Never!"

The two boys laughed, and Jacob let Ed out of the head lock.

. . .

It was a particularly dark afternoon in London. Not due to weather, but because of soot that billowed from the numerous factories. The crew was running their "Swedish Scam" in the wealthy shopping part of town. A group of men departed a suitor shop and walked toward Jacob. Spotting and deciding to target the most ornately dressed gentleman, Jacob approached. He began telling his sob story in Swedish. He told how he was lost and starving to death;

that he didn't know anyone in the city. He put a pathetic look on his face and paused, as this was the point in the story when most targets of their scam would get confused, throw up their hands, and just start giving Jacob food or money.

Jacob was stunned when the gentleman answered in Swedish. He said, "I speak some Swedish. It is limited, but I can follow what you are saying. My name is Thomas Douglas, Fifth Earl of Selkirk. I am sponsoring an expedition to North America with the Hudson's Bay Company. If you are in such a horrible situation, I offer you no handout, but rather hope. You could sign up for my expedition with the H.B.C., committing to five years. You get fare to cross the ocean and regular pay." Lord Selkirk retrieved a rolled-up paper from his pocket and handed it to Jacob. He continued in Swedish, "Here's a pamphlet with the information. My colleagues will be down at the harbor in the coming days recruiting fine young men like yourself. Now keep your chin up son and stay positive." Then, just like the conversation never happened, Lord Selkirk switched back to English and continued his conversation with the group he was walking with. Jacob looked at the pamphlet for a moment, then shoved it into his pocket. Quickly he ran across the street and pretended to fall. Right in front of a finely dressed woman. She helped Jacob up off the sidewalk and smiled. Jacob dove right into round two of the "Swedish Scam."

Chapter 10.
A Bad Day

Jacob, Otto, and Henry were playing a dice game, gambling for their individual pieces of bread. It began getting dark, and, as usual, Charlie and Elizabeth returned from their slave jobs, or as the buzzards called them, apprenticeships. Ed wasn't with them. The group carried on as normal as it wasn't out of the ordinary for the children to return late. But, as the hours passed, Jacob was becoming more concerned. He was uncharacteristically quiet as the group sang songs and played sword fights with wooden sticks. Finally, it became too late to stay awake and one by one they fell asleep. All, that is, except Jacob. Worried about Ed, he tossed, turned, and stared at the ceiling.

As the morning sun cut through the fog, Jacob was awakened by clopping hooves and the creaking wheels of a horse-drawn delivery cart. Two old men in tattered clothes lifted Ed, who was moaning, out of the back of the cart. They set him on the ground and left. Jacob looked out the window and saw Ed lying at the edge of the street. As fast as he could, he ran down the steps. Jacob knelt beside Ed. His trousers were soaked with blood on the left thigh. Jacob lifted Ed's head onto his knees to comfort him. "What happened Ed?"

"Mr. Garner was yelling at me to get to work. He told me he was going to 'knock out my brains' then he pushed me. I fell off the roof.

I think my leg broke," Ed said, gesturing to his upper thigh. "I can't stand on it." Whether Ed drifted off to sleep or whether he passed out from severe pain, Jacob was not sure. He struggled to carry Ed up the stairs and made him as comfortable as possible.

Leaning over Ed, who was lying atop a pile of hay on the floor, Jacob said, "You hang in there. I'm going for help." He jumped to his feet and ran to the door where he paused and looked back at Ed. Jacob felt sick to his stomach. He ran as fast as he could to the hospital. He burst into the hospital lobby, but he was stopped by a woman who came from behind the desk and grabbed his arm. She would not let him in. Jacob pleaded with her as she forced him out the front door and into the street. Now locked outside, Jacob pounded on doors and windows begging for help, but no one would respond. Patients and doctors paid no attention; one nurse simply closed the curtains as Jacob pounded on a side window with tears welling up in his eyes. Police officers approached and Jacob had no choice but to run off.

Ed's wound turned bright red and was filled with a yellowish puss. As Jacob dabbed sweat off his forehead, Ed said in a weak voice, "Don't die like this Jacob."

Jacob interrupted, "You're not dying. There's no way you're dying."

Ed, slurring his words due to pain and delirium, said, "Get out of this place, Jacob. Do our plan. Do anything you can to get out."

Concerned Jacob answered, "We'll do it, Ed. Just like we said. But you have to get better first."

With as much strength as he could muster into a forceful voice, Ed pleaded, "No. No, Jacob, you have to go. Listen to me. And take this." Ed pulled a caramel-colored agate stone from his pocket. He handed it to Jacob and said, "It's all I have in the world, and I want you to have it." Jacob began to say something in response, but Ed cut him off. Ed said, "Take it. And you have to go." Jacob took the agate stone and put it in his pant pocket. Ed's eyelids fluttered and, once again, he fell from consciousness.

Ed would never regain consciousness. Two days later he was gone. Jacob went into a rage when he discovered Ed, pale and no longer breathing. He punched the wall until his knuckles bled. Only Otto tackling him and holding him down made Jacob stop. Lying on the ground Jacob looked up at Otto. "We have to bury him. Where can we bury him?"

Otto answered, "We just put the body in the street and collectors will take him when they come by."

"They're not taking him. We're not letting them throw Ed onto a smelly pile of dead vagrants and burn him. We can't let that happen. We can't."

"We are vagrants," Otto said.

"Maybe we are, but Ed's not," insisted Jacob. Otto let loose of his arm, and Jacob rose to his feet. He stood with his back to Otto looking out through the dangling chards of a broken window.

Otto put a hand on Jacob's shoulder. "You're right. We're going to do this. For Ed."

Chapter 11.
A Place to Say Goodbye

Jacob leaned against an old shack and whistled, indicating it was safe for Otto and Elizabeth to cross the street. The late afternoon sun was low in the sky. Their bodies cast long shadows as they quietly crawled up beside a street cleaner's cart. The street cleaner was distracted getting a bucket of oats for his horse. Jacob grabbed a spoke on the cart's wheel and pulled himself up. There, protruding from a pile of horse shit, was a long-handled shovel. Slowly Jacob reached out, grabbed it, and the three of them ran off. Their sudden movements startled the horse, causing a snort and whinny. They ran for two blocks, then feeling safe, slowed and began walking. Then, from behind a door stoop, out popped the street cleaner. He was a tall muscular man with dark hair. Jacob tried to run off, but the man was quick. He grabbed Jacob by the shirt collar. The street cleaner pried the shovel from his hands. "Why would you steal a poor man's shovel? Isn't it bad enough I have to shovel horse shit all day to feed my children?"

"I'm sorry, I didn't mean ..." stuttered Jacob, his voice cracking slightly.

Now quite angry, the man said, "I should turn you over to the buzzards. You deserve it for what you've done."

"We needed the shovel ..."

Cutting Jacob off, the man questioned, "What could possibly make you need a shovel so bad you'd be willin' to starve a man's family?"

Jacob wiped the sweat out of his eyes and looked up at the man. "My friend Ed, a boy like me, died. We live in the alleys down by the Thames. We don't want the street crews to burn him in a pile of dead people. He deserves a proper burial. To do that ... we needed a shovel." Jacob hung his head and sniffled. The man, taken aback, paused for a long time then responded, "Where's the boy?"

The street cleaner emptied the cart's foul contents then Jacob led him to the docks and into their alley fortress. There, cold and pale, laid Ed. His eyes wide open as if he was focusing on something across the room. But there was nothing behind those eyes. The spark was gone. Ed was gone. The street cleaner reached for a blanket that hung from a clothesline and yanked it down. He gently moved Ed's body as he wrapped him in the blanket then lifted him up. He carried Ed over and gently placed him into the cart.

The sun was setting, and smokestacks billowed steam in the distance. Jacob sat in the back of the cart, his legs dangling and bouncing from side to side, as it bumped its way along the cobblestone street.

It was somber and silent for a long time when Jacob turned toward the street cleaner and asked, "Where are we taking Ed?"

"I know where there's a grove of trees and some open land between factories." After a moment with no response from Jacob, the street cleaner continued, "It's a nice place to lay Ed to rest. I promise."

Jacob looked down at the shape under the blanket still not quite believing his friend was gone. *How could he be gone? He just laughed with him a few days ago.* Jacob turned to the street cleaner and said, "Thank you for helping us." Then his voice trailed off, "No one helps us."

"What's your name?" asked the street cleaner.

"I'm Jacob Fahlstrom."

"You have an odd accent. You're not from England, are you?"

"I was born in Sweden. I was on my uncle's ship when we wrecked off the coast near Herne Bay."

The man questioned, "Where's your uncle now?"

"He went back to Stockholm," answered Jacob, giving no further detail.

The man questioned, "He left you here? How could he leave you here?"

"He didn't. I ran away. It's complicated," Jacob answered.

The street cleaner, now beginning to get a better picture of what was going on, probed further. "Your parents?"

"Gone," answered Jacob abruptly, then continued, "They died two years ago so I went with my uncle ... but he was too unbearable to stay with. I was better off taking my chances in the streets. I do miss the ship life, though. I was pretty good at it."

"I bet you're quite a sailor indeed, Jacob. We have to get you off these streets. London isn't a good place for orphan children, or pretty much anyone who's not rich. Have you tried to get on with any of the ships down at the docks?"

"No. I've been living with the other kids. But I do need to find a way out. Me and Ed, we had a plan to get out. Well, really more like a dream."

The man suggested, "I've received letters from my brother in Glasgow. He told me about a journey to America that will depart Stornoway, Scotland this June. They're recruiting men to work for the Hudson's Bay Company. I have a mind to go myself."

Jacob asked, "Why don't you?"

The street cleaner shrugged and turned back toward Jacob. "I have a family here and the journey would be too difficult for a family. But, not for you Jacob. You're young and strong with your whole life ahead of you. Hell, if you can survive the beasts on the East End, you have nothing to worry about in the wilderness of North America. Right now, you're livin' a life just as frightening as a pack of wolves or a war party of Indians. What have you got to lose?"

Jacob shrugged and the two went silent for the next several minutes. Jacob pulled the pamphlet Lord Selkirk had given him out of his pocket. Jacob studied it more carefully this time and thought about it more seriously than he had to this point.

The cart wobbled up a dirt path into a grove of trees. Once they were deep enough in the wooded area, where they would not be discovered, the man pulled on the reins and stopped the horse. The man jumped off the side of the cart grabbed the shovel and began digging. Jacob walked over and stared for a very long time contemplating the finality of that hole in the ground. This was the end for Ed. Nothing more. No more laughs or good times. No more Viking stories. The thought of it made Jacob tear up. But, on the good side, no more bad times. No more working for that vile chimney sweep. Such an abrupt end to a life. How much time did Jacob himself have left? After all, this was certainly not the first ending Jacob had witnessed. His little baby brother, his mother, his father ... now, Ed. It was incredible how much more important every day—every second in fact—seemed when he contemplated the finality of that hole in the ground.

The man walked past Jacob, approached the cart, and reached in.

"No," said Jacob. "Can I put him in the ground? I feel like I should be the one to do it."

"Sure, Jacob."

Jacob reached up into the cart grabbing the edges of the blanket. He slid Ed's body closer to the edge where he was able to lift. It was incredible how heavy even a tiny person like Ed could be. Struggling a bit, with sweat beading up on his forehead, Jacob slowly walked to the hole in the ground. He went down on one knee and as gently as possible lowered Ed into the four-foot-deep hole. Jacob turned, looked up at the street cleaner, and asked, "What should we say?"

"You just say what you feel. How you cared about him. Why you'll miss him. Stuff like that," suggested the man, fighting back tears of his own.

For a long time, Jacob struggled to find the words, worrying he might say the wrong thing. Then he turned back to the hole in the ground and looked down at the shape beneath the blanket. In a soft, barely audible voice he said, "You took care of me when I didn't know what to do. I'd be dead if you wouldn't have found me. You convinced the crew to take me in. You shared your food, even when it meant you had to go hungry. You protected me from the buzzards. You made me laugh harder than anybody. Oh, man, you made me laugh." Jacob wiped a tear off his cheek with the sleeve of his jacket. "I never told you. I wish I would have. I pretended in my mind that you were my brother. I should've told you that." Jacob sniffled loudly and went silent for several seconds. "Damn it, Ed, get up out of there and come home with me." There was another long pause, and the street cleaner was just about to speak when Jacob continued. "You were my friend when I didn't have any in the world. Now what am I supposed to do? What the hell am I supposed to do?" Jacob, finding more words too painful, simply left it at that. There was a long silence, then to the street cleaner, Jacob said, "Ya' know, I don't even know Ed's last name. Do you think it will be okay for Ed in heaven if they don't know his last name?"

"Ed will be just fine, Jacob. God knows his name."

Jacob looked up at the street cleaner, not certain he had done well. The man smiled with the corner of his mouth and nodded to Jacob affirming that he did a good job. The street cleaner was touched by this young boy so lost in a city so overcrowded and so polluted.

Deeply moved the street cleaner offered, "You want to shovel some?"

"You can do it," answered Jacob. He stood motionless, listening to the repetitive sound of metal thrusting into the ground and earth thumping into the bottom of the hole. Jacob watched, one shovel-full at a time, as the blanket and the life of Edmund disappeared forever. No one else in the world noticed, except for a soft-hearted street cleaner and a homeless blond-haired orphan from Sweden.

Chapter 12.
Hudson's Bay House

May 22, 1811
London, England

Horse-drawn carriages clicked across cobblestone on a morning warmer than most with white puffy clouds floating overhead. Frenchurch Street was abuzz with activity. The city's upper crust had places to be. Men navigated their way amongst the commotion sporting dapper woolen coats, ruffled white shirts, and top hats made of the finest beaver pelts. Ladies dressed in high society gowns strolled along the walkways. The heavy dew of late spring glistened on the finely maintained grass of the public square. Just across the street was Hudson's Bay House. The opulent brick and stone headquarters of the Hudson's Bay Company.

Inside the four-story structure, several men sat at a very large table loaded with a bounty of food and drink. These men were among the wealthiest of London's elite society. Senior executives of the largest fur trading company in the world. Across the table from the H.B.C. executives were representatives of the North West Company, their largest rival. Some might say, more than rivals. The two companies were engaged in something more akin to war than a business dispute. The Nor'Westers, led by Edward Ellice and Sir Alexander Mackenzie, joined the meeting in an attempt to obstruct

Lord Selkirk's plans for his farming settlement on the Red and Assiniboia Rivers. A location that is today Winnipeg, Manitoba, Canada. The Nor'Westers currently had a strong foothold in the Assiniboia region, so though they knew this attempt to block Selkirk's plans had little chance of success, they were intent on doing everything possible to interfere and slow things down. Lord Selkirk had applied for a grant through the General Court of the H.B.C. The agreement was basically this: Lord Selkirk was to transport recruits to a farming settlement to be created and, in exchange for land, the settlers would provide York Factory with the food the H.B.C. required to expand trade operations throughout the region. The H.B.C. saw this as a key initiative that would help them expand trade further to the west.

As the plans of Selkirk were read to the General Court, the Nor'Westers held a united front of sour faces. As the clerk continued reading, William Mainwaring, the Governor of the H.B.C. , leaned back in his chair with a pleasant smile on his face. It looked promising that he would provide his signature and finalize the deal.

It was now time to hear the Nor'Westers rebuttal. They noted the difficulty of populating a wilderness so distant from a seaport. They then went on to insist that Selkirk's settlers would compete directly with the North West Company.

Simon McGillivray, of the North West Company, stood up and without a shred of evidence said, "It has been found that this form of colonization is unfavorable to the fur trade." Given the fact the opposition had this opportunity to go on the record, one might have thought they'd be more thorough. This, however, was nothing more than fearmongering and an attempt to sink the scheme on procedural grounds. The weak performance scarcely did justice to the serious predicament being faced by the North West Company.

The reading of the Selkirk agreement followed. Among those present, only Sir Alexander Mackenzie had any real comprehension of the vastness of the 116,000 square miles of territory on both sides of the present Canadian American border, which Selkirk was being granted in return for a nominal rent and some services to the Company. This primarily involved the recruiting and transport of up to 200 effective laborers annually for ten years. After discussion the matter was put to a vote.

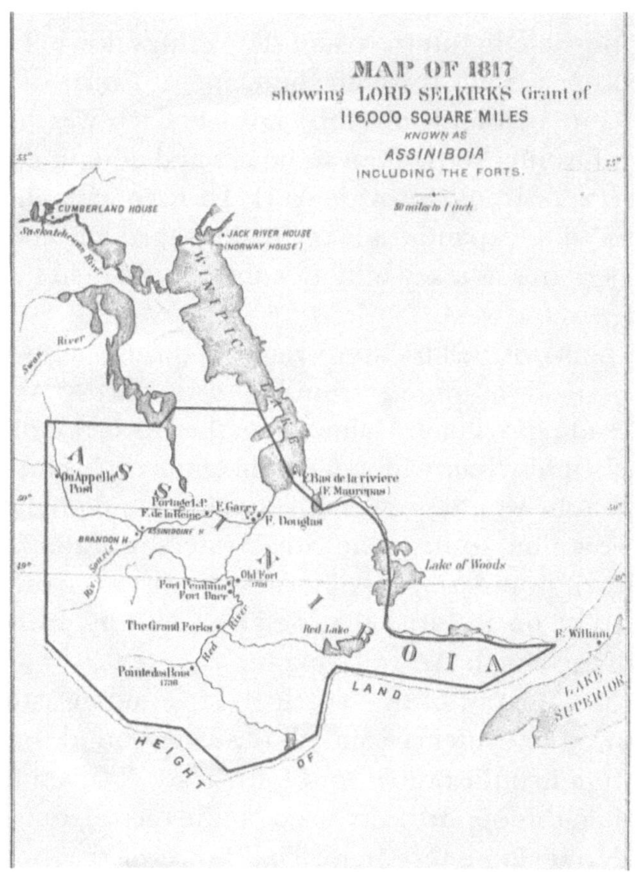

Outside the door, Selkirk's chief agent, Miles Macdonell, paced the hall anxiously. The lunch and meeting had drug on for more than three hours. Macdonell passed the time straightening paintings and obsessively rearranging flowers that sat atop pedestals along the hallway. He leaned against a table to rest his legs then adjusted the collar of his suit and the cuffs of his shirt. Suddenly, the large wooden doors flung open as Sir Alexander Mackenzie stormed out. Two Nor'Westers walked at his side. Macdonell stepped back around a corner and could hear Mackenzie speaking.

He said, "This Selkirk scheme strikes at the very root of the North West Company. They intend to ruin us. It's a crazy plan to locate a farm settlement out in the middle of nowhere. Farm settlement, my ass! This plan will lead to a violent competition in the fur trade in a place far removed from the protection of justice. Just one of our interpreters could set the natives of the region against the settlers at any moment of our choosing. The H.B.C. better know that I will do it. Damn right I will."

The threats were bold, but unfortunately, the Nor'Westers operated under the false belief that their dominance in the west, particularly the rich Athabasca region, gave them some kind of ownership when, in fact, much of the region was the property of the H.B.C. by royal charter. These conflicting realities made negotiations virtually impossible. It would foster extreme conflict from this day forward. The spark had been set in the kindling.

Chapter 13.
H.B.C. Contract

A batch of oatmeal bubbled and steamed over a cast iron stove in a small soot-covered kitchen. The scent of burning pine and sweet honey filled the air. A tall, thin woman wearing a woolen shawl and twelve years of motherhood opened the stove door and tossed in another log. Candles lit the early morning darkness.

Preceded by the clatter of multiple unseen footsteps, six children swarmed the large table and wreaked havoc on the morning peace. At the end of the table sat the street cleaner. He was feeding a baby, perched on his lap, while simultaneously sliding a bowl of porridge to his four-year-old daughter with curly brown hair and large hazel eyes. Jacob, who had spent the night at the street cleaner's house, awoke. He stood up from his bunk, which was just across the room. He walked over and, following a gesture by the street cleaner's wife, took a seat at the table.

"Jacob, this is my wife, Elizabeth," said the street cleaner, having to yell over the commotion.

"Hi, Jacob, I hear you're from Sweden."

"Yes, mam," Jacob said.

Too busy with the children, Elizabeth gave a quick smile then continued her work. The street cleaner pulled a crumpled paper out of his pocket and pushed it over to Jacob who now sat beside him. Jacob opened the paper as a bowl of porridge was plunked down in front of him. He examined the pamphlet closely. There was a sketch of ships in open water, a map highlighting a settlement offering free land, and details about ships leaving Stornoway, Scotland in June. This pamphlet had much more detail than the one given to Jacob by Lord Selkirk previously. It also noted that transport was to cost nothing for the poor. No one would be rejected on account of religious belief and all creeds were to be treated alike. The colony was to be called Assiniboia, after a tribe of the Sioux nation, the Assiniboine. The Assiniboine were buffalo hunters on the Great Plains.

"Where is Assi-ni-boi-a?" asked Jacob, struggling to read the word. Jacob now spoke English well, but still struggled to read the English text.

The street cleaner leaned toward Jacob. "It's in America. Some men down at the docks were talking about it. It's hope for a better life, Jacob. Thomas Douglas, the 5th Earl of Selkirk is starting a farming colony there. Sign on for five years as a laborer with the Hudson's Bay Company and you get free passage across the Atlantic. Be part of the fur trade in America Jacob, can you imagine?"

Jacob noted, "But I don't know about fur trading."

"It's not about fur trading Jacob. It's about freedom. It's about making your own future. It's about getting away from that stinking alley you live in. Getting away from the buzzards who would have you enslaved."

Jacob looked out the window of the stone shack and paused for a very long time. Then he opened his mouth as if he was about to speak, but rather picked up his spoon and shoveled some of the sticky breakfast goop into his mouth. He chewed it slowly.

The street cleaner watched very intently and asked, "Jacob?"

Jacob swallowed then looked over at him. "How do I get on that ship?"

The street cleaner's very serious expression twisted up into a smile as he banged a fist on the table in joy. "What a bricky boy you are Jacob. Oh, the adventures you'll have. Yesterday there were men recruiting down at the docks. Ships depart London for Stornoway in a few days. That's the gathering point for all the recruits. You better get down to the docks before the other wharf rats beat ya' to it."

As he silently finished his bowl of oatmeal, Jacob pondered a life in the wilds of America. This was a way out of the East End, just like he and Ed talked about.

...

A dark gray sooty fog hung over London's East End as drizzle fell. Jacob ran down the street and turned into an alley. The crew's alley.

There, rolling dice against a brick wall, were Henry, Otto, and Elizabeth.

"Jacob, come play with us," urged Otto."

"Can't. I'm going to the docks to join a voyage to America. You should come."

"How are you getting to America, Jacob?" Elizabeth questioned.

"If I sign up for five years with the Hudson's Bay Company, they pay for my passage aboard a ship."

Henry chimed in, "That's great Jacob. Go from nightmare to night terror. Brilliant."

"Its gotta' be better than these stinky streets. The fresh air alone will be worth it," pleaded Jacob.

Otto laughed and put his arm around Jacob's shoulder. "Ooh, right you are. It'll smell all fresh and dandy as the wild Indians pluck the scalp off my head. Count me out."

Jacob pushed Otto's arm aside. "Are you sure? I won't ask again."

"Nope," Otto and Henry said in almost complete unison.

Elizabeth looked closely at Jacob, studying his face to capture it in memory. "I won't forget you, Jacob Fahlstrom. Come back and sweep me off my feet when you've struck it rich in America!" She stepped closer, hugged him, and gave him a gentle kiss on the lips.

"Ooooohhh, are you two getting hitched or something?" joked

Otto.

"Shut up Otto," Jacob said abruptly, but with a smile. A lull of quietness overtook the group. Jacob sighed and asked, "You're sure?"

Having returned to their game of dice, they piped, "We're sure." With that, Jacob turned and slowly walked away.

As he reached the end of the alley, Elizabeth yelled, "Goodbye Jacob Fahlstrom! Good luck!"

Otto added, "Don't get eaten by wolves!" Jacob looked back one last time before turning the corner and forever leaving the East End of London.

It was a twenty-minute walk to the docks. Jacob navigated his way across the splintered and warped boards, looking all around for signs of Selkirk's recruiters. There seemed to be a large gathering past the dockyard gates in front of the Woolwich Clock House. A short man with wavy bright orange hair was standing in the back of a horse-drawn cart. Posters were up on the brick wall behind him touting the Selkirk journey and settlement. Pamphlets were being handed out. This was it. Milling about was quite an assortment of characters. Experienced sailors wanting their next voyage, country farm workers seeking land of their own, soot-covered factory workers looking for a better life, street vagrants and criminals looking for a fresh start and wharf rats, like Jacob, seeking adventure and a way out. Even a few upper-crust society gentlemen attended, curious about their chances to expand their wealth, or in some cases, rebound from unfortunate business failings in London. Their clothing identified their status in life as blatantly as if written signs hung from their necks. The orange-haired man chattered on about the opportunities that abound in America with the Hudson's Bay Company and the Selkirk Settlement that would be located at the confluence of the Red and Assiniboine rivers. His high-pitched, but booming voice echoed off the brick buildings. Jacob struggled to follow the man's strong Scottish accent. But, after all, did the details really matter? To Jacob, this was his chance for something better. A way of keeping his promise to Ed. He was going no matter what the orange-haired man promised or didn't promise. Fact of the matter was that Jacob had nowhere else to go. He found a spot at the back of a long line that extended from a small desk with a pile of papers and several quill pens.

After a long, sweaty wait Jacob reached the front of the line. There a man with a narrow face and pointy chin peered up over the top of his spectacles. "Interested in joining the Selkirk voyage?"

"Yes, sir. What's the pay?" Jacob asked shyly, having never been paid a wage before.

"Well, as you are young, I can't pay you the wage of older men. Is that a problem?"

"No sir. I'll work hard and always be on time. What is it I'll be doing?"

"Can't say exactly, the Hudson's Bay Company will assign your work once you reach York Factory. Maybe you'll have to hunt and kill bears?"

Jacobs eyes widened. "Bears?"

"Yup, they're thick in those woods," the recruiter said, breaking into laughter. "And there are tribes of savages. Probably dog eaters and cannibals."

Jacob's mouth curled in a tentative smile. "When do we leave?"

"Ships depart London Harbor in a few days. You'll meet up with the others in Stornoway; from there, you're on your way across the North Atlantic and into Hudson Bay." The man quickly shifted from the details of the voyage. "Name and birth date here," the man instructed, pushing a paper across to Jacob and pointing with his ink-stained finger to a line at the bottom of the page. Jacob wrote his name and birth date. Noticing the date, the registrar said, "Umm, well I couldn't possibly sign up a child of eleven. I'm sorry, it's not allowed." Jacob's shoulders dropped and he slowly turned away on the verge of tears.

He walked a few steps, stopped, and turned back toward the registrar. "I've got nowhere else to go."

The registrar shook his head, looked around, rubbed his pointy chin, then said, "However ..." The pause hung in the air like the tail of a kite just waiting for Jacob to grab it. Then the registrar continued, "...if you were ... say a boy of fourteen. Now that would be altogether different."

Jacob looked the registrar in the eye and with the straightest face he could muster, said, "I am fourteen, as it turns out."

The registrar pushed the contract once more toward Jacob, "Of course you are." In his haste to do the math quickly, Jacob made an error when scrawling his date of birth. He entered 1793. Correcting Jacob, the registrar laughed. "So, now you're eighteen, are you?"

Realizing his error Jacob wrote a five over the three. "Okay, sixteen it is," the registrar said waving Jacob past as he filed the contract in a metal box sitting at his feet. "Next!"

. . .

Historical note: A Minnesota Territorial Census of 1857 listed Jacob's date of birth as 1802. This is most likely Jacob's actual birth date and is supported by additional documents that place him at the age of nine when he shipwrecked off the coast of England aboard his uncle's merchant ship. It is very unlikely that Jacob was born in 1795 or 1793, the dates most frequently noted in historical records. This author assumes it is quite likely that Jacob lied about his age to sign on with the H.B.C.

Chapter 14.
Stornoway

Selkirk appointed three men as recruiters to travel to Ireland and Scotland: Miles Macdonell, the man Selkirk had already named governor of the Selkirk colony, Roderick Macdonald, and Colin Robertson.

Miles Macdonell, who was a Catholic, headed to the western coast of Ireland where Selkirk hoped a shared religion would help in the recruiting efforts. Social and religious persecution against Catholics and devastating crop failures left Irish workers seeking new opportunity and hope. Just what Macdonell intended to deliver with the Selkirk Settlement; freedom and the chance to have land of their very own. Struggling in the midst of the great potato famine, several jumped at the chance. Along with Macdonell, they made their way to Stornoway.

Roderick Macdonald traveled to the city of Glasgow, Scotland where he recruited dirt-poor factory workers, vagrants and criminals looking for a way out of town. The men were open to joining the voyage, but they thought the pay was too low. Macdonald responded by raising the wage, keeping them interested. These men were strong from physical labor, but their moral character was weak from a wretched life. They were the kind of men who could get a lot of work done, but you'd be wise not to turn your back.

Colin Robertson sailed for the Isle of Lewis in the Highlands of

Scotland where he found many recruits open to joining the voyage. These were bad times in the Highlands. Landowners were systematically replacing their tenants with sheep, which were more profitable. Cottars and crofters were driven from their land by the Duchess of Sutherland and others. Families wept and helplessly watched as their cabin homes were burned to the ground. These "Highland Clearances" had left thousands homeless, financially devastated, and in search of a new beginning. Robertson made certain he portrayed the Selkirk Settlement opportunity as that new beginning.

...

On June 13, 1811, it was official. The Hudson's Bay Company leadership voted in favor of approving Lord Selkirk's plan for Assiniboia. Much urgency was now required as the three ships docked in London needed crew and the task of loading food and provisions onboard still had to be completed. There was little time to waste. To successfully pass through the icy waters of the North Atlantic into and across Hudson Bay they had to set sail by August.

Recruits for the settlement traveled from all parts of the U.K. to Stornoway in early June where they awaited the arrival of the Hudson's Bay Company ships from London. A camp of temporary shacks and tents formed along the shore beside the harbor. Stornoway, the largest town in the Hebrides, was founded by Vikings in the 9th century, with the Old Norse name Stjornavagr. The settlement developed around a sheltered natural harbor near the center of the island. Cooled by the North Atlantic, Stornoway was damp and chilly. Even in June seldom was the temperature warmer than sixty degrees Fahrenheit with nights in the mid-forties.

The camp grew to about 120 men, boys, and a few women. The tent village sprawled well beyond the harbor with some recruits opting to live far away from the encampment for their personal safety. The largest percentage of settlers were the Highlanders, numbering seventy. Recruits from Glasgow, western Ireland, and England made up the balance. Many of the Irish colonists were skilled workmen who would be needed to erect buildings for the eventual settlement in America.

The camp was a rowdy place upturned with excitement and anxiety for the journey to come. With a long delay of the H.B.C. ships, there was little to occupy their time. They fell into the usual vices. Drinking, grumbling about camp conditions, and fighting. The disparate backgrounds and language barriers splintered the group into cliques, causing heightened tension and frequent conflict. Sometimes they fought over card games, other times deeper issues between cultural factions ended with punches being thrown and weapons drawn.

...

Lanterns lit Stornoway harbor on a dark, cloudy night with a chill in the air. A large man wearing a tattered blue jacket ducked behind the blacksmith shop. He leaned back against the wall attempting to conceal his presence. He pulled his brimmed hat down low on his forehead, concealing his deep-set eyes. Slowly peeking around the corner, he spotted a tall, thin Irishman approaching on the dock. His long red hair was pulled back in a ponytail. He was very gaunt and could not have weighed more than 120 pounds. As he walked past on the creaking boards, the large man slowly emerged. He approached from behind then aggressively grabbed the Irishman's forehead. Moonlight glinted off the blade as a large knife slashed across the Irishman's throat. Blood spurted between his fingers as he desperately attempted to stop the flow. A look of surprise and shock was frozen on the Irishman's face as he dropped to his knees. The large man kicked him in the back, and he toppled forward onto the dock. Now nothing more than a lump of flesh and clothing.

The large man nudged a leg with his foot to make certain he was dead. Then he pulled off the Irishman's boots and flipped the body into the water. The large man casually looked around, surveying the situation, as if this was all so very normal. He walked off with no remorse, having taken a life for nothing more than a pair of old boots.

...

Sea gulls screeched over London's East End. The date was June 25, 1811. Three vessels, the *Prince of Wales*, the *Eddystone*, and the *Edward and Ann* were in the final stages of boarding cargo and crew. The *Prince of Whales*, a large, three-masted vessel led by Captain Henry Hanwell, towered over the *Eddystone* and the *Edward & Anne*. The *Edward & Anne* was well past its prime and in an awful state of disrepair.

A large and apprehensive group of men moved slowly toward the ships. British soldiers nudged them forward with the butt end of their muskets. A small reminder of what it meant to sign a contract. Among the group was Jacob. He was directed across a creaky and soaking-wet gangplank that led aboard the *Eddystone*. Hudson's Bay Company records contain a list of twenty-nine passengers of the *Eddystone*. Six were from London, twenty-two would join in the Orkney Islands of Scotland and then there was Jacob Fahlstrom, from Sweden. As the *Eddystone* pulled away from the dock it had a crew of just seven. Jacob envied the *Prince of Wales*, a majestic ship. But he did feel fortunate not to be aboard the *Edward & Anne*. This ship had weathered gray sails that were mottled, and her rigging was loose and worn. It seemed poor judgement to send a boat in this condition out to sea on the unpredictable North Atlantic with its icy waves of death.

As the three vessels set sail, the hot sun worsened an already foul odor that lingered over the harbor. The Thames, which had taken the brunt of the city's growing pains, reeked of sewage, rotting garbage, and drowned "river waifs." River waifs were the unfortunate souls caught up in the underbelly of the overpopulated, disease infested, and crime riddled city of London. It was not uncommon to daily see two or three bodies floating in the river. Victims of foul play, suicide, or sometimes members of a family that simply couldn't afford a proper burial. Of all the nose wrenching smells on the journey up-river, by far the most offensive came from the many "dead-houses" along the shore. At any given time five or six bodies in advanced stages of decomposition would be lying inside. These wooden shacks produced a stench most unbearable. Jacob pulled the collar of his shirt up over his nose and mouth to block the smell as the *Eddystone* made her way toward the North Sea. So much for feeling hungry.

The North Sea connects major European countries to Scandinavia. Throughout history, it has been a waterway of trade and tyranny. Just 900 years before Jacob's birth, Vikings sailed these waters to pillage, conquer and inhabit large portions of Europe. The three Selkirk ships headed up the east coast of England but were delayed near Yarmouth by squalls. Jacob was terrified because it was in these same waters where he had previously been shipwrecked on his uncle's vessel the Uppsala. The ships battled the turbulent waves as they sought safe harbor. As Jacob scrambled to get inside, the rain seemed to fall horizontally. Violent gusts of wind almost blew him off his feet.

It was mid-July when the ships reached the Orkneys on the northern tip of Scotland where they added twenty-two more sailors and several servants to the *Eddystone.* Then, on the evening of July 16, Jacob caught sight of distant smoke and the glow of many campfires on the dark treeless shore of Stornoway. Finally, after several delays, the Selkirk ships had arrived. But, for now, the settlers would have to wait. They dropped anchor a significant distance from shore until morning light.

...

The rising sun splashed a thousand shades of orange over Stornoway Harbor as it split the billowy clouds. Crofter's huts made of stacked stone with straw rooftops speckled the countryside. Large hills of dark rock with occasional tufts of tall grass rolled off into the distance. Large buildings, evidence of commerce and trade, towered near the docks. A narrow clearing beside the harbor was cluttered with tents and shacks of the many Selkirk recruits. As smaller boats from the three ships rowed their way toward the docks, settlers began to gather.

Many were in a foul mood as agents of the North West Company had published a news article in the Inverness Journal spreading exaggerations about the perils of the arduous voyage, extremes of climate, and hostile Indians.

Jacob pulled on an oar with all his strength as his boat neared the dock. It was at this moment he caught his first glimpse of the appointed governor of Assiniboia, Miles Macdonell. Macdonell was a tall, broad-shouldered man with dark hair, stern eyebrows, and a rugged chin. He was a career military man from a family lineage of military men. His commanding presence seemed embedded in his DNA. Macdonell's family and friends, most of whom had a long association with the North West Company, could not have been thrilled when he took this appointment by the London committee of the Hudson's Bay Company. But it meant a regular salary, a large tract of land in America, plus five shares in a joint stock with the H.B.C. In short, it gave him a way out of debt. Perhaps he was also seeking a way out of the melancholy brought on by the death of two wives in the late 1790s. Macdonell was a highly qualified soldier and commander but, much to the misfortune of the settlers, an arrogant son-of-a-bitch. Not to mention his frequent bouts of depression and breaks from reality.

A group of Highlander recruits intercepted Macdonell as the boats came ashore. One of the men, his shirt filthy from weeks encamped on the harbor, stepped forward and shouted, "Governor Macdonell, we've heard the Glasgow men are being paid a higher wage than what was offered to us."

"Move aside," muttered Macdonell as he pushed past.

The man continued defiantly, "Well ... what are you gonna' do about it, captain? You going to raise our pay or not?"

Macdonell spat on the ground near the man's feet. He looked him up and down. Then straight into the eyes, and said, "You'll get what you were promised. Not a penny more."

With that, Macdonell walked off toward the temporary headquarters, never once looking back to give the protesters a second thought. British soldiers had to step in as scuffles between the Highlander's and the Glasgow men erupted into full blown fistfights. Later, Macdonell would address the issue, not by raising the Highlanders pay, but rather by lowering the pay of the recruits from Glasgow. He also refused to fulfill promises made to others, resulting in deep mistrust and conflict that ultimately delayed the journey even further.

As Jacob made his way down the dock, he got a closer look at the recruits of Stornoway. They wore torn, filthy clothing. Most had more teeth missing than were present. Every chapter of their hard lives was written on their faces in scars and deep cratered wrinkles. But most striking to Jacob was just "that look." They had that look of despair and defeat. *Is this my future?* Jacob wondered. *Is this the adventure I signed up for?*

It was then that a man amongst the group noticed Jacob's stare. He had frizzy brown hair, his ear was half-gone, and the thumb of his right hand was missing.

"What is you lookin' at?" He didn't necessarily speak the words. It was more like he spat them out at Jacob.

Jacob answered, "Nothing. I was just ..."

"I've been to York Factory. It's a shite hole. Those ships might as well fall off the edge of the earth, because in that place, behind every tree is death."

Jacob couldn't help but ask, "Well then ... why are you going back?"

"I got nothin' else, kid. Just like every other bottom-feeding bastard here."

"I'm sorry it didn't work out, but I'm going to make it. I'm gonna be something."

"How many years you sign up for?"

"Five," answered Jacob.

"Shit. You won't make it three months." The man with the frizzy brown hair waved his hand dismissively at Jacob.

A group of men approached Jacob and the man. They were less disheveled and in much higher spirits. In fact, they sang happy songs of voyage and victory.

They sang, "We'll find enough riches to fill up our britches. That's what we've come here for. Starting each day with the morning dew, now I'm even richer than you!"

As the group marched happily past, the frizzy-haired man shook his head, turned to Jacob, and said, "Them people ain't coming back." Then he shuffled away.

As Jacob continued down the dock, a large man wearing a tattered blue jacket bumped into him. Jacob stumbled a bit, then said, "I'm sorry."

"Watch where you're going. Someone's liable to throw your ass in the drink," grunted the man in a deep growl of a voice.

"I didn't ..." Jacob began to speak again but was rendered speechless as he noticed blood stains on the large man's boots. He looked up and their eyes met briefly. There was a vacant pit behind the man's eyes. No spark of life. Just cold and empty. Jacob turned and swiftly walked down the dock.

...

One small boat at a time, the recruits boarded the ships. But this voyage seemed to have nothing but problems. Firstly, Macdonell had to meet with the captain on board a man-of-war cannon ship, which was to accompany and protect the H.B.C. vessels on the journey.

This led to a lot of haggling and offering up men to put on board the man-of-war. Secondly, while the captain of the *Edward and Anne* was on shore reporting to the customs authority, a military representative, Captain McKenzie, boarded the vessel with a military recruiting party, offering enlisting money to some of the men. On this vessel were seventy-six men from Glasgow, Ireland, and a few from the Orkneys. Macdonell was livid. His hair wildly blew in the wind as he took several long strides across the deck, stopping inches from McKenzie's nose. "I greatly respect military men who fight under the Union Jack. But if you don't leave this ship, you'll be swimmin' back to England." With that the British soldiers were forced from the ship. But this didn't dissuade McKenzie who patiently awaited the arrival of Mr. Reid, the collector of customs. Reid was a scrawny man with thick spectacles hanging off the end of his unusually long nose. Though he tried to talk a good game and fain friendliness, his beady eyes revealed his lack of moral compass, betraying his false persona. Mr. Reid boarded the ship and, no doubt with bribe money from the North West Company in pocket, delayed the sailing even further while he minutely examined papers and cargo. Reid and his four-man crew of bureaucrats meticulously scrutinized and demanded documentation of every barrel, every crate, and every provision. At one point, Macdonell asked Reid if he would care to examine the crack of his ass for hidden weapons and undocumented cargo. This went on for hours.

Once the inspection was complete, Reid gathered all passengers on deck. Reid said, "Selkirk settlers, I am here on behalf of the government of Scotland and the Landlords of Stornoway with the authority as customs collector..." His speech was interrupted by murmuring and laughter amongst the crowd which was very aware that Reid had been paid off. After all, it was well known that Mr. Reid's wife was the aunt of Sir Alexander McKenzie, a high-ranking official of the North West Company. "Quiet. Quiet now," Reid urged, then continued, "I find that, as I am burdened with this heavy weight of responsibility and as a man of conscience, I feel that I must make you aware of your personal freedoms and rights in this situation in which you find yourselves." Macdonell attempted to approach Reid, but two red-coated soldiers impeded his path. Reid, who had paused in fear of Macdonell's approach, now continued, "This clause is from the Emigration Act, which regulates the provisions for wayfaring passengers. It states that if any persons are unwilling to depart port on any voyage they must not be compelled to do so and they are free to go ashore."

This caused another murmur amongst the crowd. The murmur soon turned into arguing, then chaos. A large contingent of the men leapt over the ship's side, plunging into the cold water, then swimming their way to Captain McKenzie's boat where marines pulled their shivering bodies aboard. Others attempted to get away in a lifeboat, but they were stopped, and the boat was brought back.

Macdonell pleaded with Reid, "These men have signed contracts with the Hudson's Bay Company. Therefore, they are obligated by law to follow through on our journey to York Factory." With the shouts falling on deaf ears Reid tucked his paperwork under his arm, turned, and left the ship. Another seven settlers were assisted by marines along with Reid into Captain McKenzie's boat which remained alongside the *Edward and Anne.*

McKenzie taunted those still aboard. "Just think Macdonell, now there'll be more biscuits for you and your, uh, crew." A laugh erupted from the Glasgow men in McKenzie's boat. Macdonell, showing no reaction that might give McKenzie satisfaction, calmly picked up a cannonball, extended it outward, and let it drop. The iron ball plunged thirty feet and in a splintering crash, blasted through the bottom of McKenzie's boat.

"Enjoy the swim," Macdonell said as the remaining settlers on board cheered this mode of punishment for the deserters and agitators who were clearly backed by the rival North West Company.

Jacob watched this mayhem from the deck of the *Eddystone* which was loaded with passengers and waiting to depart. In the days of waiting the crew had nothing to eat but burgoo (oatmeal porridge). This caused discontent among the passengers. A laboring class passenger approached the skipper of the *Eddystone*, Thomas Gull, who was repairing worn rigging. The passenger said, "No more."

Somewhat taken aback, the skipper responded, "Pardon?"

"No more will we eat this mush! We have all had our fill and we say no more."

"Damn my buttons," Gull said. "If you don't like the food, you may jump overboard." The recruit handed his hat to skipper Gull, removed his coat and boots, and took him up on his offer. He flipped himself over the rail plunging into the water below. He was quickly followed by five others, and they swam for shore. Quite a desperate measure as the shore was a good distance away. The skipper ordered the ship's boats lowered to retrieve the swimmers. At the same time people on shore witnessing the commotion rowed out fearing their friends needed rescue. All boats reached the swimmers at the same time. It was quite a hilarious sight as the swimmer's arms and legs were pulled in opposite directions as if they were a wishbone after Thanksgiving dinner. Eventually, the Stornoway group won and made their way to shore. Jacob never saw those men again, because within a few hours, fearing a further loss of men, the skipper weighed anchor, and started for York Factory. Thereafter the food took a turn for the better, and burgoo was almost entirely banished from the tables.

It was July 26, 1811, the latest departure destined for Hudson Bay recorded up to that time. Sails were finally hoisted, and the ships set off for the icy waters of the North Atlantic. Had they been delayed even a week longer the voyage would have been canceled until the following spring. With eyes fixed on the gradually shrinking shoreline, many a Scotsman shed a tear or two. Sadness filled their hearts as they watched the stone houses of Stornoway disappear across dark waters. They bid farewell to the land that was their home. The hills which rose and fell in the distance were treeless and black. Sighs and sniffles could be heard as the settlers came to the full realization that they were perhaps observing for the last time this dark and rolling landscape with tall grass blowing in the wind. Their final glimpse of Scotland was the Butt of Lewis with its wave-worn caverns. Some settlers openly wept as their former home faded away in the distant fog forever.

The English man-of-war, which escorted the vessels out to sea had been appointed because France had been harassing British ships. At a point some 400 miles off the Irish coast, the man-of-war turned back, leaving the three H.B.C. ships to battle the turbulent sea alone. Storm-tossed and sick from motion, the recruits were on their way into the wild Atlantic destined to expand Great Britain's colonial reach and determined to re-write their life's history.

Chapter 15.
The Voyage to Hudson Bay

Jacob felt most at home on the water. Having grown up in the harbor of Stockholm he felt connected to ships and the sea. In fact, Jacob's earliest memory was watching sails ripple in the wind while standing on the nautical rope ladder of his father's merchant ship.

On the *Eddystone*, Jacob walked the deck every morning, preferring the fresh salty breeze to the dank, musty smells in the hull cabins below. A collection of people in a confined space over time can generate quite a nose-curdling aroma. Being on deck kept Jacob's mind alert. There's a fine line between peace and boredom when on a cross-ocean voyage. Leaning on the starboard rail, Jacob noticed activity on the *Edward & Anne*. Men were carrying bodies wrapped in white sheets and dropping them overboard. One after another, nine bodies splashed into the white-capped water and slowly floated down, never to reach their destination in America. The greatest danger of the sea, in fact, was not storms, nor pirates. It was sickness. Huddled together on bare wooden floors with no ventilation, breathing a stench of vomit, and what they didn't realize, bacteria and viruses. With the overcrowded quarters disease spread quickly. The passengers were helpless in the situation not knowing the cause of the sickness and death. All they could do was wait it out until they reached dry land. Their only defense against the spreading disease was hope and luck. If they were old or weak, they had little or no chance of avoiding the death toll. Did the *Edward & Anne* get hit harder with disease than the other two ships because it was old and filthy? Or were the passengers of that ship simply the unfortunate recipients of a disease carried aboard by vermin or one of the other passengers? Much speculation among the passengers questioned what was causing all the misery and death. Mostly, they blamed the victims, who they believed were being punished for sins they had committed. Some questioned whether the sickness was God's disapproval of this voyage.

What is known today is that the cause of so much death aboard these seagoing vessels in the 19th century was typhus. Typhus was carried on-board by rats and mice. It was the lice and fleas living in the hair of these vermin that would then jump to passengers and spread the disease. After an incubation period of seven to ten days, the sick experience fever, then delirium, dysentery, headaches and a rash. After the second week, eruptions form on the skin and internal organs begin to swell. The brain, spinal cord, liver and spleen. Without scientific knowledge and available treatments, in this pre-antibiotic era, fifty to seventy-five percent of victims would die. Passengers who recovered or were able to avoid becoming sick lived in a constant state of fear. Who would die next?

Jacob contemplated life's chaotic twists of fate. It was puzzling and heart breaking how death could be so random. He thought of the passengers of the *Edward & Anne*, his mother, his brother, his father, and Ed. They all seemed to be caught helplessly in the cruel lottery of death.

The parade of bodies wrapped in white sheets aboard the *Edward & Anne* continued for weeks. By the time death's hunger subsided more than thirty souls were dropped into their watery resting place.

One particularly frigid morning, Jacob was on deck for one of his walks. He took a seat on the quarterdeck to watch the crew in action.

Men were moving rapidly in all directions. Across the deck, and up and down the masts. Noticing Jacob's interest with the workings of the ship, Skipper Gull decided to test this young Swedish lad. Due to particularly quiet winds, the ships had anchored off the southern tip of Greenland. Now, finally there was a nice breeze blowing. Over the wind noise Gull yelled, "Swede Boy! Lay aloft and loose all sails." Jacob sprung to his feet and without hesitation climbed aloft and cast off the gussets, carefully and skillfully coiling them to avoid their getting caught in the rigging. He loosed the sails then came down the masts rope ladder with ease and prepared to set the sails. The skipper looked over at Jacob with a raised eyebrow, exhibiting a *holy shit* level of surprise. He yelled, "Sheet home lower topsails." Jacob let go the clewlines and buntlines for the lower topsail and held tight the topsail sheets. Skipper called out, "Hoist upper topsail." With a precision that only comes with frequent practice and a natural aptitude, Jacob cast off the upper topsail downhauls and buntlines, eased the braces, then hauled the halyard heaving both the yard and the sail. Now without command Jacob carried on. He set the top gallant and royal masts. Again, clewlines and buntlines were let go, sheets hauled tight, and finally the halyards manned and yards hoisted until the sails were set.

Now the ship was ready to weigh anchor. "Swede Boy! Get over here," Gull yelled. Several of the crewmembers cheered Jacob's efforts as he walked over to Skipper Gull who stood at the wheel. The skipper made a gesture to Jacob indicating he should take over.

Somewhat timid, Jacob called out, his voice squeaking with the onset of adolescence. "Starboard fore braces. Port, main, and mizzen braces." The crew jumped to attention and scurried to the braces, grabbed the ropes, and began pulling aggressively. Suddenly the deck was abuzz with activity in all directions as the Eddystone came to life. Jacob called, "Brace up fore and aft." With that the aft and the fore masts were braced around to starboard and those on the main and mizzen were pulled round to port. The crew in unison pulled, leaning way forward then heaving back, pulling and moving ropes with grimaces of strain. Jacob yelled, "Weigh anchor!"

A dozen men, two per wooden beam extending from an inner post, began to walk the spoke around in a circle, the anchor could be heard twisting up with a loud metal clanking. Now, with the anchor aweigh, the bow began to fall off to port due to the way the yards on the fore mast were trimmed. Jacob, with voice cracking, yelled, "Starboard rudder!"

Now wearing a smile so huge laughter was almost spilling out the edges of his mouth, Skipper Gull engaged the rudder and the ship smoothly turned round to stern. After some time, the anchor was housed.

"Hoist out the jib," called Jacob. Again, the crew began working and pulling as if cogs in a single machine set the sail. This increased the effective sail area forward and resulted in the bow falling off more quickly. As the wind blew, the sail on the main and mizzen masts filled with a hearty snap. The ship was now on course and a further falling off of the bow was not desired, so Jacob called, "Haul out the spanker." The crew set the spanker to keep her from falling off any further. "Brace round forward!" The yards on the fore mast were swung round. Rapidly the ship gained headway. "Set the courses," Jacob squeaked with all the gusto his young voice could muster.

The courses were set to increase speed. And with that, the *Eddystone* was on her way. Water now crashed off the bow giving scale to the rapid movement of the ship. Four crewmen from the seaport city of Stornoway raised Jacob up on their shoulders and paraded him around. The Skipper offered Jacob a sip of whiskey, which he gulped back a bit too fast and choked. His eyes watered and whiskey dribbled from the corner of his mouth. This led to an even heartier cheer and laughter from all aboard. The skipper patted Jacob on the back to help relieve his choking. Jacob bolted over to the rope ladder to climb up and get a better view. On the way up, with a loud snap, the rope tore apart, and Jacob fell backward. Only his leg getting tangled in the rope prevented a much worse fall. The crew laughed at Jacob's folly, and he was embarrassed. His heroic pride, so fleeting.

Skipper Gull said, "I know you want to prove yourself, but you can't always rush into things Jacob." After helping Jacob get untangled, Gull became quite serious and added, "Guys lose a leg that way, or worse. You could've smashed your skull." Jacob picked up his hat from the deck and walked off. The skipper shouted, "You'll make a good captain someday, Swede Boy. But remember, don't rush into things. Proceed with smart caution and a steady pace."

It was an atypical late summers journey. The wind seemed to come in only two sorts. Too much or too little. On some days the wind was so strong the three ships bounced and twisted through storms with rumbling clouds and massive waves. On other days the wind was so weak that the ships had to change course to provide forward motion. These conditions slowed the progress of the fleet. The many delays were not good for morale amongst the settlers and crew. Particularly aboard the *Edward & Anne* which carried the Irish and the Glasgow men. A motley crew that seemed to resemble a mix of flint and gunpowder. Arguments and physical fighting were common. Things were different on the *Eddystone*. The passengers, being mostly from the Orkney Islands, got along well and were an effective crew.

Somewhere in the middle of the North Atlantic, to occupy time, Skipper Gull trained the passengers how to load and shoot a musket. Many had never put a gun to their shoulder and the scene was nothing short of utter incompetence. After weeks of repetitive training drills, however, the settlers became quite proficient with the weapons. Jacob proved to be a skilled marksman. In a competition of accuracy, the final round came down to Jacob and a Scot who had been in the English military. The objective was to shoot your ball closest to the center of the target; a large red circle painted on cloth from an old sail. The Scot fired and ripped a hole less than an inch from the center. Jacob loaded his musket, then raised it to his shoulder. He had one eye squinted slightly as he looked down the barrel. Sparks flew as the hammer ignited the powder in the pan. The gun recoiled expelling its projectile and punching a hole in the cloth. When Gull examined the target, it looked like there was just one large hole, but with a closer look he was able to determine that Jacob's ball hit just to the outside part of the hole created by the Scot's ball. Jacob lost the competition but won a bit of respect. It was a good day.

Jacob sat on deck slicing potatoes and dropping them into a bucket. He breathed in the salty air and hummed a tune that he recalled from the streets of London. The level of boredom with weeks at sea is difficult to match. One day blends into the next and the only sight to be seen is water, more water, and still more water after that. *Thank God the sky changes*, Jacob thought. Looking up, admiring the clouds Jacob did not notice a large rat had climbed into the potato bucket. When he reached over to grab another the rat clamped onto his right hand between the thumb and forefinger. The rat would not let go. Jacob stood up and tried to shake the rat loose. Still holding tight, the rat sunk its teeth in deeper. Jacob was now screaming with pain. He tried unsuccessfully to get the rat off his hand by banging the rat against the ships rail. Jacob reached down and grabbed the knife from the potato bucket. He stabbed the rat several times until finally its jaws let loose. Jacob picked up the dead rat and threw it overboard. Blood dripped from his hand onto the deck. Tearing a piece of cloth from his shirt, Jacob wrapped it around his hand and pressed hard to stop the bleeding. Jacob thought to himself about what the skipper told him. *Don't rush things, proceed with attentive caution. Ugh. I need to do more of that. Next time it could be a bear, not a rat.*

Days later, Jacob walked the deck. It was night. Jacob encountered a group of Orkney men. It was clear they had been drinking. He tried to walk past unnoticed, but one of the men grabbed him by the shoulder and put Jacob in a headlock. He slapped the side of Jacob's head.

"Stop," pleaded Jacob.

"Come on Swede Boy. Just funnin' you a bit," said a dark-haired man with an unkempt beard.

"Stop, let me go."

"What? Don't you want to be with us?"

"Stop."

"What's the matter orphan?" The man continued to harass Jacob. He repeated, "What's wrong Orphan ... orphan ..." Each time the dark-haired man said the word he slapped the side of Jacob's head. Jacob was on the verge of tears but knew he had to hold them back or the harassment would only intensify.

"Let him be," urged one of the other men. "Come on, he's had enough."

"I'll decide when the orphan's had enough," hissed the dark-haired man. "Oh look, the orphan's gonna cry. Is that a tear, orphan?"

Jacob pulled loose from the dark-haired man's grasp and ran off. Once behind some boxes and out of sight of the men, he sat down on deck and sobbed. He thought to himself, *what a massive mistake. What wretched adventure had I signed up for?*

Jacob remained up on deck all night. He was emotionally spent. Anything more and he swore to himself he would jump overboard and simply sink to the bottom.

As the sun rose, the squawking of a seagull woke Jacob. It had landed on the rail nearby. Jacob looked at the bird, not immediately assigning any special meaning to this visitor, but then sprung to his feet and ran to the front of the ship. There off in the distance he could see a small hill on the horizon. It was land.

"Land!" someone on deck screamed and rang the ship's bell. From every door and hatch crew members emerged. They climbed up from below deck like ants fleeing a poisoned mound. It had been sixty-one long days since they left Stornoway. The most ever required for an H.B.C. vessel to make the journey to York Factory. The shallow waters near the fort required the ships to drop anchor miles offshore. Passengers and cargo would be transferred on smaller boats.

Chapter 16.
York Factory

The ships reached York Factory on September 24, 1811. The term "factory" was carried over from the seventeenth century. It was a designation given to important overseas trading stations. York Factory, a primary fur trading post of the Hudson's Bay Company, was located on a large peninsula bordered by two rivers and Hudson Bay at its point. To its south was the Hayes River and to the north was the Nelson, a much wider river. Jacob was now twelve years old.

Wind blew, carrying a light drizzle. Pine smoke and the aroma of roasting deer meat filled the air. The Selkirk settlers paddled to shore in jolly boats. They were in the new world now. The wild expanse of North America with all its hope, promise, and danger. The York Factory buildings rose from an area of cleared timber. A tiny square of civilization carved out of unending wilderness. Jacob's mind raced with thoughts of what might be out in that great unknown. He pictured himself hunting bear and wading in rivers teeming with so many fish he could catch them with his bare hands. He imagined climbing the tallest tree he could find just to see where he might go next. A spark of exploration had been ignited in his heart. Jacob didn't know exactly what he was searching for. Maybe he was seeking meaning in his life. A purpose ... belonging.

There was a large presence of British soldiers at the factory, their bright red uniforms were difficult to miss against the backdrop of mud-covered ground and dark brown log buildings.

Birch bark canoes lined the shore. A group of men wearing deerskin leggings and leather moccasins walked toward the trading cabin carrying large bundles of beaver and other furs. These men were different than the British soldiers, different it seemed than all men in London. They were wild and hairy. Jacob had never seen such overgrown beards and unruly long matted hair. A pungent odor from hard paddling and campfire smoke wafted as they passed. It was the kind of odor only months in the wilderness could cultivate. A Cree brave joined the group. Jacob had never seen an Indian before. His skin was dark walnut, and his eyes were deep brown like that of a deer. His long black hair was split into two braids, one hanging over each shoulder. The Cree's eyes were accentuated by deep lines at the corners, as if he had spent a lifetime squinting in the sun. It gave him a piercing look that seemed in disagreement with his happy smile. He laughed heartily as he threw an arm over a fur trader's shoulder and gladly shared his bottle of Irish whiskey. Jacob wondered why people continued referring to the native people as Indians when it was well known that this new land was certainly not India. And there are so many different tribes across the continent. Why were they all lumped into one mass group?

Several huskies barked and ran in circles, greeting the settlers as they stepped off the boats. They sniffed curiously, taking in the scents from the many different places the settlers came from. Jacob crouched down on one knee, petting the head of a particularly large dog with one brown eye and one blue eye. The huskie's eyes of different colors looked up at Jacob, happy to have the affectionate rubbing of his head. That special spot, just behind the ears. Noticing he had fallen behind the other settlers, Jacob popped up and ran to catch up. The huskie tilted his head curiously watching Jacob as he ran. Jacob stopped and turned back. "See ya' later, ummm ... you need a name. How about Two-Eye?" The dog barked. "Well, that's it then. Two-Eye it is!" With that, Jacob hustled off to catch the others. The settlers made their way across the sandy beach and headed up the grassy hill toward the fort.

Many buildings made up York Factory. Several were in in a state of disrepair due to the swampiness of the land, a characteristic of the entire coast. As a remedy for the soggy, pudding-like topsoil there were wooden planks all around the fort to walk on. When looking north from the Hayes River, where the settlers arrived, the building farthest to the left was a blacksmith shop and a provision store. Next to that was the main factory building. It was the only building with white siding. Flying the Union Jack and H.B.C. colors, it towered over all others. It was built partly on pillars and was within a large oblong enclosure walled by a timber stockade. Just to the right of the stockade entrance gate were a large barracks and a boat repair shed. Further to the right, with a good deal of separation, was the trading post. Right beside the post was a large grassy area with a few scattered lodges constructed of wooden branches covered with birch bark and animal skins. This was where natives from the Cree, Inuit, Assiniboine, and Ojibwe tribes stayed while trading a season of furs. In summer this area was bustling and crowded with more than fifty lodges. But, now in late September, only a few remained. A cluster of four lodges, each billowing campfire smoke stood near the forest's edge. Just north of the lodges was a graveyard with more bodies than gravestones.

Jacob caught up with the Selkirk settlers just outside the fort's entrance, near the stockade. Lookout towers at each corner, manned with redcoats, stood as a reminder that this was indeed a wild and hostile place. The large timber doors creaked open revealing dozens of laborers scurrying about hauling furs, tanning hides, and chopping wood to keep the fur trade humming. Standing just inside the gate, ready to greet the group, was the officer in charge, William Cook. Cook was a native of London who had entered the service of the Hudson's Bay Company in 1786 and took over the management of York Factory in 1809. Standing at his side was William Auld, a Scot, and superintendent of the northern H.B.C. factories. Auld was able to translate English into Gaelic for many of the settlers from the Hebrides. Cook was civil enough, but certainly didn't offer a hearty welcome. He provided instructions in a very unenthused manner. Already viewing Selkirk's settlers as a distraction from York Factory business, he was angry that the ships arrived so late in the season. With the calendar now teetering on the verge of October, there would be no way for the settlers to make it down the Hayes River to the Athabasca region. Winter's icy breath would soon freeze all the waterways. This meant it would be June, eight long months before the settlers would be out of his hair. Cook, being English, felt a sense of superiority to these recruits. To him, the simple fact they were Irish and Scottish, was reason enough for him to thumb his nose at the settlers. Secondly, the settlers bore the appearance of those living on the bottom rung of society. To Cook, they were nothing but a bunch of backwater farmers, commoners and worse, criminals. He handled the entire situation with frustrated grunts, huffs, and a large amount of eye-rolling. Cook said, "You have arrived at York Factory. While here you will follow all orders or suffer the consequences. I am in charge. Do not challenge my authority. We will provide you with rations in the short term, but you will be expected to hunt game and make biscuits to feed your group through the winter." Cook unceremoniously turned and walked back toward the main factory building. He stopped, then turned back to the settlers. "Almost forgot. Don't go in the woods alone. We lose way too many recruits that way."

Significantly uninspired, the group was led to a large mess hall. The ninety-five settlers ate their meal alone. No one else from the fort joined. It was interesting how the group was still splintered primarily by country of origin. The Irish sat with the Irish, Orkney men sat with Orkney men, Glasgow men sat with Glasgow men, and those from the Hebridean Islands sat together. This left Jacob a bit isolated. He had no countrymen to join. With a piece of stale bread in one hand and plate of venison in the other, Jacob scanned the room with row after row of tables.

Luckily Skipper Gull rescued him, yelling, "Jacob, come join us."

Squeezing in between two very large Scotsmen, Jacob took his place at the table. Gull did his best to introduce Jacob, but most of the men at the table spoke Gaelic, so with that and a lot of empty stomachs, the conversation didn't go far. It was amusing for Jacob to listen to the banter between the men. A string of words Jacob didn't understand followed by a punch line he didn't understand and then much laughter. Sprinkled in here and there were a few vulgar curse words Jacob recognized from his time aboard the *Eddystone*. Jacob discovered on the journey that, across England, Scotland, and Ireland, there was a certain set of vulgar words that everyone, no matter their primary language, could understand. All else was incomprehensible, but shit, asshole, and wanker were pretty much understood by all, no matter if you spoke Irish, English, Gaelic, Celtic ... or, as it turns out, even Swedish.

Jacob spent much of mealtime scanning the room. The massive timbers from which the hall was constructed were impressive. *How did they build something this massive in the middle of nowhere? How did they even move those huge things?* Jacob wondered. All these people were white-skinned, but they were all so different. These settlers were so unlike the fur traders and the Cree man Jacob saw at the river. That group, though vastly different in appearance, were virtually identical in behavior, mannerism, and demeanor. It was notable the way they interacted. How they were able to speak a common language and share the same humor. They all had that sharp edge to them. Like they were always on a higher state of alert. Jacob wondered, *Why do people think skin makes you the same or different? When it really doesn't seem to be that at all. That's only skin. That's not what counts. It's your spirit, what's inside, that defines who you are.*

Jacob pulled a small bible from his pocket and read as the others finished eating. He softly touched the words that were scrawled on the inside cover as if feeling them would bring him closer to Sweden, closer to his mother. The words were, *No matter what.*

As he read, a Cree boy, a bit younger than Jacob, walked up and placed a lump of paper on the table directly in front of him. The boy smiled, then shyly ran off. Jacob picked up the paper and unwrapped its contents. Inside was a slice of an orange. He smiled and looked around to thank the boy, but he was nowhere in sight. Jacob put the wedge of orange in his mouth and enjoyed its sweetness.

That night the settlers were put up in a large building right beside the main depot. It was a trader's quarters, which may have been comfortable for a group about half the size of the Selkirk settlers. But, for this group, it was clearly overcrowded. This prompted the leader of the settlers and Governor of the Selkirk Colony, Miles Macdonell, to bring up the need to construct proper accommodations for the winter.

Later, Mr. Auld, the H.B.C. northern factories superintendent, came around to reminisce with his fellow Scotchmen. Drinks were shared and all were having a good time until Auld told a joke about how the H.B.C. captured Scotchmen in the hills by having the recruiter carry a bag of oatmeal in one hand and a box of snuff in the other. The room, previously filled with laughter, went awkwardly silent. The joke seemed to hit a bit too close to home. Auld, reading the room, finished his glass, politely excused himself, and retired for the night.

Chapter 17.
Settling In

October 1, 1811. Jacob awoke to numb toes and frost covered windows. In northern Manitoba, once October arrives temperatures can remain below freezing until May. The factory was now under the icy veil of winter. Jacob walked over and admired the beautiful star shapes magically engraved in frost on the pane. He reached out and felt the window. Quickly, he had to pull his finger away as it was very cold. He leaned closer and blew on the window, melting a small circle, and looked out. Beyond the stockade wall, children were playing a game of chase with the huskies. He noticed that one of them was the Cree boy that shared his orange slice. Like all children, Jacob just wanted to join in and have fun. He slipped on his boots, pulled a wool sweater over his head, and grabbed a jacket as he ran out the door. One of the kids noticed Jacob's arrival and asked in Cree, "Want to play?" Jacob didn't understand a word the boy said. He smiled and his extended hand, holding a tattered old ball about the size of his palm. This was an invitation to play. Jacob nodded his head in the affirmative, so the boy tossed Jacob the ball. Not knowing what to do, Jacob tossed the ball back to the boy. The boy laughed and shook his head from side to side, indicating that Jacob was doing it wrong. He then demonstrated how to play. First, he held the ball up, getting everyone's attention. He then threw the ball toward the dogs. As soon as he threw it, all the children ran to the ball, trying to get it before the dogs did. Almost every time the dogs would get the ball first which prompted a game of chase until finally one of the kids was able to wrestle the ball from the dog's mouth. This always prompted a huge cheer from the others. On one attempt, Jacob ran fast to the ball after it was thrown. He dove and just barely beat one of the dogs. The entire group cheered his impressive dive. They played like this for a long time. A pointless game, really. But, when you're a kid, who cares if it's pointless. That's why they call it play. The game would've gone even longer, but it came to an end when an old Cree man called his grandchildren over to eat their morning meal. He waved for Jacob to come over as well. When they approached, the old man said something to Jacob in Cree. After reading the confused look on Jacob's face, the old man seamlessly shifted into English. "You are new to York?"

"Got here a few days ago," answered Jacob.

"You speak with an odd accent? Where are you from?"

"Sweden"

"Hmm. Never heard of Sweden," said the old Cree man.

"It's many miles to the north of England."

The old man smiled and nodded, then extended his hand to a pot boiling over the fire. It was a bubbling, brown liquid broth containing floating vegetables and chunks of meat. It smelled good.

As the old Cree man dumped a ladle full into a bowl for Jacob, he urged, "Go ahead. It's good."

Eager to please his new friends, Jacob plunged his spoon into the broth, blew to cool it, and slowly took a bite. It was good. No, it was more than good, it was delicious. Quite possibly the tastiest thing Jacob had eaten since his mother's cooking in Sweden. Quickly he finished the entire bowl. Just then, the old man's daughter walked up. She was pointing at the huskies one at a time, as if counting.

"Hey, didn't there used to be nine dogs?" she asked in English. Jacob's eyes widened and the woman punched him in the shoulder. "Just kidding. The stew is deer meat, goofball. We don't eat dogs ... well, at least not these dogs." The entire group laughed. Jacob hadn't had such a good time since he was with the kids in London. He felt sad for a moment, wondering how Otto, Henry, Charley, and Elizabeth were doing. He also thought of Ed. He really didn't feel much like playing anymore.

...

Days later, a group of about thirty men were gathered in the main depot of the factory. Miles Macdonell was giving them instructions about life in the wilderness of North America. His presentation was delivered in military fashion. It was straight to the point and all business.

"For winter living, we need to build cabins. My men have located an appropriate spot north of the Nelson River, about six miles west of York Factory. There is a large clearing and many spruce trees nearby for construction. We'll go out tomorrow, but first every man needs to be equipped for wilderness survival. Supply number one, a weapon." Macdonell picked up an H.B.C. Trade Gun. "Here it is, gentlemen. The London fusil, also known as the Barnett musket. Also known as the Hudson's Bay fuke. Whatever you call it, it's forty-five inches in length with thirty inches of blue steel barreled death. I will train you 'pork eaters' to use it for hunting food, killing an enemy and, most pertinent to tomorrow's activities, protecting yourself against predatory animals, of which these woods are bursting. This beauty will take down a 1500-pound polar bear. It can turn a wolf into a pile of red guts at 30 paces. Manufactured in Birmingham, England, this musket is muzzle loaded and flintlock fired. It will project a lead ball 100 yards with accuracy. It can be identified as a Hudson's Bay Company weapon by the sitting fox located on the stock and the brass serpent on the side plate. An oversized trigger guard will allow you to use your weapon wearing large gloves, and with the coming extreme cold, trust me, you will need. Probably next week. Every man will be issued an H.B.C. fuke, a powder horn and two pounds of gunpowder. This afternoon I will train you in the use of this weapon. Every man will also be supplied with boots, winter jacket, gloves, hat, skinning knife and an essentials kit. I suggest you use your musket to hunt the woods in the coming months and accumulate enough skins to trade so you can more fully supply yourself as you see fit." Macdonell scanned the room, surveying the uninspired group. "Any questions?" Quiet hung over the room. Macdonell looked left, then right. He was extremely disappointed by this sorry group of recruits. "Okay, then." With that, Miles Macdonell, the son of a colonel from Inverness, Scotland, and former military hero of the King's Royal Regiment in the Mohawk Valley of New York, pivoted on his heels, turned precisely 180 degrees, and exited. His bootsteps echoed down the hall.

The training of this splintered group of misfits, scallywags, and criminals began. Weapon use, remote lodge building, wilderness survival, skinning and prepping animal pelts, open fire cooking and basic Algonquin language skills were all taught. However, the days of October and a good part of November were filled mostly with cutting down and stripping trees into wooden beams to construct the cabins that would make up the "northern barracks" for the Selkirk settlers. Jacob had been working diligently one day stripping a log of its branches when Macdonell walked by, stopped, turned back, and approached him. He was red-faced and angry.

Macdonell asked, "Why did we let a boy join these men? Every one of those branches needs to be re-cut. They're all wrong." Macdonell seemed unstable in his actions. Jacob's work seemed just as good as the other settlers. Macdonell grabbed Jacob by the shirt and began slapping him on the side of the head. He slapped repeatedly, until Jacob was able to twist loose and run off into the woods. Jacob often found solace in the woods. It was his respite from beatings and abuse at the hand of Macdonell. This was not the first time, and it wouldn't be the last. It seemed to be getting worse. Macdonell's violent outbursts and breaks from reality were becoming more frequent. The longer he was in the wilderness, the worse it seemed to get. Jacob became a master at navigating and hiding in the woods. Being 12, he was not strong enough to stand and fight.

A safe distance away, Jacob stopped and sat amongst the pines. Deserved or not, Jacob took criticism very hard. He was trying to do well and to be accepted as an equal to the other men. Arms on his knees, Jacob rested his head on his forearms. Tears were soaking his jacket sleeves. Suddenly, Jacob could feel a wet tongue licking his hands. It was Two-Eye, the huskie he met on the beach. It seemed the dog was trying to console him. He whined a couple times, offering friendship. This managed to curl the sides of Jacob's lips into a smile.

Jacob said, "At least you like me, but you're just a dog." He closed his eyes for a moment, but then continued, "Awe dang. I guess I shouldn't say that. Being a dog is plenty. You treat me better than everyone else here. They think I don't pull my weight. The Scotsmen are nice sometimes, but the Irishmen can't stand my guts. Macdonell wishes they would've left me back in London." Jacob stood and walked down the trail. Two-Eye followed along. Jacob continued his conversation with Two-Eye. "I wish everything could be more like your eyes. They look different, but they work perfectly together. Here at York, especially with the English, different is always considered bad. They act like there's something wrong with you simply because you're different or doing things different than their way. Should it really matter if I have yellow hair or if the Cree children have dark hair? Should the darkness of your skin really matter more than the color of your shirt?"

Leaves crunched underfoot as the two continued back to York Factory. Before going inside the temporary barracks Jacob looked back at Two-Eye, who was patiently sitting at attention. "I'm glad I met you, Two-Eye. It's been good talking with ya'. Hopefully we can do it again sometime." In response Two-Eye barked and a cloud of steam escaped his mouth and floated up into the Manitoba sky.

...

In his free time, Jacob would find his way over to the Cree encampment to play with the children and talk with the old Cree. His name was Ahtohtew Akami, or Walks on The Lake in English. Jacob always called him Akami because he struggled with the pronunciation of Ahtohtew. Akami spoke pretty good English and Jacob worked hard to pick up Akami's language. At Jacob's insistence, they frequently spoke Cree. This would become Jacob's third fluent language, though his Swedish was beginning to fade due to lack of use.

Akami lost his family when he was a young boy. His mother, father and two brothers were all brutally killed when their village was ambushed by Sioux warriors. This gave Akami a keen understanding of what Jacob was going through. It gave them a connection. They knew and felt things many others could not relate to. They had long discussions about being alone in the world and the similarities of their lives. The pain they both experienced on entirely different sides of the world. During the attack on his village, Akami escaped and hid in the woods. This left profound sadness and tremendous guilt clinging to his heart. Something he had now been carrying for more than seventy years. He felt like he deserted his family. He explained to Jacob that it was very painful, even today. Jacob completely understood. He knew that same pain. Often, they cried together. It made Jacob's heart ache to see Akami hang his head with tears dripping from his cheeks. He did his best to console him. These discussions were good for the spirit of both Jacob and Akami. A kind of therapy, perhaps. The sad days were a small part of the time they spent together. Ninety percent of their time was spent telling stories, making jokes, and learning skills.

Almost every night Jacob and Akami would sit by the campfire, warm themselves, and talk. Often Two-Eye would show up. Initially because Jacob always slipped him scraps of food, but later because Two-Eye had a genuine bond with the blond-haired boy. He seemed to completely understand when Jacob spoke to him. Or maybe Jacob just wished that to be the case?

Jacob taught Akami about sailing. Akami taught Jacob about fur trapping, hunting and how to become the woods—how to be invisible. Akami's favorite joke was the one Jacob told about his London buddy Otto who would put horse poop in Ed's hand then tickle his nose with a feather. Oh man, how Akami would laugh. He would literally fall off his stump laughing so hard. Seeing Akami completely amused made Jacob laugh even harder. Jacob had one of those laughs that pulls people in. It was this magical, guttural sound from deep in his belly. It was infectious. It just made funny things funnier. It touched your heart.

One evening, just before sunset, Jacob was teaching Akami about sailor's knots. Akami was amazed at how many ways there were to tie knots. Jacob taught him dozens.

Jacob joked, "Sailing is less about water, and mostly about ropes and knots." Akami chuckled, then Jacob got very serious and placed his hand on Akami's shoulder and looked him right in the eye. Jacob asked, "Can you keep a secret?"

"I think so?"

Jacob laughed a bit but was still serious. "No, you can't just think, you gotta' know for sure."

"Okay. I will keep the secret."

Jacob looked around as if checking to make sure no one was within earshot. He said, "I'll show you the Fahlstrom knot, but you've gotta' swear you won't tell anyone. You gotta' take this to your grave."

In deadpan fashion, Akami replied, "That's easy. I won't have to keep the secret long. I'm old."

They both laughed, then Jacob said, "Hey don't joke about that, Akami. It makes me sad."

"Okay. Then shut up and teach me the Fahlstrom knot."

They worked for a couple hours until Akami could tie the Fahlstrom knot perfectly. Akami looked closely at the knot and noted, "It's a lot like a classic sheepshank, but it has that extra loop on the bottom side."

"Exactly," Jacob confirmed. Akami studied the knot carefully, then realizing it was very late, they called it a night.

A few nights later, Jacob taught Akami about wind patterns and stormy weather predictions. Jacob began to explain, "There's an old sailors proverb my uncle taught me. It says, 'Mare's tails and mackerel scales make lofty ships carry low sails.' This means when there are small clumpy clouds resembling fish scales in the sky along with wispy clouds like that of a horse's tail, a storm is approaching. When this happens, the sails should be lowered to protect the ship from the high winds. It's right almost all the time. I know it works."

"I'm sure it does Jacob, you're a very smart boy," said Akami nodding. "Tomorrow before you work, I will show you how to make a fish trap. And, we will have fish for dinner," added Akami with a chuckle.

Jacob poked at the fire a few more times with a long driftwood stick, then excused himself. "I'm getting tired. I'll see you tomorrow."

As Jacob walked off toward the barracks Akami yelled, "Early Jacob, before the sun. Meet me by the Hayes, west of the factory."

...

There was a pre-dawn glow on the horizon, but it was still quite dark. Akami sat on a log that was half above water and half submerged in the Hayes. On his lap he held a device he was creating with long flexible branches. Carefully he weaved the branches together. He would work a bit, then hold the device up and examine it. After some minor adjustments to the branches, he would work on the contraption a bit more. He was a bit startled when out of the darkness came a voice. "Akami, I'm here to catch fish." It was Jacob, his eyes still a bit sleepy and his voice slightly out of wind after running all the way down from the barracks.

Akami held up his wooden device with pride. He said in Cree, "Jacob! Look what I'm making. See how I'm weaving the branches together? I'm making it long and narrow. Closed on this end and open on this end."

"How does it work?" Jacob asked, continuing the conversation in Cree.

"I build my trap, I put a shiny piece of metal in the closed end like this, then I put it in the water attached to two sticks that are jammed into the bottom of the river like this. And the trap is set."

"But how does it work?" Jacob questioned, still puzzled.

"The fish swim down river and as they approach, they're drawn by the piece of metal reflecting light. The fish swims into the trap and is caught."

"Why don't they just swim out the open end?" challenged Jacob.

"They can't. Fish don't swim backwards, Jacob. You see, the trap is too narrow for it to turn around. Just like that, my device magically transforms a swimming fish into dinner!"

Jacob laughed and smiled at Akami.

"After you finish working over at the Nelson we'll come down and see if we've caught anything," promised Akami, pulling Jacob in for a small one-armed side hug.

Chapter 18.
Winter Prep

The hours passed slowly as Jacob and the crew of settlers cut branches off large white spruce trees so they could be used to build the cabins. The shifts were long, with few breaks. The work began at sun-up, about 7 a.m. and they worked until sundown. The instant the foreman, Jack Finley, announced an end to the day by ringing a large iron bell Jacob made a dash for the Hayes River to meet Akami.

Wading into the cold water up to his knees he approached the fish trap. He instantly began yelling when he discovered a large fish struggling inside. "Akami! Akami! We caught one! Hurry!" The monster was mostly golden colored with an orange underbelly. Akami shuffled across the beach and into the frigid water joining Jacob.

"Ah, brook trout. Looks like fifteen pounds," Akami said. Jacob carried the trap with the brook trout still inside up to Akami's lodge. There Akami taught Jacob how to filet the fish and prep it for cooking. He got a roaring fire going, then allowed it to burn down to hot red coals. The fish filets were laid on a plank of pine which Akami suspended just above the hot embers. The two spent the rest of the evening grabbing tender pieces of fish by hand and eating them with wild rice Akami had brought from the Lake Superior territory. Jacob thought this a welcome respite from the monotony of salted pork and mush dinners served nightly in the factory mess hall. It was a particularly clear night and stars dominated the sky. Akami stood up from the log on which he and Jacob were sitting. He then laid down on the ground. Jacob did the same. They looked up at the beautiful sky in silence for a long time. Then Akami spoke. "The stars, *atchakosuk* are important to my people. They've been here for thousands and thousands of years. We come from those stars. We are related to those stars. Soon, when I finish what I came here to do, I will go back up to those stars." Jacob looked over at Akami. He was just about to speak when Akami put his finger against his lips indicating that Jacob should remain silent and listen. He then continued, "See that one? That's Keewatin, the 'going home star.' The English traders call it the North Star." Again, Jacob looked over. Akami just shook his head. Jacob took the hint and kept his mouth shut. "See that group of stars over there? That's Wesakaychak, the trickster. Don't trust that one." Akami took a break from speaking and sat up to light his pipe. He took a couple puffs. Jacob resisted the urge to look over at him and remained silent as instructed by Akami. Akami continued, "Low on the horizon, over there, that's Ochekatchakosuk. The weasel. According to Cree teaching, a long time ago there were years with no summer. The animals were desperate to find where summer went and bring it back. The weasel, Ochek, was chosen for the task. After he succeeded, he escaped into the sky, and The Creator stamped his shape into the stars."

Jacob, unable to remain silent any longer, said, "It does look like a weasel. Can I tell you a Viking star story?"

"Okay, of course."

"It's a story my mother told me often, about where the stars came from. The world was created from the body of a Viking giant named Ymer. His skull forms the sky and the heavens. The skull was held in place by four dwarves, where sparks from the realm of fire form the stars. Each star was given the paths they were to roam by the gods." Akami looked over at Jacob. Jacob put his finger to his lips. Akami chuckled. Jacob pointed up and said, "Look up that way.

Those seven stars are Aurvandil's toe."

"Why do Vikings worship a toe?" asked Akami.

"It's not worship. It's based on what happened in a story. Thor and an ugly giant Hrungne got into a fight."

"Over whiskey or a woman?" asked Akami.

Jacob sighed an annoyed sigh. "I was quiet the whole time you were telling Cree stories. Come on Akami."

Akami laughed so hard he snorted a bit. Then said, "I'm sorry. I will tie my mouth shut with a sailor's knot."

"Thank you. Okay, here goes. So, Thor and Hrungne got in a fight. Thor was injured and got a piece of stone stuck in his head. To get it out, he got the help of an Oracle named Groa. Thankful for the help, Thor told Groa about when he helped her husband Aurvandil escape from the land of the giants. During the escape Aurvandil froze his big toe, which Thor broke off and threw up into the sky to become the constellation, Aurvandil's toe. This made Groa so happy that she forgot her magic, and to this day Thor has that piece of stone in his head."

"That's a dumb story. Weird ending," noted Akami.

"I didn't call your story dumb," Jacob said. There was then a quiet pause, and Jacob added, "You're right, though. The ending is kinda' dumb."

Akami laughed.

The star stories went on for another hour. Of course, there were always jokes sprinkled in. Akami always said, "Without laughter, life is quiet."

So simple, but so true, Jacob thought.

For Jacob, this fragile old man was a brother, father and grandfather all wrapped into one person. They shared a pipe of tobacco, a gesture of great respect from Akami. For an elder to share a pipe with a mere boy was quite a gesture indeed. It meant he accepted him as a man, with the skills of a hunter and warrior.

Soon the evening became too cold to remain outside by the campfire. Jacob and Akami decided to retreat inside the lodge that

Akami shared with his daughter, her husband and their four children. This shifted the dynamic from that of mentor and student to more of a family interaction. They accepted Jacob as if he were one of their own. Akami's daughter was married to an Ojibwe man named White Deer. He was from Broken Head River, just south of what they described as large body of water several days journey inland. The Cree called it Lake Winipek, which means "muddy waters." They described this lake as being near the area where Jacob and the recruits were to build the Selkirk Settlement. Today this lake is known as Lake Winnipeg. Akami boasted that White Deer's brother Peguis was a powerful chief of the Salteaux of the Prairies, a band of Ojibwe with more than 300 members. White Deer, a large but soft-spoken man, always downplayed the boasting. Through conversations with White Deer, Jacob was able to practice speaking Ojibwe. He picked up the language quickly due to its similarity to the Cree language. Red Deer explained to Jacob how they call themselves Anishinaabeg, which means the "true people or "original people." It was only other tribes or Europeans that call them Ojibwe or Chippewa.

One night by the campfire with White Deer, Jacob asked, "Why is your family still here at the factory? Shouldn't you be trapping?"

White Deer nodded a bit, then responded, "We stay because, before you came, Akami was very sick. We thought he would die, but he pulled through. By the time he got better it was too late and we were stuck."

Jacob was a bit surprised. "Akami never told me he was sick."

"Akami is a proud man. He doesn't show weakness. He was a great warrior. He wanted us to leave him behind. We refused. This made him very angry, but luckily, he was too sick to fight about it. So, here we are." There was a pause in the conversation, then White Deer looked over at Jacob and cocked his head to the side. "What happened to your head to make your hair that color?"

Jacob laughed then answered, "It's always been this way. Nothing happened. Where I come from, many people have hair like this."

White Deer pondered for a minute. "Where are your people?"

"Sweden. To the other side of Hudson Bay and then all the way across the ocean."

"The Ocean?" asked White Deer.

"The Ocean is water that is ten, maybe 100 times bigger than the largest lake you've ever seen. It takes many sunsets travel to get there by ship."

"Why would you want to leave your home? Why do you come here?" asked White Deer.

"Where I come from there are so many people that all the land and water is owned by others. We come here to have something for ourselves," answered Jacob, trying hard to help White Deer understand.

"How can you own the land? The land just *IS*," said White Deer with a puzzled look on his face.

"I know, it's different. Where I come from, men own the land. It's theirs, like ... the way a gun is yours. Does that make sense?" said Jacob.

"No," he blurted with a hearty laugh. He then continued, "You yellow-hair-people are strange."

"Yeah, I guess we are a bit different." Answered Jacob.

...

North of York Factory at the cabin site by the Nelson River the Selkirk settlers were completing a roof. The sun was sinking slowly into the towering pines. Akami had come over to see Jacob's handiwork. As he approached, he looked up and yelled hello in Cree. Jacob, from one of the rooftops, answered the greeting in Cree which caught the attention of a very large Scotsman wearing a brimmed hat, a tattered blue overcoat, and worn-out, blood-stained boots. His scowl indicated his displeasure with the exchange.

The large man took a last swig from his bottle of whisky and slurred, "Well look here. We've got ourselves a white savage." There was a moment of silence as no one dared speak. The large man continued, "What happened, Swede Boy? Did you see a ghost that scared the red skin right off ya?" The large man walked across the roof until he was right next to Jacob. He sniffed the air, then went on, "All I know is that nose is telling me that you do smell like one of 'em." This got a mixed reaction from the crowd that was gathering. Some laughed. Others stood in fearful silence. The large Scotsman continued his harassment. He scooped a handful of tar from a nearby bucket then said, "Here, I'll fix you up Swede boy. I'll make you all dark again." He plopped the tar on top of Jacob's head and smeared what was left on his cheeks. Suddenly, he grabbed Jacob by the shirt between the shoulder blades. With brute strength he extended his arm out. This had Jacob dangling over the edge of the rooftop, thirty feet above the ground. The crowd, surprised by the sudden escalation, gasped. The large Scotsman laughed. He slurred, "Look, I'm gonna' do a little experiment. I'm gonna' find out if the white savage can fly!" The straw roof gave way under the Scotsman's foot, causing him to stumble and almost drop Jacob. Again, a gasp came from the onlookers.

From the back of the crowd came a booming voice, "Put the boy down. Now!" It was Akami. Jacob had never heard this gentle old man use such a powerful tone in his voice.

The Scotsman laughed at Akami and yelled back, "What are you going to do old man? You gonna' waddle up here and get me?"

Akami, never once taking his glare off the Scotsman, replied in a very measured tone, "You will set the boy down on the roof, have another drink of whisky and walk home. That way no one has to die today."

This comment flustered the drunken Scotsman a bit. A look of what resembled fear came across his face for a moment before he regained his bully composure. "Maybe I just let go and the little white savage can come down on his own."

Akami answered, "You don't want to do that." The Scotsman

laughed again. Then, before anyone could blink an eye, Akami raised his bow, retrieved an arrow from his quiver, and fired, hitting the Scotsman in the shoulder. The thrust of the impact caused the Scotsman to stagger back a few steps. He then dropped Jacob on the roof, stumbled a couple more steps, and fell. Jacob quickly scurried across the roof to a ladder and rushed down. The Scotsman, now sitting on the roof, broke off the feather side of the arrow and pushed the head side out the back of his shoulder.

He took another swig of whisky and yelled, "You better be on the watch, old man! I'm going to bring a lot of pain into your life." He coughed, then took one last drink as the crowd nervously disbursed.

Chapter 19.
Bitter Cold

York Factory. December 18, 1811.

Growing up in Stockholm, Jacob was used to the temperature never getting very warm, but it also was never very cold. The ocean breeze on Sweden's east coast kept Stockholm winter temperatures quite mild and seldom falling below twenty degrees Fahrenheit. Jacob had no idea what was coming, even though the brutal winter was a daily topic of discussion in the mess hall. This was a whole new kind of frigid. A winter at York Factory delivered sixty below zero temperatures, blizzard white outs, and in mid-winter, very little sunlight. In December, half of every day would be spent, not only below freezing, but below zero Fahrenheit. It was cold. Arctic cold. Jacob and the Cree children would often perform experiments with winter's frigid chill. They discovered that when you throw hot coffee into the air at thirty below zero, the water turns to ice instantly and floats off as a cloud of vapor. It never hits the ground. Kind of like it turns into a coffee ghost and flies away. That's the way Jacob described it.

In addition to suffering from the brutal cold, a lack of fresh vegetables and fruit led to an outbreak of scurvy. More than twenty men suffered terribly from general weakness, anemia, inflamed gums, and skin blisters. Miles Macdonell, who had seen the symptoms before, was aware of remedies for scurvy. Plentiful white spruce trees north of the Nelson River allowed Macdonell to order the making of a special tea created from the sap. After several days of treatment, the settler's symptoms subsided, and the scurvy outbreak was under control. The settlers did all they could to simply stay fed, stay warm, and stay alive.

...

It was a wicked cold day, just like the three wicked-damned cold days before that. Jacob was delivering a sled of supplies and food rations to the group of Orkney men living in the cabins north of the Nelson. A blue glow on the horizon lit the structures constructed of spruce logs stacked eight feet high topped with a straw roof. Every cabin belched smoke from the burning fires that prevented certain death of the settlers within. Jacob took some pride knowing he helped build the structures that provided shelter and warmth. Today was a particularly icy cold morning with a strong wind and snow pellets blowing harshly in Jacob's face. They were not flakes of snow, but rather little shards of sharp ice. The cold stung his cheeks. Jacob wished he had a team of sled dogs as he struggled to pull the heavy wooden sled against the wind, through the deep snow. His feet were now completely numb and had been that way for several minutes. The upside of the cold was that the rivers were frozen over, making it easier to cross the Nelson. Two-Eye barked and ran alongside as Jacob struggled to pull the heavy sled. The gusting wind was almost freezing his lungs when he tried to breathe. He had to stop many times and turn his back. His cheeks were numb and tingling so he pulled the wool scarf up from around his neck. He tried to cover as much of his face as he could.

As Jacob brought food rations inside a cabin, the large Scotsman with the tattered blue jacket approached Jacob's sled. With an axe he broke two of the cross beams that supported the skids of the sled. He then ran off into the woods and hid behind a large pine. Unaware,

Jacob came running out of the cabin, grabbed the lead rope and pulled the sled. Excited to get back to the barracks, Jacob ran. About 100 feet from the barracks the weakened sled skid hit a rock under the snow and broke. This made pulling the sled very difficult and Jacob crouched down to examine the damage. "Shit!" Jacob yelled as he ran his glove over the split piece of wood. Jacob strained, trying to pull the broken sled. He was fading. It was taking him too long to cross the Nelson. As he approached the main camp, Jacob was so cold he felt a bit woozy, and his feet were now in pain. He stumbled to a stop and decided to rest a bit. He sat on the blankets piled on the sled and nodded off. The wind blew gusts of snow, and it began to drift up on the sled.

At the camp, a birch bark door flap swung open. Akami grabbed a few pieces of firewood, turned, and headed back inside his lodge. But something caught his attention. He could hear a dog barking. As he surveyed more closely, Akami noticed a sled across the snow-covered meadow. On top of it there seemed to be a slumped body. Akami dropped the pieces of firewood and began running. As he approached, he recognized it was Jacob and became gravely concerned. Two-Eye, who was licking Jacob's forehead stopped, looked up at Akami, and barked. Akami had seen many men die in frigid temperatures like this. He knelt beside Jacob, put his arms around him and tried to urge him to consciousness. It was no use. Jacob was unresponsive. Akami tucked Jacob under the wool blankets and pulled the broken sled as fast as he could to his camp. The whole way, he couldn't figure out why it was so difficult to pull. As he got closer to the wigwam, he yelled to White Deer, "Get a fire burning. It's Jacob."

Akami's daughter came out of the wigwam and helped carry Jacob inside. They laid him beside the fire.

"Now we wait and hope he is okay," said Akami. He tried to be calm, but his daughter knew that little crack in his voice indicated he was not calm at all. He was nervous and fearful.

It was several hours before Jacob sat up abruptly and began

screaming in pain. He had tears in his eyes as he grabbed for his feet. He yelled, "My feet. It feels like someone's pouring hot tar on 'em." Jacob looked up and noticed he was in Akami's lodge. In a weak voice, burdened with confusion, he asked, "How did I get here?"

"Jacob, calm down. It's okay. Your feet are frozen. This pain happens when they thaw. It will hurt for a while." Handing Jacob a whisky bottle, Akami said, "Drink this, it will help with the pain."

Jacob took two big gulps, then curled into a ball. He reached down holding his feet with his hands to warm them. Jacob scooted a bit and moved his feet toward the fire.

Akami said, "Be careful, Jacob. You don't want to warm them too fast."

For several hours Jacob drifted in and out of consciousness. Akami's daughter put Jacob's head on her knees and rubbed his forehead. She pushed his long wavy blonde hair aside.

She asked, "How did they put a boy on that ship to come here? He's just a boy."

Akami shook his head and answered, "I don't know."

The heat in the lodge was making Jacob sweat. Jacob thought it strange that he was sweating like crazy while his feet and hands were still frozen. He lay shivering for about an hour, then drifted off to sleep.

Still curious about why the sled was so hard to pull, Akami walked outside and approached it. He crouched down and closely examined the broken crossbeams. He thought it odd that the beams were broken in two different directions. How was that possible? That break could not have happened on the trail. Also, there appeared to be unusual cuts next to the break. Akami's head tilted with curiosity, then his eyes squinted with anger as he felt the cuts in the cross beams that were clearly made by a hatchet.

Over the next few weeks, parts of Jacob's toes and the pinky finger on his left hand turned black. Eventually, the skin peeled off, but it regenerated, and he didn't lose any body parts. He was very lucky. Jacob could easily have become one of the many York Factory residents who lost an ear, nose, fingers, or other body parts to the brutal cold.

...

In January the nights were very long. Sunrise was about nine a.m., and it was getting dark by two in the afternoon. The upside was there wasn't enough light for work. So, groups of people would gather in cabins to play cards and dice games. Singing and telling stories were also popular pastimes in winter. Jacob enjoyed the men from Ireland. They were boisterous and loved to sing. The Irish settlers didn't really know what to make of Jacob. He was a nice boy but was often the recipient of crossways looks because he hung out with the Cree children and Akami. They didn't understand that Jacob was just seeking a place to fit in. He gravitated to the Cree because they were the only group at the fort with children and Jacob found their sense of humor amusing. Furthermore, they accepted Jacob most openly. They welcomed him.

One particularly cold evening Jacob was with the Cree family. They were huddled closely in the wigwam.

"If you are brave, I will tell you a story," challenged White Deer, speaking in Ojibwe. He looked around at the children's faces. "No, I can't tell it. You are but children and will run off in fear."

"Tell us," insisted the children, including Jacob.

White Deer squinted his eye skeptically. "I don't know. I shouldn't." He turned and walked out of the wigwam. The group of Cree children murmured. They were disappointed. Then suddenly, the door flap swung open, and he reappeared. "Okay. Gichi manidoo has told me you are ready. So, I will tell my story." White Deer pulled a blanket up over his head covering every part of his body except his face. "It happened to me many years ago. When I was just a boy, not much older than you. Very late on a summer night I was awakened by the hoot of an owl. Hoo ... hoo ... hoo. I tried to ignore it, but it continued. My mother and father both snored loudly as I got up and walked out of our wigwam. Then, just before I left, my father farted ... a really loud ripper of a fart." The Cree children giggled. White Deer held a finger to his mouth, indicating for them to shush. He continued, "The owl continued to hoot, and I followed the sound across the village, through the meadow, and over to the edge of the woods. My mother always told me, 'don't go in the woods.' So, I hesitated. I looked back toward the village as if checking to see if Mother was watching. Then I did it. I went into the woods ... at night. The glow of a full moon cast just enough light for me to find my way. In the daytime I had walked this trail many times. But it was different at night. It felt odd out there. Like I wasn't alone. I was more curious than frightened, so I continued deeper and deeper into the woods. Whatever else was there with me didn't feel, normal. I got a whiff of a foul odor. *Was there a dead animal nearby*, I wondered? I heard some rustling in the bushes not far from me. I thought about going back, but curiosity got the best of me. I kept going, my eyes were darting left and right as I scanned for danger. When I got to the top of a hill, I saw something that made my heart stop. There was a figure. At first, I thought it was a person, but then I noticed how it moved. It twitched in short jerky movements. Its bones popped as they moved. The head seemed human but had a much larger than normal jaw. Bones protruded from underneath the thing's ashen gray skin, but its powerful movements did not seem weak. Just the opposite. I felt like it had the power to rip the limbs from my body. It had long legs that looked like that of a dog. The creature's long bony fingers were tipped with very long sharp claws. They looked like long pointy deer antlers. The creature was hunched over a wild boar and was pulling something out of the carcass and chewing on it. Oh man, it was eating the wild boar's intestines. As a gust of wind blew from behind me, its head popped up and the creature appeared to be sniffing. Slowly its head turned until it was looking right at me. It had picked up my scent. The ghoulish face had eyes that glowed red. It did not appear to have a nose, more like a skull. Now, getting a closer look,

I realized what it was. It was the Windigo. I turned and began to run as fast as I could. I could hear the creature running on all fours behind me. The steps were becoming louder as it got closer ... and closer. It was about to pounce when I made it out of the woods and the Windigo just vanished into thin air. As I walked home, I realized there was a cut on my arm. Was that from a tree branch? Or was it from the sharp antler-like claws of the Windigo? I guess I'll never know." White Deer looked right at the Cree children. They were all frozen with fear. Abruptly he continued, "But sometimes on the night of the full moon. Nights exactly like tonight. I feel a ravenous craving for raw meat and intestines." White Deer reached into his mouth and felt his canine teeth. "My teeth seem sharper. Often a growl escapes from my chest and my hands gnarl and twist into long, bony, sharp ... claws!" The Cree children screamed. Some got up and ran as White Deer pulled his arm out from under the blanket. Extending from his shirtsleeve, where his hand should be, was a deer antler. He held it up, then toward the children and pretended he could not control himself. Jacob and the other children burst from the wigwam out into the cold. Right after them, White Deer came outside. He laughed hysterically. "Come back, it's just a story. See, my hand is fine." White Deer extended his hand showing it was normal while displaying the deer antler with his other hand. Akami tumbled from the wigwam laughing so hard he couldn't stand.

Jacob shook his head. "That wasn't scary."

Akami said, "You might have to check your britches."

"Not funny. Not funny at all," said Jacob.

The full moon emitted a reddish glow against the charcoal black sky. The Cree children waved to Jacob as he walked back to the barracks, then they went back into the wigwam. They murmured and giggled about the story. It took more than an hour for them to settle down and drift off to sleep.

...

As the winter drug on, the bitter cold led to a bitter mood. The work foreman, Finlay, was becoming a real problem. He would not obey orders and refused to do any work. Ultimately, Miles Macdonell had enough, and Finlay was confined to a small cabin near the Hayes. After weeks in confinement, Finlay's fellow Glasgow crew gathered in protest and burnt the cabin to the ground, allowing Finlay to escape. The insurgents were summoned to appear before Mr. Hillier, the magistrate, who accompanied the settlers and Captain Macdonell on the journey. Hillier, Macdonell and Mr. Auld, the superintendent of the H.B.C., sat behind a large table that was up on a wooden platform. Finlay and the group of eleven insurgents were ushered in, then seated in small wooden chairs in front of the large table. The inquiry had barely begun when the men caused a disturbance, refusing to submit to the authority of the magistrate. One of the malcontents took to his feet, stepped forward and addressed Mr. Hillier directly. The man spoke in English with a thick Scottish accent. "We ain't gotta' listen to the likes of you. Firstly, who gave you jurisdiction over us? We're in America now, not Scotland. Your authority is thousands of miles away. And you ain't my momma, and you certainly ain't me pops. Me pops would scrub the floor with a scrawny shit-sucker like you. Secondly, we've not been treated the way we were promised by your agent in Glasgow. As soon as we signed your stupid papers the awful treatment began. I spit on all of ya for draggin' me across an ocean to this horrible frozen place If I took all of your broken promises and piled them up, they'd be piled as high as the huskie shit behind the dog shed."

There was a moment of silence. The kind of silence that exists when a fuse is lit, and everyone is just watching, listening ... waiting for the dynamite to blow. Then, red in the face with a huge vein bulging at his temple, Macdonell stood. Macdonell was a large intimidating man. The muscles of his forearms stretched his cotton shirt sleeves tight. His knuckles cracked as he clinched both fists, then calmly in a voice ready to deliver an ass whipping, said, "So, you think you're free men, do ya?" The room breathed a sigh of relief after Macdonell's calm response but wondered where this was heading. "Go ahead, you're free." Faces across the room wore puzzled looks. Heads turned in all directions, looking curiously around the room. Were the Glasgow men really going to get off that easy? A low chatter among the insurgents began, then Macdonell continued, "As free men you don't have to worry about work duty at York Factory anymore..." The Glasgow men chuckled and interrupted with a small cheer, then quickly went silent as Macdonell said, "... as you are hereby ejected by Mr. Auld's authority with the Hudson's Bay Company. If you appear on York Factory grounds, you will be shot on sight. Also, as free men, you will have no need for York Factory provisions or your firearms. Sargent, please confiscate their weapons and return them to the factory arsenal. For the remainder of the winter, we shall be generous enough to allow you 'free men' to stay at the Nelson camp, where perhaps your fellow settlers will find it in their hearts to assist you. If not, you're on your own. After all, you are free men, right? In the spring you will have a choice. You can leave the fort on your own, or you will be sent back to Scotland, where Mr. Hillier does have the unquestioned authority to put you on trial for arson and mutiny." Macdonell smashed the wooden gavel down hard on the table. The sound echoed through the large empty room as the malcontented men from Glasgow exited. Once outside, the men approached their sleds and were about to mush their dog teams when, once again, Macdonell interrupted. "Free men, what are you doing with those sleds and dog teams? They're H.B.C. property. Free men certainly wouldn't have a need for the property of the H.B.C. You can walk." With this, he tilted his head to the soldiers beside him who approached and took possession of the sleds. "Oh, and the snowshoes too." The malcontents from Glasgow who were strapping their snowshoes to their feet dropped them to the ground and began their long walk to the Nelson camp, often sinking up to their crotch in the deep snowdrifts.

...

By staying clear of the warring factions, as Jacob called them, he didn't have to deal with all the arguing and fighting. On New Year's Eve, several Irishmen crashed a party being thrown by Orkney men. A fight broke out and three Orkney men were beaten so badly, it was not certain they would live. Akami was at the party enjoying his share of whiskey, but the fight soured his mood, and he staggered out the front door. He slipped on his snowshoes and began the walk to his lodge through the woods. While walking, he heard the soft crunching of snow on the trail behind him. Even an ample supply of whiskey in his belly couldn't dampen Akami's keen senses. He quickly ran forward, then backtracked covering his tracks by smoothing snow with a small branch. These woods were Akami's hunting grounds and he knew every tree, every hill ... every inch. He tucked himself behind a large pine as the crunching sound of snowshoes approached.

Then a yell bellowed out. "Time to die, old savage!" It was the large Scotsman with the tattered blue overcoat and bloody boots. He had followed Akami from the party with bad intentions. "Where are ya', you red-skinned devil?" questioned the Scotsman. Akami quickly ran across the trail. He crouched down behind a large stone pile. The Scotsman caught sight of Akami and made his way toward him. As he approached, Akami stood up behind the rock pile and stared blankly at the Scotsman for a long time, then smiled. The Scotsman raised the hatchet he was carrying and ran toward Akami. He yelled loudly. Akami just stood there and smiled. The large Scotsman was just feet away when suddenly the noose of a deer snare closed on his ankle and sprung him upward. The Scotsman's brimmed hat and hatchet fell as he hung upside down about four feet off the ground. There was confusion and horror on the Scotsman's face as Akami walked past. He stood silently behind the Scotsman for a long time. The Scotsman pleaded, "Just let me down, we can forget the whole thing. I promise."

Akami responded in a calm voice, "The mind doesn't forget. The Creator made it so." Akami sighed deeply then continued, "You have pushed and pushed. You threaten me. Worse, you threatened those I love. That can only end one way."

"No. Stop. You can let me go. I'll forget everything," begged the Scotsman. His true character was now on display. He was nothing but a shuddering coward. Which seems to be the dominant make-up of most all bullies.

Akami grabbed the Scotsman's mouth with one hand and pinched off his nose with the other. The Scotsman's arms flailed helplessly as he fought to breathe. After a few seconds of gurgling sounds and struggle, the Scotsman's body went limp. Akami walked around and looked closely at the Scotsman's face. He reached out and felt his neck for a heartbeat. No pulse. He is gone.

Aloud to the lifeless corpse, Akami said, "Well, the world is rid of you now." He danced around the lifeless body as it dangled by the deer snare, rope creaking. It was difficult for Akami to resist the temptation of taking his scalp. But he restrained himself, shook his head, and picked up a small tree branch. All around the body and as he headed through the woods, Akami used the branch to carefully cover his tracks in the snow. Returning it to its undisturbed fluffy white consistency. It was as if he were never there.

It was 3 a.m. by the time Akami arrived at his wigwam. Jacob was sound asleep inside. Blue moonlight shined in with the opening of the door flap. Akami chuckled a bit as he heard Jacob snoring. It wasn't the loud obnoxious snore of a grown man, but a cute little snore of a young boy. Akami thought it adorable. He touched Jacob's hair, closely examining it as if he had never seen it before. He believed that this unusual hair made Jacob a mamahtawisiwin—someone spiritually gifted or magic to the Cree people. But mostly, he loved Jacob as if he was a grandson. Akami, feeling a bit mischievous, yelled, "Jacob, wake up. Your britches are on fire!" Jacob popped up, a bit startled. "Jacob, I wanted to tell you something," said Akami. Jacob rubbed his eyes and became a bit more alert. "There was a fight tonight at the Nelson camp. Some of the Irish beat three Orkney men. Why do men do this to each other?"

Jacob, half asleep, struggled to process the information. He asked, "Huh? Akami I was sleeping, what?"

"All men do this to one another, and they have done it for thousands of years. From as far back to when time began men beat and killed each other. Why?" For a long time Akami sat staring up at the open hole in the top of the lodge. "Revenge follows revenge, follows revenge. It never stops. It doesn't make you feel better. Maybe for a moment, until they take revenge for the revenge you took. Then they kill your family."

Jacob, now realizing the heavy odor of whisky on his breath, placed a hand on Akami's hanging head, "It's okay Akami. Men do really bad things to one another. But they do good things too. You do good things. You forgive. And love."

Slurring, Akami added, "This life has taken from me things I can never get back. I try, but that empty place is there. Always there." He took a breath and sniffled a couple times.

Jacob urged, "It's okay, Akami. Just lay down. Go to sleep. You've had too much whisky. We'll talk in the morning."
Akami lay down and Jacob covered him with a large buffalo hide blanket. Tucking it gently under his chin. It began to snow, and the full moon flickered through the falling curtain of white.

Chapter 20.
The Thaw

May 1812. It was a sunny and warm afternoon at York Factory. For the first time in a long time, Jacob was able to take off his jacket and gloves while outside. He and Akami were in the woods building fences and setting deer snares. Akami turned to Jacob and explained, "Now that it's warming, the whitetails will become active. It's time to get food for summer." They set several snares about 400 feet into the woods from Akami's camp. Akami continued, "The Hayes has fast-moving water and will soon be open. The deer will hear the rushing water, then they will run through these woods to quench their thirst. Large herds of them will come. Right through our snares."

"You're a good teacher, Akami. Every day I learn something from you," Jacob said, feeling a bit of sadness knowing that, with the coming thaw, he would be leaving soon. Akami simply shrugged his shoulders and smiled.

As they walked together among the spruce, Akami noted, "Often you just move through the trees not listening to the earth. That's wandering. If you venture out deep in the woods and really look ... really listen, then you are exploring. Most white men just wander."

A few nights later, Jacob discovered just how great a teacher Akami was. Exactly as he predicted, deer came in a massive herd through the woods, toward the Hayes. There were hundreds them. Jacob had never seen so many animals in one place at one time. For the next month, maybe longer, there would be a continuous feasting on venison.

...

The smell of fresh-cut timber filled the air as Jacob opened the creaking door of the boat shed. The large building, made of rough-cut pine trees, was lit by a rising sun. Shards of light found their way through gaps in the wall. The sawdust floating in the air made the shards even more prominent. Men were chopping and carving white pine and birch into boat ribs and sideboards needed to build four bateaux for the journey inland to Assiniboia. A bateau is a long boat that sits very low to the water. Their advantage, compared to a canoe, is that the wide flat bottom makes it much more stable. The stability and size make it possible for the bateau to carry large amounts of cargo. The boats were constructed with a removable mast and a sail that could be stored neatly at the side of the boat when not in use and hoisted to catch advantageous winds. Miles Macdonell pushed for weeks to build this style of boat and eventually won the debate with other leaders of the Selkirk settlers. The boat shed had a high ceiling, about twenty feet, from which ropes and pulley systems hung. Along the side wall were several work benches with cutting, carving, and rasping tools. A half-constructed boat about twenty-eight feet long was in the middle of the room. It sat on four planks suspended on both sides by a simple scaffolding system of squared and stacked black spruce. Seven men worked vigorously as the timber skeleton of bateau number one took form. Jacob, who had a love for sailing and knew his way around a boat, was excited by the prospect of learning to build a bateau. For the most part the men ignored this boy hanging about, but to his good fortune, Skipper Gull from the *Eddystone* had been appointed head of the bateau project by Macdonell.

"Jacob," Gull yelled from across the room. When Jacob did not respond, Gull yelled, "Swede Boy!" Finally able to separate Gull's voice from the loud sawing, hammering, and chopping, Jacob turned and recognized the ship's skipper. He had not seen Gull since before the winter freeze. A huge smile popped onto Jacob's face as he ran to greet his friend.

"Thomas! I haven't seen you for so long. I missed you." The skipper hugged Jacob so hard that his feet came up off the ground.

"Your English has gotten quite good," noted the skipper.

"Yes, sir," Jacob answered then spoke to Thomas in Ojibwe. The skipper did not speak the language and had no idea what Jacob was saying, but he did recognize it.

"So, you also speak Ojibwe?"

Jacob answered, "Not great, but I can communicate okay. My Cree is better."

Gull said, "That's a great skill for a man to have in the Assiniboia territory." There was a pause in the conversation as they both caught their breath. Then the skipper continued in a very business-like tone. "Ya' know, I've been looking for an expert sea captain to help me build masts and sails for the bateaux. Do you know anyone like that?"

Jacob chuckled, "I might?"

The skipper went further, "Indeed, I saw a man on the York peninsula fitting that description. Strong, blond hair, full-blooded Viking. He's a bit young, but he's pretty smart for a Swede and is a highly skilled sailor." Jacob's laugh was cut short when the skipper shifted to a very serious tone. "There's just one problem though. It's a very serious problem." The skipper paused for dramatic effect and Jacob's expression sank. Then the skipper continued, "Ya' see, this Viking lad is a terrible farter. He just can't keep 'em in." Jacob was now full-blown hysterical laughing. The skipper, laughing hard himself, with tears rolling down his face went even further, "It's like he's playing the drums with his buttocks. I've seen a lotta' cabbage eaters wield some impressive cheek snappers in my time, but they can't out-fart this fart wielding lad. Neigh, they can't hold a candle to him. Well, in fact no one can hold a candle around this boy, 'cause his arse-wind keeps blowin' the bloody things out." Proud of his humor, the skipper laughed loudly and pushed Jacob's shoulder in a friendly gesture. Several of the builders who had been listening also laughed. Jacob was a good sport about the whole thing. He was experienced enough to realize that, if a crew was teasing you, it meant they like you. "Seriously though, Jacob, I need you to help me. You know pully systems, ropes, and sails better than anyone at York."

Jacob smiled and responded, "Yes sir, when can I start?"

The skipper handed Jacob a pair of boots and leather work gloves. "Right now," he answered. Then the skipper gestured to Jacob's backside. "But don't aim that thing at anyone, especially if you've had pickled rutabagas for breakfast." The crew again laughed. Thomas Gull, the skipper, was the kind of man who told a story with the skill of a trained actor, extracting every ounce of drama, suspense, or humor.

Three weeks into bateau construction much progress had been made and Jacob was now very familiar with the crew. Jacob spent this particularly warm and sunny morning threading rope and rigging sails. He and two of the wood carvers took a break to have lunch. They found a comfortable spot outside the boat shed. As they sat eating salt-pork and cold beans, six British soldiers walked past at a brisk pace. The wood carver yelled, "What's the hurry, lieutenant?"

The soldier stopped momentarily and said, "Dead body found in the woods." Jacob and the two wood carvers looked at each other with surprised silence.

Jacob stood and said, "I've got to check it out."

He then trailed the soldiers into the woods for more than a mile before reaching the location of the dead body. The afternoon sun blasted through the tall white pines. The British soldiers and Miles Macdonell looked on silently as the York doctor approached the body that hung from a tree by a deer snare. He pulled on a pair of gloves and covered his nose with a handkerchief as the body was in an advanced state of decomposition.

Miles Macdonell asked, "Did he freeze to death?"

"Not sure. Maybe? Might have also starved to death, being caught up here like this," answered the doctor.

"Who is it?" questioned Macdonell.

The doctor thought for a moment, then answered, "I can't state for certain. But, based on height and overall size, plus the blue jacket he's wearing ... it's the Scotsman that went missing New Year's Eve." There was a momentary pause, then the doctor continued, "The one everyone suspected to be a deserter."

Macdonell took a few steps away, then turned back toward the doctor. He said, "I can't believe anyone in this camp could kill the Scotsman. He was a boxing champion, and just look at the size of him." The doctor and most of the soldiers nodded in agreement.

The doctor tilted his head in thought then answered, "Well, it's hard to know with the body in such bad shape. That's really all I can tell right now. I don't see any signs of gunshot or stabbing."

Macdonell nodded then yelled to the soldiers, "Get a cart out here and bring the body in for a proper burial."

Jacob watched the entire exchange. His eyes squinted a bit as he examined the rope around the Scotsman's ankle. He approached and looked more closely. The odor was horrible. He raised his arm and buried his nose in his crook of his elbow. At a quick glance the knot in the rope looked like a normal sheepshank, but it had an extra loop on the bottom side. The knot was unmistakable to Jacob. It was the Fahlstrom knot. No one else here knew how to tie a knot like that. Except Akami. Jacob was stunned. He continued staring at the knot in frozen silence.

"What's the matter, Swede Boy?" asked Macdonell. "Looks like you've seen a ghost."

"No, it's nothin," insisted Jacob. "I just remembered I gotta' get back to the boat shed." Jacob turned and ran off through tall purple flowering plants and into woods.

"That was odd," Macdonell said to the doctor as he looked up at the snare around the Scotsman's bloated and purple ankle. Then he looked over at Jacob running down the trail. He repeated under his breath, "Very odd."

...

It was a particularly dark night and the stars shone bright in the sky. Jacob lay on the cargo dock by the Hayes River. In the water, to his left, floated the four bateaux or, as they were now being called, York boats. Jacob stared up at the sky. He was quietly observing and learning the way Akami had taught. Jacob admired Akami and wanted to be like him. With this in mind, Jacob's thoughts drifted to the Scotsman and what happened. That deranged, evil man would certainly have come to kill Jacob had Akami not stopped him. As Jacob watched the starry sky, he listened to the water flowing under the dock. He could hear the water lapping against the boats and the boats clunking together. He could smell the musky odor of trout. This made him want to listen more closely, the way Akami would listen. Jacob wanted to find out if he could hear fish swimming in the current. He thought he did hear a couple trout, but maybe that was just wishful thinking. From the woods many animals could be heard. Birds, deer, and insects buzzing in the trees. Even the wind had a voice. Then, Jacob heard the breathing of an animal. The breathing was getting closer. It was the panting of an animal that had been trotting. Jacob could tell it was now on the dock because it suddenly became louder. The sound was now reflecting off the wooden boards where just prior the sound was being absorbed by the soft mushy turf. Slowly Jacob picked his head up off the dock and looked between his feet. There at the end, near shore stood a dog. It was one of the huskies. Or was it? It seemed larger and not as fluffy. The hair on the back of Jacob's neck stood straight up as he realized the truth. This was a wolf. With slow movements Jacob rose to a sitting position. The muscular gray creature stepped toward Jacob, it's eyes glowing with moonlight and bad intentions. Then white teeth were exposed as the wolf growled a snarling growl. There is truly nothing more terrifying than a wild beast growling when you have no means to defend yourself or route for escape. It's a primal feeling, millions of years in the making. Thousands of generations of humans have been trained to fear beasts that would pursue, kill, and eat them. Jacob's mind was racing. What am I going to do if the wolf attacks? My path off the dock is blocked. I could hang and drop into the water, but the beast will chase right in after me. It's late at night and this wolf has probably gone all day without food. It's feeding time and the wolf is hungry. I have nothing, except maybe a shoe, to use as a weapon. I could yell for help, but no one can get here quickly enough to save me, and the noise might prompt an attack. Not looking good.

Then, to make matters worse, two more wolves came trotting up. Just as he was about to make a leap for the water, Jacob saw another wolf running at full speed across the beach. Now things were looking dire. *Wait*, thought Jacob. *That's a dog.* It was one of the huskies. The dog ran at full speed and leaped into the alpha wolf, biting at his throat. This knocked the alpha wolf into the shallow water. Both animals tumbled. Mixed sounds of snarling, yelping and growling cut through the night air. The huskie spun around and bit the wolf again. Somewhat stunned and caught off guard by this attack the wolves thought better of the whole situation and retreated to the woods. The alpha stopped momentarily to lick a wound on his shoulder, then turned back to look at the huskie that was still standing aggressively on the shore beside the dock. Defeat was a bitter pill to swallow, but the wolf thought it more advantageous to live to fight another day. He slowly turned and trotted away. The huskie now walked out on the dock and limped toward Jacob. It was then, getting a closer look, that Jacob realized it was Two-Eye. He crouched down and called the dog over. "Come on, Two-Eye. Are you okay, boy? Let me see your paw." Jacob looked closely at the dog's leg. Two-Eye was injured, but it didn't seem too serious. He probably twisted a joint during the fight. He pulled the dog close rubbed his head and ears, then looked into his blue and brown eyes and said, "You saved my life. I knew you were special that first day." Jacob again laid down on the dock to watch the stars. Two-Eye came close, laid down, and placed his head on Jacob's chest. There they lay for several minutes until lightning appeared on the horizon. Storm clouds were moving in from the Bay.

Chapter 21.
From Wild to Wilder

July 17, 1812. With temperatures now in the 70s, both the Hayes and the Nelson were entirely free of ice. All four bateaux were built and ready to go. Jacob was dragging a wooden sled from the fort to the shore. It was piled high with bags of dried beans, salt pork, oatmeal and pemmican. Provisions were being loaded for the journey up the Hayes to Assiniboia. Miles Macdonell had originally chosen seventy-two men for the journey, but only thirty-eight turned out to be competent and trustworthy. In a letter to Lord Selkirk, Macdonell despaired about the lack of quality men under his leadership. Jacob, due to his sailing skills and his ability to speak Cree and Ojibwe, was chosen to go along. In addition, a good word from Skipper Thomas Gull, certainly helped. Not that Macdonell held anything against Jacob or thought him deficit in valuable skills. It was just that he was only a boy, after all. Macdonell was concerned he wouldn't pull his own weight.

This was Jacob's chance to seek his destiny and maybe even make his fortune. A chance to get a place of his own in the world. It was also time to say goodbye to his friends. There were a select few that Jacob was going to miss severely. The skipper, White Deer, Two-Eye, and especially Akami. As the men finished loading the boats, Jacob pondered his fate. It was a bittersweet day.

Akami was clearly fighting back tears as he gave a smile to Jacob.

In Cree he said, "I am proud of you, Jacob. The fur trade is a small group in a very big place. My hope is that our paths will once again cross." Then Akami reached into his essentials kit and pulled out a necklace. He held it out to Jacob and said, "This is for you." It was a long piece of leather strung with wolf teeth. Jacob looked at Akami with a question in his eyes. Akami continued, "I caught him. No wolf is going to try to hurt my boy." Akami reached out and placed his hand on the back of Jacob's head. He pulled him into his chest and sighed. "Oh, I will miss you so. Our talks. The Viking stories. Your laugh ... your amazing laugh." Akami paused for a moment then said, "Now go, your boat is waiting." Jacob wiped a tear and looked Akami in the eye.

Jacob said softly, "Goodbye." Jacob turned and ran across the sand. "Now stop crying. Warriors don't cry," Jacob yelled to Akami as he stepped over the side of the York boat.

As the boats pulled away from the dock, Akami yelled to Jacob, "Be a good man Jacob Fahlstrom!" Jacob waved as Akami shrank in the distance.

Men began to sing a Scottish song "The Walking of the Faulds" as they began to row up the Hayes. Jacob joined in the singing, struggling at first but eventually grasping the Scottish words. Akami watched from the sandy shore with Two-Eye sitting upright at his side. There was a bloody gash across Two-Eye's snout.

The York boats disappeared on the horizon. It was 700 miles inland to Assiniboia. Their first stop in the journey would be Oxford House, an H.B.C. fur trading post on the eastern shore of Oxford Lake at the mouth of the Hayes River. It was 200 miles from York Factory. With robust paddling the settlers would make about thirteen miles a day. The long days of paddling were followed by nights on shore fighting off thirsty mosquitos, out for blood. Jacob loved being on the water, but the campfires were his favorite part of the journey. Campfire time meant a calorie-rich evening meal, a full belly, and comradery. The men would imbibe in a sip of whiskey, a bit of song, and storytelling. Jacob enjoyed watching these typically stoic highlanders cut loose and have a bit of fun. It was through their stories that he learned about the hardships they had endured. Jacob also picked up quite a bit of Scottish Gaelic. To have the ability to do what you want, when you want and have land you can call your own were the things these highlanders sought. Jacob thought deeply about this. Even at his young age he realized how important freedom truly was in a man's life, and how rare it can be in this world.

Jacob spent a good portion of his time exploring the forest watching and learning from the terrain and the animals that inhabited it. This was a quality Akami instilled in him. *Watch and nature will teach you*, Akami would say. Jacob pondered two things that he loved so much. On the one hand he loved being alone in the forest or on the water. But, on the other hand, he truly loved being in the company of others. It seemed there was a time for being alone with his thoughts and a time to share them. Jacob thought there was much to be learned from both. Maybe it wasn't so weird after all. Suddenly, Jacob's daydreaming was interrupted by the sound of loud rushing water. Rapids. For the group, this meant bringing their boats to shore and portaging. Navigating rapids while traveling against the river current would be next to impossible, especially given the large amount of cargo aboard. Shallow water and rapids would force three dozen portages on the 200-mile journey from York Factory to Oxford House. Portaging was exhausting work carrying heavy loads often for miles.

It was a cloudy, dark night. The four bateaux were pulled up on shore and the settlers were scattered around what remained of a campfire. They slept soundly after a long day of paddling. There was a sloshing of water as a birch bark canoe slid quietly into shore. A distant rumble of thunder masked the sound as an Indian stepped out of the canoe. He gestured to several more canoes to pull up and be quiet. He used sign language to communicate the location of the bateaux and the sleeping settlers. The man wore deerskin leggings, moccasins, and feathers in his hair; worn in a manner most associated with the Cree nation. A bow and animal skin quiver hung from his shoulder. He pulled a hatchet from his belt and walked forward with it at the ready. More than a dozen Cree braves followed the man along the shoreline, their faces painted black and red. They inspected the bateaux, discovering mostly food and camp supplies that didn't much interest them. Then one of the braves motioned as he uncovered several muskets and gunpowder. The others came over and they began taking the guns from the bateau and loading them into their canoes.

"What the hell is going on?" yelled a settler in Scottish Gaelic just before an arrow pierced his throat. Blood spurted as he reached up trying to remove the arrow. The Scot had a surprised look on his face as he fell to the ground, never to breathe again. The yelling caused a stir among the settlers. It was disorganized chaos as half-dressed men ran in all directions, some forgetting to grab their weapon in the commotion. After all, they were settlers, not trained soldiers. The Cree braves rushed a group near the beach and most of them scattered. One man stood his ground only to receive a hatchet in the face, followed by more blows that did nothing but mutilate the body of an already dead man. A brave, now covered with blood splatters, yelled loudly, celebrating the kill. Jacob watched the chaos in horror. He scuttled to the edge of the woods and sat with his back against the base of a large black spruce. His gun lay across his thighs; slowly, he reached over and flipped the safety, readying the weapon. The blood-covered brave and three others continued their charge into the group of settlers. Jacob turned and raised his H.B.C. trade gun, taking aim at the attacking group of Cree. He was just about to pull the trigger when Miles Macdonell fired a shot that found its mark on the forehead of a charging brave and his lifeless body fell in a heap. He was dead before he hit the ground.

More settlers fired, wounding another of the braves in the upper leg. This halted their charge and they retreated to their canoes. The Cree braves paddled down the Hayes shrieking and whooping with their cargo of stolen guns. It took several minutes before they could no longer be heard. Three dead bodies scattered about camp were a reality check for the settlers. This was a wild and dangerous place.

"Why did they do this? I thought the Cree were our friends?" Jacob asked Macdonell who was crouched next to Southerland's body, surveying the damage done to his skull by the Cree hatchet. Macdonell turned Southerland's head back on its side and pushed closed his wide open, horrified eyes. He wiped his brow, accidently smearing Southerland's blood on his forehead, then looked up at Jacob.

"It's not simple, Jacob. All men have the potential for greed and evil in their hearts. The French have been fighting with the English for centuries. The tribes out here have been killin' each other for thousands of years. You're correct, many of the Cree are friendly with us because of the fur business. This group, on the other hand, was out for themselves. In a place like this, where half of what's out there can kill you at any moment, guns are a valuable item. Guns can make these men powerful among their tribe. It could be that. Or maybe these men are just desperate and think guns are the best way to feed their hungry families. Right, wrong, valor, treachery, good, evil; it's all messed together out here. A bloody mess. Trust the wrong person and you end up with a hatchet in the face." Macdonell stood up, turned toward the campfire, and yelled, "McPherson, grab shovels from the boat. We need to bury these bodies before the wolves smell 'em." As Jacob walked away Macdonell yelled, "Swede Boy!" Jacob stopped and turned back. "The thing is, we got off easy. That attack wasn't even bad. You don't want to see bad."

For the next several days, the group was somber. The attack had shaken what little confidence they had. After a night like that, who wouldn't question their decision to come way out here beyond civilization's touch? Did they really leave their families to die out here? Jacob questioned whether he might have been better off staying at York Factory. At York Factory he had good friends and

Akami who was like a grandfather to him. Jacob was now beginning to realize that this place was even more treacherous than he imagined.

The four York boats with sails aloft moved across Lake Winnipeg. They were careful not to get too far from shore. Boats this size would never survive a storm in the deep turbulent waters. As the sun began to set, Macdonell ordered the boats ashore for the night. The men set up camp and prepared a meal. A large fire crackled as the men chewed on chunks of salt pork and dry biscuits. Macdonell was reviewing some old, tattered maps. Jacob played a flute that Akami had given to him.

Macdonell began to speak, and the group went silent. Jacob stopped playing his flute. "We're getting low on rations. A few miles south, we'll cross the Berens River. I say we take the Berens inland a few miles and hunt. Should be teeming with deer."

"Agreed," said MacPherson.

Everyone knew that going into the woods in uncharted, hostile territory was not wise, but they needed food. There wasn't much to argue about.

Early the next morning the group loaded the York boats and pushed away from shore. The sun rose on the eastern horizon as they sailed south on Lake Winnipeg. A rocky cliff wall marked the entrance to the Berens River.

Macdonell pointed and yelled, "There it is. Head left into the mouth of the river, lower your sails, and grab your oars men."

For miles they paddled down the Berens until a low flat bank provided the perfect place to go ashore. One by one, the bateaux pulled up into the wet and mushy grass.

"MacPherson, O'Flannery, Lind ... grab your muskets. Let's go get some deer," yelled Macdonell.

"Sir," said Jacob. "Sir, can I join? I'm a good hunter."

Showing a bit of frustration, Macdonell said, "Swede Boy. Not now. You're always pushin' things."

"I won't get in the way. I'll keep up and will do my best, sir."

"All right. Just keep your mouth shut and when we get a deer, you're gutting it." Macdonell rolled his eyes and the four men walked toward the woods. Jacob ran back to the bateau and grabbed his Barnett musket. He looked closely at the brass dragon side plate and rubbed it with his thumb for luck. Jacob pulled the strap of his kit and power horn up over his shoulder, spun around, and ran to catch up with the other men.

The woods were dark and foreboding. Though it was mid-day it seemed like evening. In the shadow of towering spruce trees, the men walked deeper into the darkness. The relative safety of the river was now out of sight. Birds chirped; small animals could be heard scurrying in the underbrush. The damp, musky scent of tree bark and moss filled the air.

MacPherson said, "You stay close Jacob. Not much out here that don't wanna' kill ya'."

Deeper into the woods they walked. No deer to be found. With every step the woods seemed to become darker. It was as if the woods were swallowing them. Each man became progressively more fearful. Their heads were constantly scanning left to right for signs of trouble. The bird chirping sounded more like a funeral drudge than a joyful tweet. The men walked on. Suddenly, there was a loud cracking sound behind Jacob. He spun and aimed his gun in the direction of the attack. But it wasn't an attack at all. It was just MacPherson who stepped on a dead branch.

"Dammit, Swede Boy. You're gonna' shoot somebody," scolded Macdonell. He grabbed the barrel of Jacob's gun that was pointing in MacPherson's direction and pushed it down toward the ground.

"I'm sorry. It's just it scared me, is all."

"You head back to the river. I don't trust you on this hunt any longer," said Macdonell. "Go on now. Get going back to camp."

Body slumped with disappointment, Jacob turned and followed the trail back toward the river. The other hunters continued deeper into the woods. Now more than halfway back, Jacob could hear a churning river echo in the distance. Pillars of light blasted through the branches of towering spruce trees. A massive bull moose emerged from the thick underbrush into the light. Jacob's jaw dropped and his eyes widened. This beast was twelve hundred pounds of fury with a rack six feet across. Doing everything he could to keep calm, Jacob pulled the strap of his Barnett musket off his shoulder.

Miles deeper in the woods Macdonell and the three other men approached what appeared to be a game trail. Macdonell raised his hand in the air, then brought a finger to his lips, signaling the men to be silent. They raised their muskets and slowly proceeded down the trail. A distant gunshot broke the quiet. Given the direction the sound came from, MacPherson asked, "Think that's Swede Boy?"

"We'd better head back in case he's run into trouble," suggested Macdonell. A bit of concern registered on his face. The men walked back down the trail, occasionally calling Jacob's name. They heard another distant shot as a heavy rainstorm moved in. Back at the river, the men took cover from the rain for the night. The next morning, they broke up into three separate search parties and combed the woods for a sign of Jacob. For hours they yelled his name hoping for a response. Nothing. They never found a clue of which direction Jacob may have gone. The heavy rain washed away all evidence. He was lost and alone in frontier America at just 12 years' old. By nightfall the group of settlers gave up the search and at sunrise the next morning, they continued their journey across Lake Winnipeg.

Chapter 22.
Blizzard

January 1815
Red Lake, Minnesota Territory

The sky was white with swirling snow. Moonlight glinted off a hand-woven rope that stretched off into the distance, or at least as much distance as you could see in this blizzard. The silhouette of a man emerged. He wore snowshoes, deerskin leggings and a buffalo hide overcoat with a hood that hung down halfway covering his face. He carried firewood in the crook of his left arm while keeping his right hand firmly on the rope to avoid losing his way in the blinding storm. Reaching a wigwam, to which the rope was tied, he grabbed the leather handle and flipped back the birch bark door flap. Cold wind swirled into the lodge momentarily until the flap was closed, holding back the relentless Minnesota Territory wind. Inside the wigwam, a fire burned. Beside it, Blue Jay was stitching together a pair of moccasins; she shivered and looked up toward the entrance. The man pushed back the hood of his buffalo hide overcoat spilling a pile of snow to the ground. We now see the man's striking blue eyes and long wavy blond hair draped across his forehead. It's Jacob. Now fifteen years old with the benefit of a recent growth spurt that has made him more man than boy. The tribe, as was custom for the Ojibwe people, had broken off into smaller groups for winter. It was easier to find sufficient game and survive as a smaller group in these months when days were short and bad weather made the hunt more challenging. Blue Jay and Jacob were wintering with a group near Red Lake, about fifty miles south of Lake of the Woods. Lake of the Woods was one in a series of inter-connected rivers and lakes that created a route, a virtual highway of water, from Lake Superior to Lake Winnipeg and further up to Hudson Bay. This significant waterway provided access to the British, French, and Scottish fur trade. The furs could go north to Hudson Bay where the British-owned Hudson's Bay Company shipped their cargo of furs across the Atlantic to Europe. The furs could also go to the east across Lake Superior and up the St. Lawrence River to Montreal, which also had access to the Atlantic. There, French and Scottish traders shipped furs to supply Europe's voracious demand for fine pelts. The Ojibwe, Ottawa, along with the Cree, Sioux, Assiniboine, and Metis were significant partners in trade for all fur companies on the Great Lakes and up into the Arctic north to Hudson Bay. The three dominant fur companies of the era were the Husdon's Bay Company, the North West Company and the emerging American Fur Company. The native people would hunt, snare, and trap the animals and prepare their hides, which were then traded in a variety of ways. Traders from the companies might come to the tribes to trade, however, more commonly furs were traveled to a nearby trading post, or the furs were taken to a location of rendezvous. All trading took place in summer, typically between July and August.

Jacob added wood to a crackling fire in the middle of the wigwam. The pine created a heavy white smoke that floated up and out a vent hole while filling the room with a sweet, smoky aroma. Jacob placed a metal pot, half filled with snow, over the hot flame. In Ojibwe he said, "It's bad out. You can't see three feet in front of your face. I'm glad I didn't go off on a hunt."

Blue Jay asked, "When is Thunder Bear coming?"

While cutting venison into small pieces and dumping wild rice into the pot, Jacob replied, "He'll be here when the storm calms, then we'll go to the Red River and hunt buffalo. We'll bring back enough food to get us through the rest of winter."

"What about the traps," asked Blue Jay.

"Flying Gull will check 'em once a day until we get back."

"You be careful. As you get further west, you'll be closer to Arikara and Sioux lands. They have revenge in their hearts for us. They've killed Ojibwe men for no reason at all."

"I know. Thunder Bear will be with me."

"I know, but this is your first time on a buffalo hunt. And that country is more dangerous than anywhere you've been. I worry. I know it's not fair, but I worry because your blond hair makes you a target. They might hurt you just because you're different. The Arikara are very unfriendly with white men. What if Blackfeet wandering east come across you? They hate white men. You've heard the stories of the killings and mutilations." Blue Jay's voice trailed off and she sat silent, contemplating the dangers of the Dakota Territory near the Red River.

"Blue Jay, I know you're worried, but I'm a man now. I'm ready for this. I know what I'm doing. Besides, you said skin doesn't matter."

"I know, I said that, and it doesn't matter to people with love in their heart, Jacob. But evil people will … they will …" Blue Jay shook her head and pushed the back of her hand into her mouth, holding tears.

"It's ok." Jacob pulled her tight and tried to console her.

"I'm so worried to lose you. You saved me. I thought I might kill myself when my son Flying Eagle died of smallpox. Then you came to the village. What would I do if something happened to you? I'm sorry, it's not right for me to hold you back from becoming a man. But you are my Jacob. I touch your curls and keep you safe. That's what I do. I want all the best in the world for you. Don't you see why I'm such a mess?"

"Yes, I know. I promise I'll be okay," assured Jacob.

Blue Jay broke her soft tone and became angry, "Don't you say that. You can't make a promise that you'll be okay out there. You don't know that. It's like a lie, Jacob. Don't ever lie to me."

Jacob nodded in agreement. "Okay, you're right. I can't make that promise. But I can tell you this. I'm good in the woods. I'm a good fighter. I'm a good shot with my trade gun. And I survived the streets of London." Jacob paused momentarily, looking at Blue Jay and waiting until she made eye contact with him. Once she made eye contact, Jacob continued to speak. "The east side of London was crawling with all kinds of beasts."

Blue Jay chuckled a bit and added, "It's true. If anyone can make it out there it's you Jacob."

Jacob laughed. "Ah, I knew I would make you smile." Jacob hugged Blue Jay then stoked the fire. Outside the snow relentlessly blew against the wigwam. The wind whistled through every gap.

Morning brought calmer skies, an end to the storm, and a bright sunrise. The blowing snow had drifted into large banks, in some places five feet high. The lodge flap opened, and sunlight filled the space. Jacob and his mother both squinted toward the opening. A head popped in. It was Thunder Bear. He crawled into the opening which was now very small because the snow had covered two-thirds of its height. He asked with a laugh, "Enjoying the weather?"

Jacob threw a rabbit bone at him. "No. It's been awful. Yesterday, I couldn't see two feet in front of my face. We had to string a rope to the firewood pile so we wouldn't get lost in the blizzard."

Thunder Bear rubbed his chin. "This is nothin'. Just wait 'til February." He laughed a big laugh, then continued, "Good idea with the rope, Oza. I've taught you well."

Jacob turned to his mother and said, "See, I told you I've learned a lot."

Picking up on Blue Jay's frown and the tension in the room, Thunder Bear looked closely into her eyes and asked, "Are you okay, Mother? I won't go against your wishes. I think Jacob has earned the right and is ready to come on the hunt. But I will do what you say."

Blue Jay smiled and touched her heart. She said, "I would never stop Jacob from going. I just worry. You know how I worry."

Chapter 23.
Buffalo Adventure

In the middle of the wigwam, embers crackled in the fire ring. "You awake?" Jacob asked as he poked Thunder Bear's shoulder. A groan came from underneath the heavy buffalo hide blanket, but no answer. Jacob looked around the wigwam. He could see his breath in the cold air. He threw a couple logs into the fire and pushed the embers around with a large stick. He put his face low and blew to stoke the embers back into flame. As the logs began to burn the growing fire gave off more heat and Jacob held his hands close to warm them. He pulled on his heavy boots, slipped into his jacket, and went outside. It was a mild day compared to the previous several which consisted of snowstorms and extreme temperatures well below zero. Today the sun was out and there was no wind which made the six-degree temperature feel much warmer. Jacob couldn't help but think how warm it was compared to York Factory's arctic chill. He chuckled to himself for thinking whether this cold could ever feel warm. But, to him, it did. He resolved that it's all just a matter of where you've been. In truth, the human body is incredibly resilient. The more it's exposed to extremes of any kind, the stronger it becomes.

Red Lake was far enough south to make winters a bit easier, yet still provided ample opportunity to trap beaver and other animals for fur. The cold winter temperatures made the pelts thick and lush.

These were the most desired pelts by European tailors and hat makers. In turn, they drew the highest price in trade. In summer, they would travel, with furs, pemmican, and sugar, up to Lake of the Woods and, from there east to Lake Superior where they would meet with traders from the American Fur Company at Fond du Lac, present day Duluth, MN. The traders would come west across Lake Superior from Mackinac Island. With them they would bring metal and iron implements, guns, whiskey, and other trade goods.

Thunder Bear heard from a Frenchman, who was trapping in the area, that buffalo robes were becoming popular in the American cities to the east. Thunder Bear knew buffalo would be plentiful this time of year at Red River near the forks. They would get enough food to last through the spring and they would have plenty of prime buffalo hides that would be in demand at Fond du Lac this summer. Their biggest conflict would be whether to go east to Fond du Lac or go north to trade with the H.B.C., now that Jacob was a trader under contract. This conflict was causing some tension amongst the tribe.

Now slightly bored waiting for Thunder Bear, Jacob was inspired to play a trick on his brother. He climbed a tree that was near the wigwam. Once up the tree he broke off a branch and broke it up into several smaller pieces. He threw the branch pieces, one-by-one, at the front flap of the wigwam. It took about four branches, then the flap flew open. Out came Thunder Bear, still half asleep, his hair sticking up in all directions. He looked around, listened closely, and observed his surroundings. Jacob threw one of the branch pieces into the woods just a few feet past the tree in which he was hiding. He hoped it would make Thunder Bear walk nearby. It worked. He walked over, looking into the woods curiously. Closer, then closer still until he was almost directly under Jacob. Jacob leaped from the tree down toward him. However, right before Jacob landed on his back, Thunder Bear dove and rolled out of the way and Jacob landed on the ground with a thud. Jacob pushed himself up to his knees and gasped a couple times as the fall had knocked the wind out of him. Thunder Bear laughed.

Jacob asked, "How'd you know I was up there?"

Thunder Bear sniffed a couple times then said, "The smell. Whew..." Then he pinched his nose and roared with more laughter. Jacob could not help but laugh along. Wiping a tear of laughter from his eye, Thunder Bear said, "Look at the ground, your footprints are everywhere. And they stop right there at the tree. So, I knew you either grew wings and flew away, or you were up in that tree."

Jacob smiled a bit and shook his head. "Ah. I was a bit sloppy."

Thunder Bear patted Jacob on the top of his head then said, "Now get your snowshoes and winter gear. We need to meet Kiwani and Turtle at Red River. Gonna' get some buffalo. Whoop!"

A sled, pulled by four huskies with ice clumps dangling off their fur, cut through drifts of white. The swirling winds blew snow up into opaque clouds of frozen mist. Jacob sat atop a pile of cargo while Thunder Bear stood on the back leg of the sled and rode along. The frozen, snow-covered earth was flat and open as far as the eye could see. More open than any other place on earth. Only occasional tufts of prairie grass defied winters touch. It had been snowing for hours and more than six inches had accumulated. In some areas, the blowing and drifting snow was almost three times as deep. Each time the sled struck a drift, it would be jarred sideways. Finally, a drift too large flipped the sled and both Jacob and Thunder Bear fell into the cold snow. As they slid across the ground, every open gap in their jacket and boots were filled with the frozen moisture of the northern prairie winter. Getting wet in the frozen north is a very uncomfortable, often painful experience. The storm was getting bad, it was time to make shelter. Jacob pulled off his mitten exposing his hand to the frigid cold. He reached down for the hatchet that was tucked into his belt and pulled it out. He found some bare shrubs protruding from the snow then hacked away at them, trying to free kindling for a fire. As he chopped, his hands ached from the freezing wind and wet snow shaking off the branches. While Jacob worked on the fire, Thunder Bear assembled their shelter out of tree limbs covered in deer hide and birch bark.

They always carried this gear with them when doing winter travel. Once set up, the two warmed themselves by the fire. They marveled at the abundance of stars they could see through breaks in the clouds. Being so out in the open, they felt a bit exposed to danger. But actually, in this location, they could see a threat approaching from miles away in any direction.

With very few trees and virtually no hills, this land was dominated by sky. It's a different kind of natural beauty that can't be comprehended unless you've experienced it. Flat, open land stretching for what seems like forever, entirely dwarfed by the dominating heavens above. In most places, the land rules. The majesty of mountains, forests, rolling hills, or water dominate the terrain. But here, in the Red River Valley, the sky owns the land. Stars seem brighter, clouds seem bigger, and the supernatural seems more possible. Jacob and Thunder Bear couldn't resist laying outside. They were marveled by the sky above with its uncountable stars and glowing moon. Never, even on so many open seas, had Jacob felt so small in the universe. It can break one's nerve to realize your life is so inconsequential to the sky. It's a bit haunting.

The next morning, sunlight's warm rays provided refuge from the freezing cold. Jacob and Thunder Bear broke camp and packed the sled. They continued their journey westward. It was about noon when Thunder Bear noticed a long, winding row of trees in the distance.

"Red River," he yelled.

Then, in true Ojibwe fashion, pointed with his lips. The Ojibwe people believe that it is disrespectful to point with one's hand, or even with a canoe paddle. They believe by doing so, they show respect to the spirits that inhabit the land, the forest, and the waters. For this reason, they point with their lips, using a puckering motion, in the direction to which they want to call attention.

On the prairie, large groups of trees like this only existed along the riverbank. Everything else was grassland. When Thunder Bear called out the trees, they seemed so close. But it took thirty minutes to reach them. Funny how this flat open land makes distance deceptive. This deceptive power was considered somewhat supernatural to the native people in the area.

The Red River was completely frozen over, but near the shore Jacob was able to break through with a hatchet to get water to drink and for cooking. The water was cloudy with a good amount of muddy sediment, so they opted to melt snow for their drinking water. After scarfing down some boiled potatoes and fry bread Jacob laid back and prepared to relax.

"Not time for sleep yet, Jacob. We've got work to do," said Thunder Bear as he pulled a shovel from the sled and handed it to Jacob. The two dug a large pit in the snow along the crest of the riverbank. Then, out of woven pine branches they made a cover for the pit and entirely buried it with snow. Each took a branch and brushed away all their footprints to make the area seem undisturbed. They set up their wigwam about 100 feet from their pit by the riverbank. They walked several hundred feet along the riverbank then went down into the trees. The trees grew close together, so Jacob and Thunder Bear were able to jump across from tree to tree. They did this until they reached the site of the pit they had dug. They climbed down and ran over to the pit. Being very careful, they wiped away their footprints as they climbed the riverbank and entered the pit from the river side. Once inside, Thunder Bear opened a hole in the ceiling then used his flint to start a fire to keep them warm.

The next morning they were awakened by the heavy clop of horse hooves on frozen ground. Thunder Bear reached over and covered Jacob's mouth. He put a finger to his lips, gesturing for him to be quiet. He tilted his head in the direction of the sound. Now the snort of a horse could be heard. Carefully they peeked through the pine branch roof of their snow-camouflaged pit enclosure. About thirty feet away, they could see two men slide quietly off the backs of their horses. Their clothing and hairstyle identified them as Sioux. The two Sioux braves slowly and quietly approached the decoy shelter Jacob and Thunder Bear had set up. Jacob wondered if they had come to rob them, or was it something worse? The taller Sioux brave gave a hand signal to the other and they prepared a trap near the entrance of the shelter. They laid out a rope tied in a noose and buried it in the snow to hide it. Then they snuck to the side of the shelter, carrying the length of rope with them. The shorter brave made a sound resembling that of a young bear cub. There was no response at the shelter entrance, so he made the call louder and added a little groan. The two braves looked at each other and shrugged. Still no activity at the shelter entrance. As this was going on, Jacob and Thunder Bear watched attentively, then crawled out of their underground enclosure. They snuck up behind the Sioux braves. Thunder Bear handed Jacob the end of a long piece of rope. Now, each holding one end, they slowly approached the braves then accelerated as they got closer. Running full speed with the rope dangling about a foot off the ground, it caught the Sioux braves behind the ankles, causing their feet to fly up in the air and they landed on their backs with thud. Stunned, the men scrambled to their knees trying to grab their weapons. At the sight of this, Thunder Bear burst into a loud roar of laughter. The braves looked up with fear hanging on their face. It took a moment, but now they recognized that it was their good friend Thunder Bear.

One of the Sioux braves yelled, "Thunder Bear!"

Thunder Bear screamed a primal victory cry, then laughed. The taller of the two men ran at Thunder Bear and lunged into him. They both ended up falling into the side of the shelter, entirely collapsing it. Now both men laughed as Jacob looked on somewhat puzzled by the entire situation. Turns out Thunder Bear and Kiwani had a long history of playing surprise tricks like this on one another. Kiwani was tall and lanky, with long straight hair as black and shiny as a horse's mane. His face was painted left-side red, right-side blue for the buffalo hunt. Turtle was short and round in stature. Their contrasting body types were almost humorous. They were both Oglala, Sioux. The Ojibwe and Sioux people had traditional grudges going back hundreds of years. In a conflict over fur trade, the Ojibwe pushed the Sioux westward out of the Great Lakes area many years earlier. This didn't stop Thunder Bear and Kiwani from being friends. They met in their early teens when Thunder Bear saved Kiwani from Scottish fur traders who tried to steal his pelts as he headed up the Red River to trade at Pembina. Very meek and mild-mannered, Turtle was true to his name. He seemed more likely to retreat into his shell than attack.

Jacob was a little jealous of the bond Kiwani seemed to have with Thunder Bear, but at the same time, admired the amazing love he shared so willingly. His brilliant sense of humor never ceased to crack Jacob up. The two stood and walked over to Jacob and Turtle. Kiwani looked Jacob up and down, taking in his appearance. He then looked over at Thunder Bear. "I thought you were coming with your brother?"

"He is my brother," answered Thunder Bear flatly.

Turtle, a little scared of Thunder Bear but too puzzled to resist, said, "But he's, uh ... white."

Thunder Bear reached out and touched Jacob's face, "Oh man ... oh man ... I never noticed! Oh no. He's white." At this point, Thunder Bear fell onto the snow flopping about. In mock distress he yelled, "Jacob, you never told me you were a wasicu." The group laughed, then Thunder Bear sat upright in the snow and became serious. He said, "We found Jacob lost in the woods, starving, and injured. The tribe took him in. Yes, Jacob is white." Thunder Bear looked over at Jacob, then continued, "Very white." The group again laughed. He continued in a serious tone, "But when you are with him, you'll see he's every bit as Ojibwe as I am."

Putting an arm over Jacob's shoulder Kiwani said, "Your brother is my brother. Now we celebrate!" Jacob didn't know how to receive all of this. Having Thunder Bear so openly accept him as a brother was simultaneously heartwarming and terrifying. He couldn't understand why he always felt this fear when people tried to show him love and acceptance. Jacob thought, *why do I always pull away and reject love? Maybe I don't deserve it? What if I accept it, then lose it again?*

Kiwani pulled a bottle of whiskey from his pack and the four spent the next several hours drinking, arm wrestling, joking, laughing, and dancing late into the night.

The next morning, Jacob arose later than the others. This was his first time drinking and he was in rough shape. Nauseous with a throbbing head, he stumbled over and joined the others by the roaring fire. Turtle elbowed Jacob's arm and asked, "Too much whisky wasicu?"

Jacob answered, "Yeah, I think so. Feels like there's thunder in my head." There was a momentary pause among the group. Thunder Bear looked upward.

"That's not in your head, Jacob," said Thunder Bear. The group continued to listen attentively. They could now hear and feel the distant rumble of hooves. Buffalo!

"It's a large herd, let's go," yelled Kiwani.

They grabbed their rifles, mounted two per horse, and rode in the direction of the distant rumble. They rode for about five miles when they could see a heavy fog hovering in the distance. It was the steam rising off the warm bodies of the herd. They moved as quietly as possible, carefully adjusting their course to approach the herd downwind. About 300 yards away, they dismounted. Each found their most accurate shooting position. Jacob took one knee. He cocked the hammer and sighted in on a female. He aimed at her chest, carefully targeting a spot about a fist's width above the elbow joint of her foreleg. Taking in a deep breath, then a pause, he slowly squeezed the trigger. A puff of snow exploded from the beast's shaggy coat when the fifty-caliber ball struck its mark. Hit in the lungs, the buffalo remained stationary while its life rapidly spurted and spilled to the frozen ground below. Jacob had learned from Thunder Bear that, for the group to have more than one kill, a buffalo had to be shot in the lungs, which would keep it stationary. When a buffalo is shot in the heart, it will run, often for a half mile or more, before dying. Which in turn would cause the rest of the herd to dash after it, leaving the hunters with no more targets. In contrast, a buffalo shot in the lungs will typically stand its ground until the loss of blood causes it to fall. And that's precisely what the female did. It staggered, then toppled to the ground. Jacob reloaded and fired again, dropping a large bull that was drawn closer by the injured cow. Likewise, Kiwani, Turtle, and Thunder Bear also dropped buffalo. After nine buffalo were taken, Thunder Bear signaled to stop shooting. Now began the dangerous task of taking the hides and meat. Slowly, the four approached the fallen animals. A large bull approached snorting and thumping its front hooves on the frozen ground. Jacob signaled for the group to stop. He took careful aim and shot the bull directly in the heart. As taught, the huge beast ran off and the herd, in a frenzy, followed. Kiwani whooped loudly and patted Jacob on the back. Thunder Bear cut open the 1700-pound bull taken in the hunt and Jacob was given the traditional liver. Still steaming in the cold winter air, Thunder Bear handed the liver to him. Jacob took a large bite and blood dripped from his lips as Turtle, Kiwani, and Thunder Bear lifted him onto their shoulders in celebration.

Later at camp, they feasted greatly on prime cuts of roasted meat washed down generously with whiskey. They danced to give thanks for their good fortune. Jacob had proven his worth as a buffalo hunter. In Sioux culture, this was a high honor.

Chapter 24.
Selkirk Settlement Under Attack

June 25, 1815
Selkirk Settlement, Manitoba, CA

Dark smoke billowed over the Selkirk Settlement. Flames shot out of doors and windows. The flour mill, homes, and the blacksmith shop were set ablaze. The rising smoke collided with clouds overhead, creating a murky mix of gray and white. The settlers frantically loaded up what they could carry, launched their boats, and escaped with the assistance of Peguis (Peg-wee), chief of the Salteaux, and ten of his warriors.

While taking distant gunfire from the Bois-Brûlés, Peguis and his men bandaged wounds and set broken bones as the boats were pushed northward by the fast-moving murky brown water of the Red River. The sun began to set, and from their canoes, the settlers could see light from the burning flames that were devouring three years of hard work. At the settlement, the carnage continued. Running with flaming torches from one building to the next, the Bois-Brûlés, with faces painted for war, were destroying the Selkirk colony as if wanting to erase it. The Bois-Brûlés, also called Métis, were a group of half-French, half-native men led by Cuthbert Grant.

They came from the Qu'Appelle River valley. An area of southwestern Saskatchewan where the Qu'Appelle meets the Assiniboine River. The Bois-Brûlés were stirred into battle by North West Company leader Alexander Macdonell. The North West Company considered the Selkirk settlement a ploy by the H.B.C. Another one of their efforts to dominate the fur trade in the lands along the Red River. They saw it as a direct threat to their piece of the fur trade, maybe a threat to their very existence as a viable business. The Bois-Brûlés had their own reasons for wanting to rid the valley of the Selkirk settlement. They felt the colony would drive away the buffalo, which they depended on for survival. Though the colony did pose challenges for the Bois-Brûlés, they were certainly being used by the North West Company as their conduit in this battle between the two dominant fur trading companies in North America. This was a conflict several years in the making, now ignited into full blown war. By morning, the once thriving Selkirk colony was reduced to smoldering piles of ash.

The six canoes and three bateaux continued north in darkness. The Red is one of the only rivers in North America that runs to the north, eventually draining into Hudson Bay.

"What happened back there?" asked Chief Peguis while trying to stop the bleeding of an injured man. He pushed a cloth against his shoulder. Momentarily pulling away the cloth, a gaping wound became visible. It was so deep, bone was exposed. The man was thin with dark brown eyes. His shirt was torn, and his dark hair was soaked with sweat. Blood dripped from his nose and a large bruise marred the left side of his face, evidence of a significant blow. Blood soaked the cloth and dripped down the chief's arm as the man fought to maintain consciousness. His head bobbed as he struggled to focus. Blinking a couple times, his vision cleared, and he began speaking in English with a thick Scottish brogue.

"This here shite has been going on for a long time. A year, maybe longer. Hell, it started in Scotland before we even got here. Those bastards have always seen the settlement as a threat to their stronghold on the Athabasca Country. Those Nor' Wester' arse-pieces really stepped things up this spring when they sent Duncan Cameron from Fort William. That twig-shaft shows up around Fort Gibraltar with his fancy military stitches in April. Struttin' around, showin' off like he's above us all. He sweet talked about a sixty of the settlers into relocatin' to Montreal and upper Canada for 200 acres of land and a year of provisions. Another fifty took a bit more arm twistin', but they left too. That's why there's so few of us here. Cameron arrested Governor Macdonell and took him to Montreal for trial, I guess for standin' up to his horse shite. That walloper can kiss ma fart-box. We are leavin' now, but when we can gather more men, we're goin' back to claim what's rightfully ours." Peguis was attentively listening. There was silence for a moment, nothing to be heard but oars pushing water.

Then Peguis said, "My English is not great. But I think I grasp your meaning." Peguis sighed then continued with a hybrid accent mimicking the man's Scottish brogue, "So you're tellin' me this Cameron is a turd-flavored fart lozenge."

"Pretty much," the injured Scot answered, then laughed which immediately caused him to realize the overwhelming pain in his broken jaw. He winced and began to choke and cough. Chief Peguis patted the man on top of his head and wrapped a Hudson's Bay blanket around his shoulders.

Chapter 25.
The Evil in Men

August 1815.
Jack River Trading Post. North of Lake Winnipeg, CA.

Jacob crawled out from under a buffalo blanket. Still in a state of half-sleep, he ran a hand through his wavy blond hair, making it stick straight up. He walked across the room, opened the heavy wooden door of the Jack River H.B.C. barracks, and exited. He replayed a bad dream in his head. At his home in Stockholm, Sweden, Jacob was again a young child. He pushed open a bedroom door. Inside his mother lay on the bed. He approached slowly and reached for her hand. It was cold. He squeezed it gently and her pale white face turned toward him. Her eyelids opened, but there were no eyes, just empty sockets. There was a squishing sound and two large black bugs slithered out. Jacob jumped back, letting go of his mother's hand. He watched in horror as her upper body began to rise. Once seated upright, she reached for Jacob with an extended arm. Her sockets had no eyes, but they seemed to look at him. She said, "I will never leave you Jacob. Never." Jacob began to cry as his mother continued. "Never."

Jacob, standing outside the Jack River barracks, rubbed his face attempting to wipe the dream away. His skin crawled and his heart ached thinking about it. He wondered if the loss of his mother would ever stop haunting his nights. To clear his head, he walked over and sat on the dock, next to the canoes. He stared at the water for a long time, until others from his Ojibwe tribe joined him. They had completed delivery of their pelts to the Hudson's Bay Company for the season; thirty bundles this year. Now it was time to return to Lake of the Woods.

Water churned and splashed as Jacob paddled hard to avoid large rocks that protruded from fast flowing rapids. The canoes, four in all, made their way successfully and a loud cheer of relief erupted from the Lake of the Woods Ojibwe fur traders. Earning a well-deserved rest, they laid back and let the canoes float along with the slow, smooth river current for a few miles. Suddenly, the relaxation was disturbed by a distant scream.

Jacob bolted upright assessing the direction of the source. As the four canoes floated around a bend in the river, they saw several British soldiers beating a Cree man. To the side, a Cree woman and a four-year-old boy cowered. Jacob and the other Ojibwe fur traders began rowing their canoes as fast as they could.

A soldier grabbed the woman by the waist, not allowing her to give assistance. She kicked and flailed. One of the redcoats, with a silver sword hanging at his waist, walked up and kicked the Cree man in the mouth as he was down on all fours. The other soldiers laughed as the man pleaded for the beating to stop. He writhed in pain on the ground. The redcoat looked down at him and asked, "Where are our pelts?"

"I don't have them," the Cree man said.

The redcoat used the butt-end of his sword to punch the man in the mouth. The other soldiers cheered on the beating as the Cree man again fell to the ground with blood pouring from his mouth and down his chin.

The redcoat said, "What do you mean, you savage. You owe us pelts."

"I don't have the pelts."

The redcoat grabbed the man's shirt. Pulled him by it and punched his face three times, in rapid succession. The man cried in pain as blood ran from his nose and a large cut above his eye. His face was swollen, eyes barely able to open.

Through broken teeth, the man said, "No pelts. I traded them with the French."

"You fucking savage!" yelled the redcoat with the silver sword.

He let go of the Cree's shirt, dropping him to the ground. Then he drew his flintlock pistol, walked three steps in the direction of the small child, aimed, and fired. Flame shot from the barrel and the child's lifeless body dropped to the moss-covered ground. The Cree woman shrieked, and the man screamed an inhuman yell. Overcome by the emotional pain of seeing his child murdered, the Cree man grabbed a soldier's musket, placed the barrel in his mouth and pulled the trigger. He fell to the ground in a heap, blood pouring out the top of his skull. The soldiers were ripping at the woman's clothes and assaulting her.

Jacob yelled, "Don't you touch her."

A flurry of arrows flew from the approaching canoes, killing one of the soldiers instantly. The other redcoats mounted their horses and rode off. The woman lay sobbing on the ground. Jacob struggled to console her, but it was hopeless. How could anyone be consoled after that? Jacob was in shock, looking at young child's lifeless body lying on the ground and his father close by. *I just don't understand all this senseless killing,* Jacob thought. *Over fur pelts.*

He held the woman in his arms as she whaled. It was a cry grounded in primal pain. A sound that sent a chill through your body and your soul. It was heartbreaking.

Rain began to fall, but it couldn't wash away the damage inflicted. This family was ripped to shreds. This woman will never be the same. That is, if she even survives this.

The day's devastating loss brought back pain from the old wound deep in Jacob's heart. A tear dripped off his cheek into a rain puddle beneath him. One of the Ojibwe fur traders walked over and put a hand of support on his shoulder. The gray sky turned to black as a storm cloud moved in from the north.

Chapter 26.
Pembina Trading Post

March 1816.

North West Company's Fort Pembina to the left and across the Pembina River to the right is Fort Daer (Hudson's Bay Company). The larger body of water is the Red River.

The early morning sky remained dark as the Red River flowd gently past Fort Pembina. The smell of burning oak fires hung heavy in the air. A lone wigwam sat outside the fort walls. The door flap of the wigwam flipped open, and Jacob stepped out. He stood for a moment pondering the uncountable stars of the Dakota Territory sky. Jacob and Thunder Bear were camped outside Fort Pembina, a North West Company trading post at the confluence of the Red and Pembina Rivers. Having trapped and hunted their way up the Red River, their plan was to trade their pelts, pemmican, and buffalo hides. Then head back home to Lake of the Woods.

Just across the frozen Pembina River was Fort Daer, an outpost of the Hudson's Bay Company, the company for which Jacob was currently a trading agent. It was unusual for rival trading companies to be in such close proximity. A stark reminder of the rising competition for territory and the heated conflict that was already boiling over in the Red River Valley.

Jacob started a fire and began heating water for tea in the pre-dawn glow. He placed a griddle over the flame, added lard, then several pieces of bread dough, which made it sizzle and pop. Thunder Bear walked up and patted Jacob on the head in a non-verbal gesture of good morning, then joined.

With a chuckle, he said, "Your eyes are looking further than they can see. What is it Oza Windib?" Jacob bowed his head forward and breathed in deep.

Again, Thunder Bear asked, "What is it?"

"It's nothing. I just feel like ... I don't know. Did you ever just have a bad feeling?" Jacob said staring off into the distance.

"You've been through a lot. Don't let your worries get the best of you."

"Yeah, maybe you're right," answered Jacob. Thunder Bear was not convinced.

Pembina sat between three tribes with historic grudges. The Sioux, Ojibwe, and Assiniboine. The conflict between the Hudson's Bay Company and the North West Company was now approaching full-blown war. Racial tensions seemed to be on the rise. To say things here were volatile was an understatement. Jacob and Thunder Bear just wanted to get in and out quickly.

Standing as a reminder of the volatility of this place, twenty-foot timbers surrounded Fort Pembina. At night, trading activities were ended, and the gates closed. That's why Jacob and Thunder Bear were camped outside, waiting for sunrise.

Water dripped from icicles, the first evidence of spring's approach. Chewing on a piece of fry bread and shielding his eyes to block the bright rays peeking over the horizon, Jacob noticed a cart, heaping with fur bundles, coming up the trail. It bounced in and out of grooves frozen in the mud. A massive beast unlike anything Jacob had ever seen pulled the cart. Part cow, part mythological creature. Some kind of dragon, perhaps from the Viking sagas. The huge beast had light yellow fur and long horns. As the cart neared, Jacob was wondering if it might blast flames out it's nostrils and burn him to a crisp. The cart stopped just feet from the campfire. At the reigns of the cart sat a large, broad-shouldered man wearing a black wool coat and a fur hat that sat high on his head. His mustache and beard were not long, but very thick. His piercing eyes were such a dark shade of brown they were almost black.

He began to speak, *"Pourriez-vous, les garcons epargner un petit dejeuner?"* Jacob recognized the language as French but didn't understand the words. Picking up on their puzzlement and their manner of dress, the man seamlessly shifted to Ojibwe. "Could you bucks spare a bit of breakfast for three hungry travelers? We have buffalo meat we can share later." Thunder Bear smiled, stood up, and walked over to the cart. Jacob knew that his brother was not doing this out of blind friendliness. He was doing it because the closer you are to a potential threat, the easier it is to make a counterattack if they draw their weapons. He always told Jacob that strangers are always a threat ... until they aren't. As a cautionary measure, Thunder Bear approached at such an angle to place his body between the men in the cart and Jacob.

"Where are your weapons?" Thunder Bear asked.

"In the back of the cart," answered the man as he gestured for the Indian sitting atop the fur bundles to reveal them. Calmly, the

Indian held up one hand and slowly pulled back a blanket with the other. Now Thunder Bear could see their rifles standing in the back corner.

Holding his hands in plain sight, the man with the thick beard and dark eyes spoke calmly and slowly to Thunder Bear. "We're no threat to you, just here to trade. I am Métis, half-French and half-Ojibwe, my name is Pierre Bottineau. My friends are both Ojibwe. This is Red Bear and Peguis. Red Bear is my uncle."

Relaxing his posture and gesturing with a tilt of his head toward the fire Thunder Bear said, "Join us, we have fry bread and pork belly. There's plenty." The Indians, both in their forties, climbed down from the cart and walked around for a while, trying to loosen up their cramped travel legs.

Jacob joined the conversation. "My name is Oza Windib, and this is my brother Thunder Bear. We're from the Lake of the Woods Ojibwe band."

Bottineau chuckled and noted. "Ha! My mother Clear Sky Woman was from that band."

"I do remember a Clear Sky Woman from when I was very young," noted Thunder Bear. The group paused conversation as everyone ate their morning meal.

"So, Red Bear, where is your warm weather place now?" asked Jacob.

"About one day travel to the west. I'm a buffalo hunter."

Bottineau cut in, "Red Bear is being modest. He's the chief of the Pembina band of Ojibwe. A great warrior and leader. And Peguis, is a famous chief."

Shaking his head from side to side, Peguis interrupted, "No, no."

Bottineau let out a deep rumbling laugh. "Don't let this old man fool you. He's a powerful battle chief. His tribe is the Salteaux of the Prairie. They dominate the Red River from here all the way north to Lake Winnipeg. He's willing to share, but if men try to degrade the river or take from him ..." With another deep laugh, Bottineau made a slicing motion across his forehead then pulled up on his hair, mimicking a scalping. Noticing an abrupt quietness of the group, Bottineau continued, "But Peguis has a compassionate soul. If it weren't for him those settlers would've all been killed last summer up at the Selkirk Colony."

"Wait, did you say Selkirk?" asked Jacob.

Bottineau answered, "Yes, the group connected to the H.B.C. up at Fort Douglas, on the Red River. Bunch of Irish and Highlander Scots mostly."

Jacob noted, "I came over, across the Atlantic, with those people."

Peguis turned a bit serious. "Did you have family or close friends among the settlers?"

"No, no one real close, but you don't make that kind of a journey without forming some kind of bond."

"There's been a lot of trouble. A war for trade between the H.B.C. and the North West Company. And every day it gets worse. There was an attack last summer. I was south of Fort Douglas with my hunters when we saw the heavy smoke. We got there as fast as we could. No one was killed, but the settlement was burned to the ground and there were many injured. We helped a group escape on the river to Playgreen Lake, just north of Lake Winnipeg. Many of the settlers continued to York Factory and back home for good. Several other settlers were persuaded by the promises of a more stable life by the Nor'Westers. So, they went to Quebec."

Jacob was now becoming more intrigued. "Has the settlement collapsed for good?"

"No, a large group has returned, and more are arriving this spring. But I worry for them. A group of Bois-Brûlés, under the command of Cuthbert Grant, have been riled up by bad leaders with the North West Company. They have already attacked once; I would not be surprised if they return. Duncan Cameron, a foul man, is leading all of this. He tried to recruit me, and other tribes as well, to harass and intimidate the settlers. Many nights I wake with visions of destruction and bloodshed." Jacob was shocked by what he was hearing.

Bottineau scoffed. "Awe, ignore the old chief. He goes on and on sometimes. If you listen too long, it'll spook ya'."

Peguis, with some inner ferocity revealing itself, added, "Don't joke, Frenchman. Don't joke about this." Bottineau held up his hands in a gesture of surrender and apology. Peguis continued, "Oza, where do you come from? Your manner says you are Ojibwe, but those blue eyes don't keep your secret.

"I'm from Sweden."

Peguis was somewhat puzzled. "I have not heard of this place, Sweden?"

Bottineau joined in to help explain. "Sweden is home to warriors that built great ships and traveled the ocean, they were called Vikings."

Peguis shook his head and smiled at Jacob. "I had a feeling about you Swede Boy." Jacob, somewhat taken aback, replied, "How'd you know they called me Swede Boy?"

Peguis laughed and continued, "I just know things, Jacob. Sometimes ... I just know things." Suddenly there was a loud clanking followed by the rattling and grinding of gears. The gates of Fort Pembina were opening.

Inside the trader's cabin, sitting at a small desk, a man scribbled away in his leather-bound ledger. His name was Dominic Provencalle, a former voyageur from Quebec. Having gained several pounds since his paddling days, his protruding stomach pushed against the desk in front of him. Provencalle was married to a Lakota woman from the Oglala band. They had four children together, all of whom lived with their mother among the Oglala. Provencalle would frequently travel to see them during the non-trading months. Since he could not read or write, Provencalle sketched pictographs in his ledger to record the daily transactions at the post. This coincidentally worked out better than handwriting, as the pictographs were broadly understandable. It transcended language barriers. This transparency of accounting garnered a deeper trust in Provencalle by all tribes that traded with him.

His face was flushed red, evidence of too many years with too much whiskey. He wore round spectacles that seemed permanently squished into his chubby face.

The door flung open and Provencalle, startled, almost fell off his chair. Standing in the doorway was Bottineau. He laughed heartily at the distress he caused for his old friend. Provencalle and Bottineau had worked together in the fur trade several years prior.

"Making little pictures in your book?" asked Bottineau. Provencalle dropped his pen, rose to his feet, and approached Bottineau. He put his arms around Bottineau's legs, grunted, struggled, and eventually picked him up off the floor.

"Bottineau, it has been too long. What brings you to paradise?" he asked, in reference to the poor condition of his quarters. The furniture was old and worn. The single window had broken glass and a grain sack served as a curtain. On the wall behind his desk hung Provencalle's prized possession. An old paddle from his voyageur days.

"I have buffalo hides and beaver pelts," said Bottineau.

Provencalle proceeded with the examining, weighing and meticulous recording of the fur exchanged by drawing his little pictographs. After which Bottineau was outfitted with next year's essentials. Traps, salt pork, a winter tunic, skinning knife, tomahawk, lead, gunpowder, and, of course, the all-essential barrel of whiskey.

Having sampled some of the barrel, the two old friends eventually found their way to the ale house. Basically, a large room with a few tables and chairs scattered about. In this place, stories were told, cards were played, and hell was raised. When Provencalle and Bottineau entered, the smoke-filled, dimly lit room was booming with the raucous singing of a French Voyageurs song.

C'est à l'aube que nous partirons
C'est à l'aube oui, oui, oui
C'est à l'aube non, non, non
C'est à l'aube que nous partirons
Nous navigu'rons toutes les rivières...
English:
Bearing tales of the voyageurs
Bearing tales oui, oui, oui
Bearing tales non, non, non
Bearing tales of the voyageurs
Tales of lakes and of rushing rivers...

Mud covered the floor, and a strong odor of stale beer permeated the air. Most of the men gathered near the bar while others sat at scattered tables playing cards and trying to woo the local Sioux women that hung around the fort. Although not much wooing was required. For the right price, they were quite available.

Bottineau and Provencalle were seated in the corner of the room. Bottineau leaned in toward Provencalle, not wanting others to hear. "Why are so many H.B.C.-ers hanging around across the river?"

"Things have changed in the last year. A lot of bad shit up at the Selkirk Settlement. Especially since Governor Macdonell's *Pemmican Proclamation.* You can't just forbid the transport of pemmican from the Assiniboia region. People have been doing that for hundreds of years and they'll keep doin' it. Macdonell is just pourin' grease on the flame," said Provencalle. Then he leaned back to light his pipe.

Bottineau inquired, "Why would he do that?"

Provencalle leaned back in and answered, "Basically, he wants to help the Hudson's Bay Company block the North West Company from moving furs from the Lake Athabasca region to Fort William. The H.B.C wants to squash trade for the Nor'Westers and push us out. Right now, they have a river blockade to stop the movement of furs and pemmican along the Red River. In fact, there's one just north of here and one on the Assiniboine River as well. They want to shut off all traffic of furs and pemmican from the west. Last spring Selkirk brought in paramilitary soldiers from Ireland, so don't let 'em fool ya' with all that talk about how this is just a simple farming community to supply food for York Factory. That's a cart full of buffalo shit."

Bottineau gulped down the remaining whiskey from his glass and slammed it down on the table. He looked Provencalle in the eye, "I hate those British swine. With their arrogance."

This caused a rumbling laughter from Provencalle. "Ah, my friend. You are the same old Bottineau!"

Bottineau continued, " Ya' know, I spoke with an Ojibwe kid today who was part of the Selkirk Settlement a few years back."

Curious, Provencalle asked, "How'd an Ojibwe kid get mixed up with Selkirk?"

"It's a bit of a story. This kid's not of Indian blood. He's an orphan from Sweden. Came across with the settlement group and Governor Macdonell himself. Apparently got lost in the woods, at least that's the way he tells it. He said he almost died but was rescued and taken in by the Ojibwe at Lake of the Woods."

Provencalle paused as a waitress filled his glass of whiskey, then as she walked away, he asked, "You think we can trust him?"

Bottineau rubbed his eyes, shrugged, then answered, "Peguis thinks he's good and I swear that man is never wrong. I'd trust his judgment with my life."

Provencalle urged Bottineau to continue. "Keep going, what's the kid doing here at Fort Pembina? Isn't he with the H.B.C.?"

Bottineau puffed a couple smoke rings after a long drag off his pipe, then went on. "Like I said, it's a bit of a story. He and his brother have buffalo hides to trade and don't want to transport them all the way back to their village."

Provencalle was shaking his head, losing track of the story. "Okay, wait now. Is this another kid from Sweden, his brother?"

Bottineau laughed, then asked, "Are you sure you want to

continue this?"

"Yes, go on," Provencalle begged.

"All right, the answer is no. I'm talking about his adoptive brother who is full Ojibwe. They did a buffalo hunt down in Lakota territory then trapped their way up the Red River. Now they have too many furs to carry all the way back home, so they came to Pembina to trade."

Somewhat puzzled, Provencalle asked, "If they're with Selkirk, why don't they go to Fort Daer to trade?"

"I've been tryin' to figure out that very same thing. My guess ..." Bottineau stopped as a very drunk trader stumbled past, bumping into their table. Bottineau shook his head, took a big swig of whiskey, then continued his story. "Like I was about to tell you ... my guess is the kid doesn't like the British too much either, eh? I ponder he's stuck in an indentured servant's contract."

Agreeing, Provencalle added, "As he most certainly would be in exchange for the ocean transport."

"Exactly. He must hate those bloodsuckers at the H.B.C. as much as I do," said Bottineau as he finished his glass of whiskey and slammed it down on the table.

Suddenly, Bottineau felt a splash of beer hitting his boot. He looked down at the droplets, then turned in the direction of the splash, his eyes ready to burn a hole in the poor bastard that was to blame. After all, these were his prized elk hide boots. Just one table away, Bottineau noticed a girl's face and dark hair entirely soaked and dripping whiskey. She was Sioux. The man sitting across from her held his empty glass, regretting the unfortunate deflection of the three droplets that went astray and landed on Bottineau's boot. Bottineau stood and approached the table. The man was tall for a voyageur and more lanky than usual. His greasy hair was pressed against his forehead, and he was sweaty from sitting too close to the fireplace. Now hovering over the man, Bottineau smiled.

The greasy-haired man smiled back nervously, revealing a mouth with black and rotting teeth. "You will have to pardon my horrible aim," the man whimpered. Then, so quick the movement was barely perceivable, Bottineau's canoe paddle sized hand clamped onto his throat. He lifted the greasy-haired man off the floor, his feet dangling just inches above the wooden planks. Barely able to speak, he choked out the words, "How 'bout I buy you a whiskey." Responding to the suggestion, Bottineau released his grip and the man dropped back onto his chair.

He looked down at the man and said, "Your apology and your whiskey are accepted. But first, you must apologize to the mademoiselle." Bottineau pointed to the Sioux girl.

The greasy-haired man reacted. "She's just an Indian bitch."

A low rumble emerged from Bottineau's throat. He took a step toward the man.

The greasy-haired man scrambled away in fear. Tripping on the chair leg and falling to the ground. "Okay, okay, I'm sorry!" he said as he struggled to his feet and looked at the Sioux woman. "I'm sorry. It was an unforgivable act. I shouldn't otta have thrown whiskey in your face," said the greasy-haired man. He was clearly not enjoying having to swallow his pride like this and just couldn't help the next words that slipped out of his mouth. "It was terrible of me to waste such fine rot-gut whiskey on a sleazy whore squaw."

You could hear the crunching of cartilage and cracking of bone when Bottineau's fist connected with the greasy-haired man's face and sent him crashing into the wall. The man lay there completely limp and the room, now done watching the sideshow, went back to celebration and inebriation. Bottineau offered a cloth from his pack to the girl who sat expressionless. She was clearly very drunk and not in her right mind having gone through incredible abuse and trauma over the years. A single tear dripped from her eye, rolled off her cheek, and splashed onto the dust covered floor.

Chapter 27.
Fort William –
Fortitude in Distress

Fort William sits on the western bank of Lake Superior at the river Kaministikwia. It is the center of the North West Company's universe of trade, serving as a warehousing center for more than sixty trading posts scattered about the western frontier. During peak trade season, from May to September, more than 5000 people work at the fort in a buzz of activity. Daily, canoes and bateaux arrive with trade goods from Montreal for inland barter. The boats then are loaded with the season's peltry and set out on their journey to Montreal. This happens all trading season. The voyageurs power these boats. Most of them are French and they are mostly from lower class families. The wealthy Scottish partners of the company look down their snooty nose at them. The ideal body type for paddling sixty strokes a minute, ten hours a day, is short and stocky with powerful shoulders and arms. Many voyageurs have native wives and children living out on the frontier and trade season is the only time of year they can see them. Unattached voyageurs typically spend their time getting drunk and partaking in debauchery at the fort tavern. Fort William, built on land obtained by contract from an Ojibwe tribe, is made up of wooden structures of all sizes and shapes. One building immediately catches the eye. It's at the center of the fort and is fronted by a wide veranda. Three large gable windows at the roof give it an architectural presence. In this building company elites gather to discuss the state of the fur trade and business operations. It contains a council hall which serves as the parliament chamber of the Nor'Westers. On the second floor is a great banquet hall that seats two hundred. In this hall, great feasts and celebrations take place. There is no want for fine cuisine as chefs, brought from Montreal, prepare savory dishes for the company's upper crust and anyone lucky enough to receive an invite. At one end of the room stands the bust of Simon McTavish, strategically placed so his gaze seems to rest upon the partners and servants of the company he founded.

At a thirty-foot table draped in fine white cloth sat the eighteen highest ranking partners, all members of the NWC's illustrious Beaver Club, a social organization of the NWC partners in Montreal. To be admitted, it is required that the partner pass the test of a winter in the Northwest beyond the Height of Land west of Grand Portage, which is located at the far western shore of Lake Superior. Admittance to the Beaver Club also requires a unanimous vote by all current members.

Portraits adorned the walls. One of reigning monarch George III, another of Prince Regent, a third of Admiral Lord Nelson. There was also a painting of the famous Battle of the Nile, and a large map of the fur-bearing country. In the middle of the long table, in the fort that bears his name, sat Lieutenant Colonel William McGillivray, the Chief Partner of the NWC. Directly behind him, above the fireplace, hung a large painting. A far more perfect version of himself. The painting diminished the man who sat below. It called out every imperfection and insecurity. Unlike the masterful brush strokes above, his red hair was thinning, and his head twitched intermittently with a nervous tick. His face, pocked from severe adolescent acne, possessed a sickly and unattractive appearance. He had everything money could buy and the suit he wore was no exception; hand made by the finest tailors in Montreal.

Unfortunately, his riches couldn't buy him the one thing he lacked most, greatness.

Scottish born; McGillivray rose to the Chief Partner role after the death of his uncle Simon McTavish. McTavish bore the arms of the McTavishes of Gathberg. His father John McTavish fought as an officer with the Jacobite armies at the Battles of Culloden and Falkirk Muir. William McGillivray, in his early years leading the NWC, brought rapid expansion and great prosperity, but with recent struggles and a rapid decline in revenues, rumblings began to emerge that McGillivray was not the man his uncle was and whispers about nepotism and incompetence were rampant throughout the ranks.

Cloaked in a false confidence, McGillivray rose to his feet. A gold medal hung from his neck, signifying his membership in the Beaver Club. The medal bore the image of a beaver and the words, *Fortitude in Distress*, the club's motto. On the itinerary for the week's discussion were rising tensions with the H.B.C. and input from men with first-hand awareness of the latest developments.

McGillivray raised his glass and said, "To all, elite gentlemen, members of the Beaver Club, and our esteemed guests, I offer a toast. Thank you for bringing society and civilized conversation to this remote outpost."

The group all chimed in at once, "Here, here!"

McGillivray continued with a toast that was offered at the start of every Beaver Club dinner. "To the fur trade and all its branches. To the 'Mother of all Saints.' To the King. To Voyageurs, Wives, and Children." The mention of voyageurs brought a rousing cheer from the group. Then McGillivray walked over to the bust of Simon McTavish, raised his glass, and added, "To absent members." Other Beaver Club members raised their gold medals and bowed their heads in a moment of silent memory of lost loved ones, friends, and members they did not have the pleasure to meet. McGillivray returned to his seat and gave a closing comment. "We have much to discuss. Many looming problems to be solved. But tonight, we feast!"

Suddenly, the kitchen doors burst open, and the room cheered uproariously as four bagpipers wearing traditional Scottish kilts led a celebratory procession. Their playing was very loud and almost drowned out the cheers. Following the bagpipers were two men carrying a flaming boar's head on a red velvet covered platform. The meal that followed was an exercise in extremes and extravagance. The menu included braised venison and bread sauce, Chevreuli des Guides, venison sausages with wild rice and quail, partridge du Vieux Trappeur, and pickled turnips. Then for dessert, "sweet peace" applesauce and bag pudding. Highland Scotch whiskey, Mahogany liquor, and High Wine were poured in abundance.

The pouring continued well into the night when the members re-staged 'le grand voyage.' The men, in an extreme state of inebriation, sat on the floor and used whatever was within arm's reach as a paddle; forks, knives, pistols, dinner plates, boots, a woman's brassiere, or whatever they could grab quickly. Paddling and singing the songs of the voyageurs, the member's imaginary canoe faced all manner of fictitious challenges. Invisible rapids, angry bears, treacherous waterfalls, and pretty much anything else their drunk imaginations could come up with. Drinks were splashed into faces representing the churning waves of rumbling rapids. They hoisted the imaginary canoe onto their shoulders to portage it across table and chairs. While doing this, much glassware was broken. Candles were tipped over, starting minor fires that had to be swatted out by the wait staff.

Beaver club member Frederick Thompson slipped and fell forward, bloodying his mouth on the edge of the table. This left a gaping hole where six teeth used to be. But no worries, Frederick flashed a toothless smile, pounded down some whiskey, and the games went on without a hitch. The men flipped the imaginary canoe on its side and ducked down behind it. They loaded their imagined muskets to battle hostile natives. As the faux battle raged about the room, William McGillivray pretended to be shot in the chest with an arrow. He fell to the ground and one of the club members, John Southerland, was quick to the rescue. He held McGillivray's head on his knees and asked, "Is it bad, sir?"

McGillivray examined his wound and coughed. "I'm afraid it went straight through my heart. I won't be long for this world now. Tell my cocker spaniel I will miss him."

"But sir, what of your wife?" implored Southerland.

"Awe, I hate that bitch," answered McGillivray and the two laughed hysterically.

Pulling a bottle of whiskey from his coat pocket, Southerland said, "Aye, you've got blood spurting all over the place. Look at that, you've wrecked my fine dinner jacket you swine licking arse picker."

He took a long swig, then passed the whiskey bottle it to McGillivray who also took a big gulp. "I owe you a debt," said McGillivray then promptly passed out drunk on the floor.

It was typical for the Beaver Club to announce the times of their dinners likewise; from 5p.m. until the final guest is able to sit in his chair. All the gold medal wearing members took that responsibility seriously. Alexander Mackenzie stumbled out of the room, down the corridor and outside the NWC partner's building. He placed a hand against a post on the front porch to steady himself, then vomited profusely. As he walked to his sleeping quarters, a slight glow on the horizon was beginning to break the darkness and the chirping of birds had begun. It was 4:30 a.m.

By noon the following day, McGillivray, who had no recollection of how he got to his room the night before, sat up in bed and began reading a letter with the seal of the Governor General's office for the Colonies. It read:

Dear Honorable William McGillivray,

Here in Quebec, far from the settlement at Red River and my authority there quite honestly in question, I feel compelled to consult you on a concerning manner. Some servants of the North West Company are suspected of being involved in the diabolical plot to destroy the Selkirk settlement. I was wondering if there exists in your opinion any reasonable

grounds for concern about the safety of the settlement from Indian atrocities. It would be regrettable if anything untoward did happen as the NWC would be considered responsible in the eyes of the world.
-Governor General Sir Gordon Drummond

McGillivray crumpled the letter and tossed it aside. He got out of bed and walked over to a side table that had tea and an assortment of cookies exquisitely displayed. He sat down and popped a cookie into his mouth. He then poured a cup of steaming hot tea, blew gently on the liquid, and took a sip. Still feeling the effects of the previous night's festivities, he gingerly walked across the room and took a seat at his writing desk. With his head buzzing like a June bug against a screen, he proceeded to compose his reply to Sir Gordon Drummond.

Dear Governor General,
Please excuse my abruptness, but I was very offended by your accusatory letter. I deny in the most solemn manner, the allegations where upon this shameful accusation is founded. The Nor'Westers have actually saved the Selkirk settlers from starvation during their first year at Red River. Had not the NWC given them food, there would have been no need for hostile natives to destroy the settlement because hunger alone would have speedily accomplished the task. It is a matter of astonishment that the idea of colonization in the Indian country should be tolerated by His Majesty's government. If it fails, as it must, numerous innocent individuals will fall as sacrifice to his Lordships' visionary pursuits; and if it succeeds, it must infallibly destroy the Indian trade. Furthermore, we cannot remain passive spectators to the violence used to plunder and destroy our property under any authority as was assumed by Mr. Macdonell. If this was to continue, the NWC would assuredly be justified in repelling force by force. I cannot but consider the rights and property of the NWC as equally entitled to protection of His Majesty's Government.
-Sincerely, William McGillivray, Chief Partner, North West Company

The sun shined bright yellow over blue skies speckled with a few happy white clouds. As he walked across the fort grounds, McGillivray wondered how the day could be so damn cheery when he was in such a decrepit mood. Three major problems weighed heavily on his mind. The threat from the H.B.C. at Selkirk's Red River Settlement, plunging revenues, and competition from John Jacob Astor's American Fur Company at Fort Fond du Lac and Mackinac Island.

There was a general commotion at the fort gates as canoes from the Athabasca region arrived with wintering partners Archibald McLeod and Jon Fraser. Duncan Cameron also arrived that morning with Miles Macdonell and Sheriff John Spencer from the Selkirk Settlement as prisoners. As they pulled ashore, British military guards put McDonnell and Spencer in cuffs and walked them off to the guard house. Mcdonell was clearly upset and delivered not-so-pleasant greetings to anyone within earshot.

The council hall was a large room with several windows along one wall. At the head of a table in the corner sat McGillivray. McLeod and Fraser were in intense discussion with McGillivray. Archibald McLeod, a broad-shouldered man with wavy red hair gathered at the back of his head in a ponytail, stood and said, "The bloody rascals forced us ashore and seized 600 sacks of pemmican and at least twenty bundles of pelts. They claimed it was in accordance with the pemmican proclamation under the authority of the new Governor of Assiniboia Robert Semple."

"I see they wasted no time replacing McDonell after his surrender to Cameron," noted McGillivray.

"And we're not the only ones. They seized John Pritchard's cargo as well. At the Souris River," continued McLeod.

McGillivray said, "I sent John Richardson to speak with Selkirk on these matters last fall so we might resolve this conflict. I offered a union between the North West Company and the Hudson's Bay Company. That arrogant bastard, Selkirk, insisted that we acknowledge the validity of their claim to all of Rupert's land and give them full control over it."

Fraser curiously leaned in and asked, "Well?"

McGillivray continued, "Of course, Richardson told Selkirk to shove it up his ass." Having witnessed the severe conflict and destruction of property at the Selkirk colony firsthand McLeod and Fraser were stunned by McGillivray's flippant tone.

Rubbing his forehead in disgust Fraser looked McGillivray in the eyes and said, "Begging your pardon sir, but you're still looking at this like a business negotiation." Fraser walked over to the window and looked out, observing men carrying bundles of furs from storehouse to canoes. He then continued, "This isn't business. It's a god damned war. Governor Semple and his men under the command of Colin Robertson took our Fort Gibraltar just weeks ago. He ordered all NWC men to leave the Red River. He tried to arrest Cameron, but luckily Cameron slipped away by dressing in the clothes of a voyageur. We witnessed the sight on our way here. The fort walls have been dismantled and removed. Everything else was burned to the ground. It was horrible. There were still decaying bodies lying among the torched buildings, some half-eaten by scavenging wolves."

McGillivray leaned back in his chair. His face went ashen realizing the true battle he was in. He then shared his thoughts. "What an unfortunate situation we find ourselves in. These unprincipled agents of government on one side and a speculating nobleman on the other. I blame them. This is not our fault. We have been trading and hunting in these lands for the last 100 years and now they think they can just come in and push us out of the fur trade in the Assiniboia and Athabasca regions? To hell with Selkirk, to hell with his damn colony, and to hell with the H.B.C. It's not an innocent group of farmers, it's a strategic maneuver to drive us out!" McGillivray turned away, looking up at the massive stuffed moose head that hung in the room. Then he continued, "I really wish I was decently out of it, but I shall never submit to be kicked out of it by any lord or commoner in the King's dominions."

McLeod asked, "Sir, what's our next step?"

McGillivray pondered for a moment, then spoke. "God knows what took place at Fort Gibraltar in the spring. I am shocked to learn the truth. Open hostility is inevitable, not only at Red River but throughout the western departments in which case the natives will doubtless get involved in the quarrel. I must dispatch Richardson at once to Quebec in order that he might ask that Governor Sherbrooke send officers with sufficient authority to help us regain Fort Gibraltar and keep the peace."

Later that evening, Duncan Cameron joined McGillivray for dinner. Candles lit the small dining room as the men drank French wine and dined on caribou. It was a humid and hot summer night. Through an open window, loons could be heard singing in the distance.

Duncan Cameron said, "Our work of two years is coming together, and a storm is gathering north of the Selkirk Colony. We're ready to take decisive action in response to Governor Semple's destruction of Fort Gibraltar."

"Tell me more about developments," urged McGillivray.

Cameron went on. "I have received word through courier that Cuthbert Grant has the Bois-Brûlés unified and ready to obey our commands. Many of the half-breeds have come a great distance to join their brothers, as far as the upper Saskatchewan and Cumberland House. They're gathered in numbers surpassing 120 men at the Qu'Appelle River and ready to burst onto the shit suckers who rightly deserve it. Little do they know their situation. Last year's attack at the Selkirk colony was but a joke compared to what they will see this year. The Bois-Brule are calling themselves the New Nation and are ready to clear their native soil of these intruders and assassins. They've had it with the settlement messing up their livelihood; the buffalo hunt."

"That is good, very good," noted McGillivray.

Cameron continued, "Alexander MacDonell attempted to recruit the Salteaux as well, but Chief Peguis was not willing to join our cause. He has made a choice and clearly, he thinks he's in a stronger position trading with the H.B.C. than allying with us. But I'm damn ready to prove him wrong. In fact, once we wipe out the settlement, we should burn Peguis' village to the ground and kill everyone possible."

"Duncan, don't get ahead of yourself, let's first focus our sights on Selkirk," instructed McGillivray as he finished his glass of wine. Duncan Cameron nodded his head in agreement.

Chapter 28.
Jack River

June 4, 1816
Jack River Trading Post. North of Lake Winnipeg in Manitoba,
Canada.

The Lake of the Woods band of Ojibwe, with Jacob as their trading agent, completed delivery of more than sixty bundles of pelts to the Jack River Post. This would be the last season Jacob was obligated under contract with the Hudson's Bay Company. It was a very successful season, with Jacob delivering twice as many fur bundles as the previous summer.

The chief trading agent at Jack River, Mr. Walker, was impressed. "Jacob, this is a huge load of pelts. You've done well."

"Thanks Mr. Walker," said Jacob.

"I'm looking forward to seeing what you can do next season."

"I guess we will see," answered Jacob. Jacob knew he had no intention of continuing his work with the H.B.C. He felt trapped and wanted to strike out on his own. He had heard about the emerging American Fur Company that was looking for partnerships with trappers and traders on the American side of the border at. As Jacob turned and walked away, Mr. Walker had a curious look on his face.

Too late to start the journey back to Lake of the Woods, Jacob and the others stayed the night in the company barracks. Heavy rain crashed loudly onto the roof of the structure. Ten men from the Lake of the Woods band were sound asleep inside. Jacob snored away on a lower bunk, only to be outdone by Thunder Bear who snored heavily on the upper.

The night sky was a tapestry of opaque blacks and grays. Only an occasional flash of lightning broke complete darkness. A muddy boot sloshed into a puddle as a wall of rain fell. With determination and urgency, a man moved down the water-logged boardwalk, though his progress was hindered by a significant limp. He hobbled his way to the barracks door.

He banged his fist on the door. Then, in a heavy French accent yelled, "Please open. Chief Peguis sent me." Popping out of their beds and slowly coming awake, the men grabbed their muskets and took cover, assuming a defensive posture. Rain blew in through an open window, soaking Jacob's shoulder as he took aim on the door.

"State your business, sir," yelled Jacob, trying to raise his voice above the booming thunder.

The voice on the other side of the door continued, "Bois-Brûlés from the Saskatchewan attacked the Saulteaux village at Netley Creek. They tried to force Peguis to join them in an attack on the Selkirk Settlement. When Peguis refused they opened fire. If it weren't for the heavy tree cover, they would've killed more of us." There was no answer and the man again pounded on the door. "Jacob, we saw your canoes go past a couple days ago. It is me, Bottineau."

Now recognizing the voice, Jacob nodded to the brave closest to the door. The brave cautiously pushed up on the door latch, unlocking it. Bottineau stumbled forward when the door swung open. It appeared he was about to fall when a hand, that seemed to come out of nowhere, grabbed the back of Bottineau's shirt. It was Thunder Bear. All the braves wondered how he got out there. Putting things together in his mind, Jacob looked at his rain-soaked shirtsleeve and now realized that when Bottineau first approached the door his brother had slipped off the top bunk and out the window completely undetected. As Thunder Bear helped Bottineau to a chair, Jacob couldn't help but be amazed by his brother's incredible instincts and how he always seemed to be two steps ahead of everyone else. If the person at the door had bad intentions, Thunder Bear would have put an end to it.

Jacob lit candles to illuminate the room. The light made it apparent that Bottineau's shirt was not only soaked with rain, but blood. A bullet had entered at his side, just above the waist. Bottineau grabbed Jacob's arm and, wincing pain, pleaded, "You need to get to the Selkirk settlement. Cuthbert Grant is promising a massacre. He says this attack on the settlement will be ten times worse than last year's skirmish."

Thunder Bear yelled to one of the braves, "Go quickly and get the trader, he'll have surgical supplies. We need to take out the musket ball."

Jacob intervened, "I'll go, Mr. Walker knows me. It'll be safer." With that, Jacob bolted out the door and sprinted as fast as he could through the woods from the company barracks to the trader's cabin.

Meanwhile, Bottineau went on describing the incidents at the Salteaux village. "That Peguis is a tough old son-of-a-bitch. Grant was yelling in his face about how he needs to join the native cause to reclaim their land for the buffalo hunt. Peguis never changed expression the whole time, even when Grant told him he should put on a dress and join the women if he refused to fight. When the yelling and cursing stopped, the chief said, "You talk too much. While you were yapping away, my warriors untied your horses. Enjoy your walk back to Fort Qu'Appelle." All of us laughed like crazy when Grant turned around and saw about forty of his horses running across a meadow. You should've seen his face. He was so mad. Then Peguis said, "You're a lot shorter without your horse." We all laughed right in his face. That's when a couple of his Bois-Brule soldiers started shooting. We scattered for cover in the trees, but there was too much gunfire and at least four of Peguis' warriors were killed." Bottineau winced a bit then coughed up blood.

Thunder Bear helped him over to one of the beds and began examining the entry wound. Just then, Jacob and the trader, Mr. Walker, arrived with surgical supplies. Having been in the wilderness for twenty years and in his share of scrapes, Walker was skilled with a surgical knife. Jacob fed Bottineau as much whiskey as he could get him to swallow.

Walker cut open Bottineau's flesh, then probed inside with his fingers, searching for the musket ball. "Ah, there it is," Walker said as he squinted and dug deeper. Bottineau groaned in pain, biting down on a tree branch. Through gritted teeth, Bottineau sang old voyageur songs. Then with a clank, Walker dropped the musket ball into a metal dish. He said, "Luckily it didn't hit bone, or the damned thing would've made a real mess." Walker stitched up the three-inch slice in Bottineau's side. "Don't think it hit any vital organs or he would be bleedin' way more. Let's have him get some rest and we'll sort things out in the morning." Calmly Mr. Walker closed his surgical kit and walked out of the room like it was just a normal evening.

Jacob turned to Thunder Bear and said, "We've got to get to the settlement and warn them."

"It's not your fight, Jacob," implored Thunder Bear.

Jacob insisted. "But I know those people. Most of 'em are completely innocent. They're just farmers."

Thunder Bear uttered a frustrated growl. "You don't even like those people at the settlement and the H.B.C. has treated you like a slave and they treat Indians like dog shit."

Jacob shook his head from side to side then said, "I'm not a slave Thunder Bear. I agreed to work for five years in exchange for the voyage across the Atlantic. You're right, the H.B.C. does treat Indians like dog shit, but I have a debt to repay." There was a momentary lull as Jacob looked Thunder Bear in the eye. Jacob continued, "I gave 'em my word. I can't go back on that. And, if I don't try to help, how could I live with myself? This isn't just the H.B.C., there are families ... women and children, at the settlement."

Thunder Bear rubbed his eyes with both hands in frustration. "Okay, we warn them, but we're not going to war against anybody," said Thunder Bear as he looked Jacob in the eye forcing him to make eye contact and nod in agreement.

"I know, just to save lives. That's it," promised Jacob. Outside the thunderstorm raged on. Rain poured down and the night sky flashed as lightning crackled through the clouds.

Chapter 29.
The Warning

It was just after dawn. Jacob, Thunder Bear, and the Ojibwe men loaded their trade goods into six birch bark canoes and departed Jack River. Now with the supplies needed for the coming fall and winter months, they were ready to journey home to Lake of the Woods. Jacob left the post without committing to another contract with the Hudson's Bay Company, much to the disappointment of Mr. Walker. Sailing south on Lake Winnipeg Jacob noticed a fresh campsite. He and Thunder Bear went ashore to get a closer look. Glowing embers indicated a group was there recently and many hoof prints were apparent. Thunder Bear closely examined the minute details of the individual hoof prints. He made an assessment that the prints were most likely left by the Bois-Brule. Further, he estimated there must be at least fifty men.

Jacob asked, "How do you know it's the Bois-Brûlés?"

Thunder Bear explained, "There's an odd mix of horses with metal shoes and without. Sioux or Assiniboine almost never travel this far to the northeast. Peguis' Salteaux are not a horse tribe, nor are the Cree. They're canoe Indians like us. Plus, someone forgot their hat." Thunder Bear indicated in the direction of a hat submerged in the water along the shore. It was a round, brimmed hat commonly worn by the Bois-Brule. He picked up the soaking wet hat and placed it on his head.

Jacob laughed and said, "You look ridiculous."

"Exactly. That's why this is definitely not a Sioux or Assiniboine camp," joked Thunder Bear.

As they sailed further south, they came across two encampments of similar size. Thunder Bear said, "This is a war party. They're certainly not up here hunting buffalo."

A campfire crackled and flickered yellow and red splashes of light. With a stick, Jacob poked at the embers, leaned forward, and blew, stoking the fire. Then he added two more fallen spruce branches that had been gathered from the woods. Across from Jacob sat Thunder Bear with another three warriors of the group. They wore traditional Ojibwe summer clothing. Breech cloth with doeskin leggings and moccasins. Being a hot summer month, none of the men wore a shirt except one who was particularly proud of the new white cloth shirt he had traded for at Jack River. All of them had long hair, including Jacob, as they believed long hair was an extension of the senses allowing one to be more receptive to the surrounding world, both physical and spiritual. Two or three feathers in the hair was common. The men prized intricate beadwork with animal teeth or claws as ornate neckwear. Jacob still wore with pride the wolf tooth necklace given to him by Akami at York Factory. When at the trading post, Jacob would often wear the clothing of a fur trader, but when away from the post, he always dressed like his fellow tribesmen. He did this because the trading agents and wintering partners with the H.B.C. held a misguided view of native people, considering them uncivilized and less intelligent at best, savages and sub-human at worst. Jacob understood that dressing the part gave him an advantage in the bartering, resulting in a better trade outcome for the tribe. It was much less likely that an Englishman with the H.B.C. would try to cheat a white man. Sad, disturbing and disgusting, but true. A young but very tall brave named Lone Bear was with the group. At six feet four inches he towered over most warriors of the Lake of the Woods band. Having a particularly long upper body, Lone Bear's height disparity was even more evident while seated at the campfire. The other two men at the fire had many years of experience hunting and going out on raids with Thunder Bear. They were both older but recognized Thunder Bear's superior abilities and trusted his judgment. Their close friendship and comradery were apparent in the ease with which they shared company. They constantly played jokes on one another and frequently retold stories of shared triumphs and tragedies. The bond was complex and difficult to follow. Jacob was somewhat new to the clique, but he had found acceptance and familiarity. For Lone Bear, this being his first adventure, things were still a challenge. It was hard to fit in and he was treated like a greenhorn. Having been in that position recently, Jacob understood and empathized with Lone Bear's awkwardness and his desire to fit in. For many minutes, the group sat silently around the fire, content to listen to the wind whistling through the trees, intermittent owl hooting, and the distant buzz of cicada bugs. The men were eating fresh caribou, cooked over the open flame, courtesy of Jacob's musket earlier that afternoon.

Finally, Lone Bear broke the silence by saying, "I like your shirt."

The brave wearing the white cotton shirt looked down at his sleeves and replied, "Thank you."

Thunder Bear added, "Now you can run for Governor."

The group all laughed, ribbing the brave for his white man clothes.

The brave with the shirt responded, "My wife did tell me that her mother said I'm a bit girlish."

Jacob asked, "Oh man, what did you say to her?"

I said, "Who's not girlish, compared to your mother." All laughed. Thunder Bear lit a pipe, and they all shared a smoke.

Thunder Bear exhaled a big puff of smoke then said, "Tomorrow morning we split. You will take three canoes and continue to the Winnipeg River. Jacob and I will head east to Red River with the other canoe."

The brave with the white shirt asked, "Why are we splitting

ways? A larger group is a safer group."

"I know. But there are people in danger down at the Selkirk settlement. Jacob has friends there. We must try to warn them that the Bois-Brule have been stirred up and assembled for an attack with the Nor'Westers," answered Thunder Bear.

The oldest brave was somewhat surprised by this decision, for once doubting Thunder Bear's judgment. He said, "We should all go and fight. Strength in numbers."

Thunder Bear insisted, "This is not a fight. We're just going to warn them, then we head for home ourselves."

Jacob added, "There are families there, innocent people caught in the middle of this damned fur trade war between the H.B.C. and the North West Company. We've gotta' try to help,"

"Okay, but I don't like it," said the oldest brave. The group again went silent, experiencing their inner thoughts and the sounds of nature all around them.

Before dawn, Thunder Bear and Jacob transferred trade goods from their canoe into the others to lighten their load. They kept only critical tools and weapons, a week of rations, and a barrel of gunpowder for hunting. As the sun rose in the eastern sky behind them, Jacob raised the sail, and they were on their way. Thunder Bear was asleep as they neared the point where the Red River dumps into Lake Winnipeg. Jacob noticed many walleye in the water, hundreds of them. Enough of the delicious tasting fish to eat for days. He lowered the sail, threw out an anchor, and began spearing fish. When Jacob speared his last, he held it, wet tail flapping, just over Thunder Bear's snoring nose. This startled him and he popped up, wiping water off his face and cursing at Jacob. Jacob fell back in the canoe, laughing hysterically at his reaction.

"If you weren't my brother, I would drown you right now," yelled Thunder Bear, trying to hold back his laughter, realizing how funny the whole prank was.

The Red River is the only river below the 49th parallel, today's northern border of the United States, that flows to the north. For this reason, to head south from Lake Winnipeg to Fort Douglas at the Selkirk settlement, Jacob and Thunder Bear would have to paddle upstream, against the current. They made it as far as Netley Creek and decided to make camp.

Jacob suggested, "This is going too slow. We'll never beat men on horseback to the settlement."

Thunder Bear thought about Jacob's suggestion for a bit, then added sarcastically, "Unless you have a herd of horses to pull out of your ass, I'm not sure how we get there any quicker, Oza?"

Jacob contemplated their situation then said, "I could run the woods. You've seen me, I can run all day."

Thunder Bear shook his head and protested, "Yes, but I don't like the idea of you going alone, unprotected."

Flexing his arms to bulge his biceps Jacob said, "Unprotected? What are you trying to say?"

Thunder Bear answered, "Quit joking, this is serious."

"I know. And I do know that there's no safer place to be than with you. But we'll never get there trying to paddle against the current," Jacob insisted.

Thunder Bear began to laugh. "I have an idea. You run the woods. I'll run interference with the Bois-Brûlés. I'll see if I can't slow them down and buy you a bit of time." Thunder Bear made a clicking sound with his cheek and winked at Jacob. The two spent the night swapping Viking sagas and native legends until Jacob's head tilted forward and his eyes closed. Thunder Bear laid Jacob down and covered him with a blanket. He heard a faint snore and smiled as he tucked another blanket under Jacob's head. Thunder Bear sat for a moment watching Jacob sleep, thinking about how thankful he was that the Great Spirit had brought to him this blue-eyed brother.

...

A woodpecker stopped hammering to listen as the crunching of running footsteps approached. Jacob flickered through very tall and narrow birch trees. Ducking under low hanging branches and jumping over downed trees, he moved at full speed through the woods. In some areas, it was densely packed with trees slowing Jacob down, but other areas were more open meadows and plains allowing him to keep a faster pace. Water was a blessing and a curse along the route. A blessing because it provided ample drinking water, a curse because large ponds, marshes, and swamps caused the addition of several miles to the thirty-five-mile distance to Fort Douglas.

With the repetitious sound of inhaling and exhaling inside his head, Jacob focused his eyes on the constantly changing terrain in front of him. He used his nose to anticipate what he could not yet see. A strong musty odor signaled standing water ahead, the strong scent of spruce was an unmistakable sign of thick trees coming, and the subtle scent of wildflowers indicated open meadow. Jacob's mind wandered as he ran. Thoughts of Sweden, his London friend Ed, Blue Jay, and this wretched mess between the Hudson's Bay Company and the Nor'Westers. He wondered to himself, *was he doing the right thing getting tangled up in this mess? Was the threat overblown? Did he even know any of the people who remained at the settlement? Was it even his business? Was he heading into a squabble, or was Thunder Bear, correct? Was it a war?*

Jacob stopped at a flowing creek that looked clear and clean. He crouched down and took a drink. He removed a piece of pemmican from his pack and ate it. Several birds sat on the branch of a tree above. Jacob wondered what they thought of him. He sat for a moment in the grass just watching the birds and catching his breath. Their chatter intensified the longer he lingered, as if they were carrying on a full conversation about this curious beast drinking at the stream. On a regular day, it would be a deer, caribou, or maybe a wolf that drank at the creek. Not today. Today it was this odd creature. Many parts of this vast wilderness had never been visited by man, so Jacob could only imagine how surprised the birds were to see him.

Thunder Bear crawled on his stomach through heavy brush. Rain fell, soaking the ground and causing water to puddle. Cautiously, he approached an ox cart trail, listening attentively for anyone approaching in the distance. Determining it was safe, he began gathering large fallen branches and dragging them onto the trail. He piled the branches high like a beaver dam. Once satisfied it was large enough, he ran through the woods back to his canoe where he emptied twelve tin boxes that held tobacco and began filing them with gunpowder. Thunder Bear filled his pack with musket balls and topped off two powder horns, hung them from his shoulder and ran back into the woods. He placed the tin boxes in trees, on the ground, and in bushes along the trail. Thunder Bear crossed to the other side of the trail where he loaded three muskets and leaned them against a large boulder. He covered the muskets with a buffalo blanket to keep them dry and began to wait. Thunder Bear knew that a large group on horseback wouldn't be able to make it from Peguis' village on Lake Winnipeg to the Selkirk settlement without using this ox cart trail. Eventually they'd arrive at this spot unless he was too late. But that wasn't likely as a group that large would've left many hoofprints in a wide swath, which did not seem to be the case.

Thunder Bear was quite certain the Bois-Brûlés war party would arrive soon. So, he waited. He listened to the sounds of the woods, like the game he used to always play with Jacob. What sound was right and what sound was out of place. Birds whistled in the branches and the scurrying of small animals was evident. If he listened closely, he could hear the slithering of snakes in the brush. Then, the first clue arrived. It was not a specific sound, but rather a lack of sound that triggered Thunder Bear's senses. A large group of men traveling through the forest startles woodland animals. Birds fly off, rabbits freeze in their tracks and gophers go underground. Slowly and quietly, Thunder Bear uncovered the muskets and prepared himself. Affirming his suspicion, he heard distant horses snort and whinny, then the voices of men speaking French became audible. Coming down the trail was a group of at least twenty men on horseback that looked like a native tribe, but some of the men wore European clothes, others dressed like Indians but had short hair, mustaches, and beards. All wore the war paint of their ancestors.

As the Bois-Brûlés neared the eight-foot pile of branches Thunder Bear created, a man with a thick black beard barked out an order in French. "Dismount! It's a trap. Prepare for battle!"

Thunder Bear took aim at the first tin box across the trail then pulled the trigger. Horses reared up and men scrambled for cover as gunshots were coming from all directions, or so it appeared. Thunder Bear continued to fire his musket into the ground just in front of the horses and then at another tin box across the trail, then another and another.

"Retreat! We've got H.B.C. soldiers all around us. Retreat," yelled the bearded man. The men jumped up on their horses and rode off in the direction from which they had come. Wasting no time, Thunder Bear shot one last tin box then sprinted through the woods to his canoe. He threw in the muskets and paddled quickly down the creek. Thunder Bear chuckled to himself as he paddled. This delay and change of route would add hours if not days to their journey. Jacob now had a bit more time.

A squirrel gnawed on an acorn at the base of a large oak tree. Suddenly he darted away as footsteps approached. Jacob, his hair entirely drenched with sweat, sped past. He continued running well into the night until complete exhaustion forced him to take a seat in a grassy meadow. Almost immediately, he nodded off. A couple hours later, a mosquito buzzed in Jacob's ear, waking him. Startled, not knowing how long he had slept, Jacob popped to his feet and again began to run. He ran for several miles when his vision began to blur, and his legs became weak. Going down to one knee, Jacob tried to recover. He attempted to get up but stumbled, fell over and lost consciousness. Fortunately, a group of Chief Peguis' warriors had already been trailing Jacob wondering who he was and what he was doing in their territory. One of the men lifted Jacob's head and pushed the long hair away from his face. He looked at the other warriors with surprise that this was a white man. Propping his head up a bit higher, the man poured water into Jacob's mouth. Jacob began choking as he regained consciousness. Rising to his feet and with barely enough wind in his lungs to get the words out, Jacob said, "Fort Douglas. Bois-Brules are gonna' attack. Have to warn the Selkirk settlers."

...

June 16, 1816. The sun was low in the sky when two men approached Fort Douglas on horseback. Mud splashed as hooves navigated the rain-soaked trail. They cast long shadows as they neared the gate. It was Peguis and Jacob.

Peguis turned to Jacob and gave him instructions in Ojibwe. "Let me speak. The settlers know me."

In a strong Scottish accent, a man yelled from the watch tower, "State your business or I'll be puttin' a hole through ya?" The man had his musket pointed right at Jacob.

In English, Peguis said, "I'm Peguis, chief of the Salteaux of the Prairie. Governor Semple knows me, as do most of the settlers. I come with a warning."

Somewhat impatient, the Scot in the watch tower added, "Keep talkin'."

Peguis continued, "The Nor'Westers have again roused the Bois-Brûlés. A war party of more than fifty men, led by Cuthbert Grant, are headed this way. They plan to destroy the settlement. They want it gone and they're willing to spill blood to accomplish it."

"Stay there," the Scot said curtly. He turned and walked away from the opening in the watch tower. Jacob and Peguis could hear his footsteps running down the wooden stairs and across muddy ground. The gate opened slowly and the Scot from the watch tower stood very casually in the opening.

Noticing the man was no longer carrying his weapon, Peguis asked, "Shouldn't you have your musket?"

"Yes, you've got a bloody good point there," said the Scot, laughing. It was clear that, though there were several rumors circulating of another Bois-Brûlés attack, the settlers were in a state of denial. It seemed they had a bit of false confidence because of Colin Robertson's actions last spring when he took Fort Gibraltar by force. With everything he had been taught by Thunder Bear, Jacob couldn't believe the lack of preparedness.

He said to Peguis in Ojibwe, "They have no idea of the storm that's coming." Peguis simply nodded his head in agreement. They dismounted and followed the man to the Governor's residence where they were greeted on the front porch by Robert Semple.

Semple cleared his throat and said, "Chief. How's your day?"

Peguis paused a moment then said, "You have a serious problem. The Bois-Brûlés have plans to wipe you out and they have the numbers to do it. More than 50, all armed and on horseback. Could be tomorrow, no longer than a week."

"Peguis, I have authority here. The law is on my side. Besides, if they want a fight, let's have it. The Bois-Brûlés can't handle my men."

Peguis looked around the fort. One man was petting a cat, and another was using a pitchfork to unload a cart of cow shit onto a garden. Leaning up against a fence were six unattended muskets. Peguis sighed and suggested, "I'm not so sure."

Insulted, Semple blurted, "Whatever do you mean?"

Impatient, like a schoolteacher having to repeat instructions on a very simple lesson, Peguis continued, "For starters, the fort's gate is still open and it's unattended. The man in the watch tower is asleep. Your military commander Robertson and eight of his men headed up to York Factory a week ago, meaning everyone north of here knows they're out. Don't get me wrong Governor, you have able-bodied men here. Good men. But they're not warriors ... and a war is coming." Now in a position where it was difficult to deny the wisdom of Peguis, Semple took pause. His hand nervously covered his mouth and chin. Peguis continued, "I can provide thirty warriors to help defend the fort. Discourage an attack. The Bois-Brules are unlikely to attack their native brothers."

"Nah, this will all blow over. The North West Company is just trying to put a scare in us. They've been playing this charade since the settlement's founding. It's all show," defended Semple.

"Please take the men," urged Peguis.

Now a bit angered, Semple barked, "I said no, god damn it! Now get the hell out of my fort, before I have the two of you thrown into the brig."

Peguis dropped his head in disappointment. One final time he urged, "You don't want to do this, Governor. I'm trying to save your life. Take the men."

Semple yelled, "Mackenzie! Whittingham! Show the chief and his friend the way out." Peguis looked Semple in the eyes non-verbally pleading with him to reconsider. But Semple averted his gaze, went back into his residence, and slammed the door. That was it. There was nothing more Peguis could do.

Chapter 30.
Storm Clouds Gather

At Portage la Prairie, about sixty miles west of the settlement, another group of Bois-Brûlés was encamped. The day prior, they had captured six H.B.C. York boats and stole their entire supply of pemmican. It was their intent to get this supply of pemmican north to Lake Winnipeg to supply a NWC canoe brigade arriving from Fort William. It was a cold morning for June, below forty degrees. A large group of men had gathered around Alexander Macgregor who stood on a large boulder. The chill in the air caused white steam to float from his mouth as he spoke. "My friends, I address you regrettably, for I have not a pipe of tobacco to give you. All our goods have been taken by the English. They've been destroying these lands which belong to you, the Bois-Brûlés. By who's right? Did you say to the English ... to the Hudson's Bay Company, go ahead, drive away the buffalo? Go ahead, take food from the mouths of our children. Go ahead, look down upon us. Treat us less than human. Is that what you said the English could do?"

A rousing and angry roar came from the group. "No!"

Macgregor continued, "Damn right, no! This is indeed the time to say no, because if you don't, you'll soon be in a bad position. Are you going to let the English tell you that you can't hunt, trade, and travel—on *your* land?"

The group again yelled, "No!"

Macgregor went on. "It's time to end this. If the Indian tribes won't drive the English away, then we will damn sure make it happen. The North West Company and the Bois-Brules are one!"

A loud cheer came from the crowd. Increasing his volume and passion even further Macgregor yelled, "We will take Fort Douglas and uproot this damned Selkirk settlement once and for all. I don't want to have a repeat of the shit we had last summer where we leave something for those bastards to come back to. Every building ... burn it to the ground. Every crop ... up in flames. Every settler ... run off for good. And if they fight, well, then you have to do what is necessary. In that unfortunate case, the land shall be drenched with their blood." Macgregor had to wait for a long time as the group would not stop cheering. "If they take to the fort for protection, we lock it down and starve 'em out. If any of them come out to fish or to get water, I want them shot." Macgregor paused momentarily as his words sank in. He then continued, "The HBC wants complete control of YOUR land. What do you say to the English? Do you say yes? Or no?"

"NO!" Birds screeched and flew out of the trees as the response from the Bois-Brules was so overwhelming and loud.

Later that day, as the group prepared to depart, Alexander Macgregor approached Cuthbert Grant who was seated aloft a fine brown horse with white speckles and a well-groomed mane. Grant, who typically dressed in the clothing of Montreal society, now wore the attire of his mother's Assiniboine people. He wore a fringed doeskin shirt, breach cloth and leggings. Two eagle feathers were woven into a braid at the side of his head. His face was painted entirely red with a black circle around his left eye.

Macgregor said, "Now, Grant, when you get near Fort Douglas it would be best to pass in the plains as far distant as possible to avoid causing alarm. There you should wait at Frog Plain for the arrival of the canoes from Fort William."

Grant chimed in, "I know. We spoke of the plan nights ago."

Somewhat annoyed, Macgregor added, "This is the direction from Montreal, and I have to make assurances that this goes correctly. There will be several Fort Williams canoes arriving at Frog Plain. They are on their way north to the Athabasca country and need pemmican for the journey. It is critical that you supply them these necessary provisions. After the canoes are provisioned, and on their way, you are to blockade Fort Douglas and starve Semple out."

"Yes, sir, we'll turn the tables on these scoundrels," affirmed Grant as he turned his horse and rode off to the river's edge where a large group of Bois-Brûlés had gathered. Part of the group drifted down the Assiniboine River with weapons, gun powder, and provisions while the majority of them rode on horseback. The group had two carts and canoes carrying fifteen bags, over 1000 pounds, of pemmican. Their faces were painted in hideous fashion to instill fear, and they were well armed with guns, pistols, lances, tomahawks and bows & arrows. A man on a black horse flew the Bois-Brûlés flag. It was royal blue, about four feet square and in its middle a white figure eight was placed horizontally. Flapping in the wind as they rode, the flag reflected yellow light from the sunset at their backs.

...

An old man pushed a cartload of torches to the front gate of Fort William, headquarters of the NWC, on Lake Superior. He dipped each torch in whale oil, placed them in their brackets and lit them ablaze. Inside the guardhouse. Miles Macdonell, former governor of the Selkirk settlement and now captive of the Nor'Westers, sat on a straw filled mattress in the corner of his cell. In his right hand was a clump of his gray hair. He set the clump of hair on the mattress, then reached up to his head, grabbing another handful. It made a horrible ripping sound as he uprooted the hair, taking much skin and follicles with it. Blood dripped down his face as his eyes stared vacantly. A small rat scurried across the floor. Macdonell stomped it with the heel of his boot, leaned forward and picked up the blood-soaked rodent. Ripping open a hole in the end of his mattress, he stuffed the rat inside. His body rocked from side to side, and he seemed completely unaware of a large wisp of drool dripping from his mouth.

Across the room, a very drunk Frenchman slurred his way through a voyageur song.

"Shut the hell up," yelled Macdonell. This caused the Frenchman to come out of his stupor and he approached Macdonell who was still seated on his mattress.

"No piece of *merde* Irishman gonna' talk to me in that tone," the Frenchman said.

With drool still handing from his lip, Macdonell looked up at the man.

The Frenchman slurred further, "I believe you were about to apologize."

Macdonell slowly stood and looked the Frenchman in the eye. The Frenchman was somewhat taken aback by these strange eyes looking at him, but at the same time looking at nothing. The Frenchman said, "There ya' go. Now get on your knees, beg for mercy, and I won't knock you out." The Frenchman laughed as he pushed on Macdonell's shoulders and forced him down on his knees.

Suddenly, Macdonell delivered a powerful upper cut to the groin. The Frenchman fell over onto the ground in pain. Macdonell stood up and kicked the Frenchman in the face. Blood and spit flew against the wall. The Frenchman tried to get up, but Macdonell grabbed his shirt and punched the man in the face four times in rapid succession. He then grabbed the Frenchman's head and banged it on the stone floor repeatedly until a crack in his skull exposed the gray matter within and blood began to pool beneath. Macdonell stared blankly at the pool of blood for a moment, then simply walked back to his mattress, sat down, and began to again rock from side to side.

It wasn't until the next morning that the guards discovered the carnage in Macdonell's cell. They put him in ankle and wrist shackles, then took him in front of William McGillivray, Chief Partner of the NWC. Macdonell was chained to a bench in front of

McGillivray's desk. Two soldiers stood watch behind Macdonell.

McGillivray questioned, "Seems there was a bit of a problem last night with your cellmate?"

Macdonell blurted, "I'm the governor of this fort and I will conduct its business the way I see fit. I demand my prompt release."

McGillivray shifted in his chair and said, "You realize you're at Fort William, correct? This is not the Selkirk settlement at Fort Douglas, and you resigned your position as governor months ago. They say due to 'severe emotional instability' ..." McGillivray took off his glasses and glared curiously at Macdonell.

Macdonell answered, "I am Miles Macdonell Governor of all Assiniboia. I have supreme power ascribed to me by royal charter of the British government. This land, Rupert's Land, was granted by King Charles II in 1670, making me the true and absolute lord. That means, I can do whatever I think is fit and requisite."

McGillivray was becoming noticeably frustrated. He continued, "Like I said, you're not in Rupert's Land, you're at Fort William on Lake Superior."

Macdonell threatened, "You best not raise your tone with me. I rule over an army of soldiers who become invisible at the full moon."

"You've lost your senses, man. I am William McGillivray, Chief Partner of the North West Company. You've been apprehended by my men for crimes against my traders on the Red River. We will be transporting you to Montreal for trial. Firstly, your *Pemmican Proclamation* was without cause and has led to much criminal mischief by you and the H.B.C. Plus, you directly participated in attacks on Fort Gibraltar, where you committed foul acts. The willful destruction of property, theft, murder, and the illegal apprehension and detention of my officer, Duncan Cameron."

Macdonell glanced up at the ceiling, his neck and eye twitching in a disturbing manner. He giggled and said, "In twelve days, when the moon is again full, my army will walk through these walls, spill the blood of your men, and string you up. In the gallows, you will hang as an exhibition of my supreme power." Macdonell then gazed off into the corner of the room and began a conversation with an unseen person.

McGillivray cut in, "Be that as it may, I will inform you, Mister Macdonell, that the NWC has privilege to the lands of Assiniboia and the Athabasca territory by right of discovery. It was Alexander McKenzie that opened these lands for trade. Not the British. Not the H.B.C. We have every right, as do the Bois-Brûlés, to trap, hunt, and trade these lands unfettered by your provocation and obstruction. No wonder the Bois-Brûlés are ready to descend upon the settlement and vanquish these lands of the H.B.C."

Macdonell, completely oblivious to what MacGillivray was saying, suddenly seemed to realize that he was in chains and screamed, "Why are these chains on me? I need to get out of here! My soldiers need me! They're dying ... they're dying." Then, once again, looking into the corner of the room Macdonell resumed his conversation with the unseen person. He said, "Ye...ye...Yes, sir. I will get to the front." A look of horror come over Macdonell's face and he began to cry. He was experiencing a vision of one of his men being burned alive during his military days with the King's Royal Regiment in the Mohawk Valley of New York. He continued talking to himself, "Why is your face melting? Help! He's burning! He's burning!"

McGillivray looked up at the guards standing behind Macdonell, making eye contact with them. He then made a waving motion with his hand, prompting them to remove Macdonell.

"He's lost his wits, sir," one of the guards offered.

McGillivray responded, "Wet gunpowder on the brain. Prepare his transfer to Montreal immediately. I want this lunatic out of my fort." Macdonell's body hung limp and his legs slid along the stone floor as the two guards drug him away.

...

Firelight illuminated the faces of Chief Peguis and Jacob.

Behind them, several wigwams dotted the prairie near Netley Creek.

"You can't protect people who don't want protection. You can't save people who reject being saved," said the chief. Jacob was attentive but his face showed a lack of satisfaction with Peguis' thoughts.

Jacob offered, "We could still try to do something. Help the Selkirk settlers in some way?"

"I am proud of your desire to help your friends. Your heart is good, Jacob ... but it is also reckless. There is danger in these things. This is a war that is way bigger than you and your friends."

Jacob again tried to offer a suggestion. "But maybe ..."

Peguis interrupted, "Be quiet, Jacob. You talk too much. Ears don't work when your mouth is moving."

"You're right, I'm sorry," Jacob said apologetically. Then, realizing he was talking again quickly cut himself off.

Peguis looked Jacob closely in the eye, scolding him with his gaze. He took a moment to pack his pipe with tobacco, lit it, took a deep drag, then passed it over to Jacob.

Peguis said, "Let me tell you a story. There was a wolf, a leader of his pack. The pack hunted well and lived well. Then one day the leader came across another wolf pack. This wolf pack was under attack by a bear. The wolf jumped in to help and he succeeded by ripping out the throat of the bear. He felt good about his actions, but he was injured in the battle. Now he was not able to help his own pack hunt. So, his pack did not hunt well, and many died of starvation. You see, Jacob, the wolf thought he was doing the right thing. And yes, he did a good thing. But actually, he was being selfish. He put his emotions before the welfare of his pack. He did not have Humility. Jacob, it is a good thing to help people. But it is not always the right thing."

Jacob nodded in agreement. Peguis reached over, pushed Jacob's shoulder, and smiled. Jacob chuckled, then threw a couple more pieces of wood into the fire. Sparks rose to the endless sky above.

Chapter 31.
Battle of the Seven Oaks

It was June 19, 1816, and several Bois-Brûlés on horseback, including Cuthbert Grant, trotted alongside the Assiniboine River. When they reached a shallow creek, they stopped, dismounted, and filled their canteens with water. Grant scooped water from the creek with his hands and drank as they waited for the carts and canoes to catch up. Two hours later, the canoes came around a bend in the river. The carts trailed closely behind. Perrault, who led the canoes, waved to Cuthbert Grant and greeted him as they came ashore. Perrault said, "We are all present. No troubles. Why have you waited here for us?"

Grant replied, "We spotted an H.B.C. river blockade at the forks. We'll have to go by land to Frog Plain from here."

"Ah, doesn't surprise me," acknowledged Perrault.

"Load all the pemmican into the carts and make it quick. We need to get there well before sundown," ordered Grant. Once the carts were loaded, the group proceeded north until the ground was so swampy their horses were sinking to their bellies.

Grant yelled, "Too muddy. Got to head east." The group changed direction, abandoning the swamp route, eventually finding ground a couple miles to the east that was more traversable by horse and cart. However, they were now more at risk of being discovered since they were within one and a half miles of Fort Douglas and the Selkirk settlement.

Inside its wooden palisade walls, Fort Douglas was abuzz with the activity of daily chores. A boy, about ten years old, stood in the watch tower holding a spyglass to his eye. He scanned the horizon and saw settlers working their fields while others fished from the shore of the Red River. He put down the spyglass to play with a spinning top. He got down on his knees and twisted hard and the top spun on the wooden floor. He did this several times, trying to see how long he could make it spin. Then, suddenly becoming aware that he was neglecting his duties, he returned to the large opening in the watchtower. He placed the spyglass to his eye, scanning the horizon from the Red River to the west. His jaw dropped as he saw dozens of men on horseback crossing an area the settlers called Seven Oaks. Near Seven Oaks by the Red River, eight NWC canoes had pulled ashore and were awaiting delivery of pemmican from Grant. The boy in the watchtower carefully set down the spyglass, descended the stairs, and ran at full speed.

"Indians! There's Indians gathering for an attack," yelled the boy as he ran to Governor Semple's quarters. Having heard the yelling, Semple met the boy outside on his front porch. The boy was so winded that he could barely get the words out. "Indians. Must be a 50 of 'em. They have guns ... war paint."

Semple asked, "Where did you see them?"

"North, past Inkster Creek." There was a pause then the boy continued, "They've got Mr. Bannerman and Alexander Sutherland held prisoner." The Governor ran toward the watchtower, yelling instructions for Lieutenant Holt to gather the men, fetch the muskets and a cannon from the artillery. From the watchtower, Semple surveyed Seven Oaks.

Speaking to himself Semple said, "It's the half-breeds." He came down the steps and met Holt and twenty-six armed men at the front gate of Fort Douglas. Captain Rogers handed the Governor a double barrel musket as the gate opened and the group departed. Semple yelled to Captain Rogers, "It's the half-breeds. They've got two carts full of pemmican and I'm sure they're supplying that Nor'Wester canoe brigade on the river. They're either going to give up that pemmican or they're going to give up their lives."

Semple and his men walked north through the farm of John McLean where they met fleeing settlers running south toward Fort Douglas. The settlers were yelling, "Half-breeds! It's the half-breeds!"

As the group approached Semple, one of the farmers, Alex McBeath, said, "You're gonna' need at least two cannons if you're gonna' confront that bunch. It's a bloody war party. I saw at least a 50. Many on horseback."

Semple scoffed, "Nonsense, ten Englishmen could take on a hundred half-breeds." "Beggin' your pardon, but don't you think it's the other way around, Governor," questioned McBeath. Semple gave no reply, so McBeath continued running toward the fort.

The Bois-Brûlés completed loading the NWC canoes with pemmican and the sun began its descent toward the horizon when Cuthbert Grant noticed the approaching group led by Semple. He called over the French-Canadian interpreter, Francois Boucher, instructing him to ride forward and negotiate with Semple. "Go to them. Tell them to ground their weapons and surrender. Or we will fire upon them," said Grant. Boucher was a nineteen-year-old clerk of the North West Company. His rapid advance was somewhat due to his father being a respected landowner in Montreal, but in large part it could be attributed to his cockiness. The long mane of his dark brown horse blew in the summer breeze as he trotted forward to meet Semple and his entourage.

"What's your business here?" he asked Semple in English.

"Shouldn't I be asking you what your business is here?" Semple replied.

"We want our fort," said Boucher.

"Well then! Go to your fort," replied Governor Semple, pointing in the direction of Fort Gibraltar.

"That's a bit difficult now, isn't it? Since you burned it to the ground you son-of-a-bitch," cursed Boucher.

"No, to the contrary, I've met your mother. You are certainly the one who is a true son-of-a-bitch," said Semple, then spat on the ground. Semple continued, "I just witnessed you transporting a thousand pounds of pemmican across my lands in violation of the *Pemmican Proclamation of 1814.* Worse yet, I have communication that says this pemmican was stolen from H.B.C. York boats on the Assiniboine River a few days back."

Boucher's horse took a few steps closer to Semple. In a very angry tone he yelled, "This is Bois-Brules land, and my native brothers are simply doing what they've been doing for thousands of years."

Semple laughed smugly, "Well, Frenchman, you seem to find yourself on the wrong side of the facts ... and the law. I am Governor of all of Assiniboia. The dirt you're standing on, is mine. I'm the law here." Semple stepped toward Boucher, prompting him to raise his musket and point it at Semple. In reaction, all of Semple's men raised their weapons. Semple continued in a calm tone. "Go easy, Frenchman. Lieutenant Holt, please inform this gentleman ... no wait, we clearly established earlier that he is a 'son-of-a-bitch' so let's go with that. Please inform this son-of-a-bitch that he needs to dismount his horse and surrender immediately, or we will have no choice but to put a hole in his head where one ought not be."

Boucher responded, "If your men make a move, you'll be digging a lot of holes tomorrow." With this, Semple grabbed the reigns of Boucher's horse with his left hand and with his right hand pushed away the barrel of his gun.

"Shoot him now," yelled Semple. Not obeying him, the H.B.C. entourage simply watched in shock. Semple continued, "If you don't fire, you're all dead men! Now fire, cowards!"

Boucher jumped down from his horse but continued holding its mane. Smoke rose from muskets as two shots rang out from the H.B.C. men and a bullet grazed Boucher's ear. The shots startled

Boucher's horse, causing it to rear up and run. The horse drug Boucher who was still holding onto its mane. Witnessing the confrontation, the Bois-Brûlés approached and from this instant forward, the gunfire became general between the H.B.C. entourage from Fort Douglas and the Bois-Brûlés. A shot rang out and a small red dot appeared in the middle of Lieutenant Holt's forehead. He slumped to his knees and fell forward on his face, dead. After the first round of gunfire, a great number of the Bois-Brûlés dropped to the ground. This inspired Semple's men and, thinking they had killed several of them, they cheered loudly.

One man stood tall, waving his hat "Woo-hoo!" he yelled. Then an arrow went right through his neck, and another pierced his chest knocking him over backward. Unfortunately for Semple's over-ecstatic men, the Bois-Brûlés had simply dropped to the ground to reload their weapons. Now they popped up from the long grass all around and began firing. Shots came from every direction and Semple's men, who stood out in the open, dropped one after the other.

Semple himself was shot in the leg and he fell onto the body of Lieutenant Holt. A horse rode up to Semple. Recognizing that it was Cuthbert Grant, he begged for his life. "I am injured, but it is not fatal. If you get me to the fort, I shall recover," he pleaded.

"Watch the governor. If you can, get him to the fort for treatment," Grant yelled reluctantly to one of his men, then rode away. He chased down a man running toward the river and split open the back of his skull with a crushing blow from his tomahawk.

Governor Semple struggled to get to his feet with the assistance of a Bois-Brûlés man. As this happened, an Ojibwe man approached. It was Maugegawbow, chief and medicine man for the Leech Lake band of Ojibwe. The chief yelled to Semple as he walked toward him, "My child died at Fort Gibraltar when you attacked. Now you must follow my child." Maugegawbow raised his pistol and shot Semple in the chest. He then descended upon him, stabbing him several times, and taking his scalp. Jumping back onto his horse, Maugegawbow held the bloody patch of Semple's hair high above his head and uttered a bone-chilling war whoop.

The gunshots stopped and it was all over in less than fifteen minutes. Many horses and men lay on the ground scattered about. Only one Bois-Brûlés was killed. On the other side, twenty men, including Semple, lay dead and wounded. Only six of the Fort Douglas men were able to escape. They ran to the river and swam across to the east for safety. Moaning could be heard from the injured H.B.C. men. Captain Rogers, who had fallen, rose up and staggered toward a Nor'Wester he recognized. The man advised him to give himself up, which he attempted to do. Rogers raised his hands and called out in broken French for mercy.

Francois Deschamps, a Bois-Brûlés yelled to his fifteen-year-old son, Grossetete, "No pardon!" After which Grossetete raised his weapon and shot Captain Rogers at close range through the temple. Another of the Bois-Brûlés ran up and cut open Rogers' stomach with a knife, spilling his intestines onto the grass. Deschamps and his three sons then proceeded to kill the survivors, shooting and stabbing them as they walked through the carnage. When all evidence of life was gone, Deschamps, his sons, and a few others looted, then mutilated the bodies. Seven Oaks was now a horrible display of scattered body parts and blood spatters in the tall yellow grass. As the sun began to set, the peaceful sound of birds singing returned to the prairie. Several Bois-Brûlés left the scene wearing articles of clothing taken from the dead.

Chapter 32.
Blood-Soaked Prairie

A man named John Pritchard was taken prisoner by the Bois-Brûlés during the battle. For some reason he was not finished off like the others. Most likely it was random luck. They took Pritchard to their camp at Frog Plain where he encountered other settlers, a group of six, who were captured before the battle took place. Several tents made up the camp and many fires burned, illuminating the night.

"What happened?" asked a man with a strong Scottish accent.

Pritchard answered, "It was a massacre. They killed us all. We went out with Semple to confront the half-breeds. Shots erupted and all holy shit-fire broke loose. I might be the only one alive from the group that went out with Semple."

The Scottish man pressed further, "What of the fort?"

"I'm not certain. One of the Nor'Westers gave me a taste of the butt-end of his rifle and knocked me out. I woke up here with my hands tied," answered Pritchard. There was a long pause as the shock set in, then Pritchard went on. "Semple started the whole damned thing by ordering the men to open fire. They had us surrounded on horseback. We were outnumbered. Semple had to know that we were all dead men once we fired those first shots." The group hushed their conversation as one of the Bois-Brûlés walked up to Pritchard who sat on the ground. He was wearing Governor Semple's hat and the chain of a gold pocket watch dangled from his waistband. From his pocket he retrieved a stone and proceeded to sharpen his very large hunting knife. The grinding sound sent chills up Pritchard's spine. In a harsh tone, the man wearing Semple's hat said something in Sioux then spat in the face of Pritchard.

Another man yelled at the Sioux brave in French. It was Cuthbert Grant. Switching to English, Grant turned to Pritchard and asked, "Why are you alive?" Confused, Pritchard didn't know how to reply so he remained silent. Grant raised his voice, "Why are you alive, you English pig?"

"I, I don't know, sir?" stuttered Pritchard.

Grant continued, "You're alive because I let you be alive." He then crouched down to get eye to eye. "You're gonna' to be my carrier pigeon. I need you to go to Fort Douglas with my instructions for the settlers. Quite simple really. They surrender, or I dump their bodies in the river."

Pritchard spoke, "That man had Semple's watch. I beg that you let me return it to Semple's wife and family." Grant did a half smile, surprised by Pritchard's boldness. He turned to notice the Bois-Brûlés man winding the watch. Without saying a word, Grant simply stood up and walked away.

At Fort Douglas, intermittent shrill screams and crying for the dead broke the night's silence. Fearing for their lives, men, women, and children crowded into houses within the fort walls. Mr. Bourke and five other survivors who had escaped the battle to the river now returned to Fort Douglas. They took charge and set up cannons for its defense. Their stories of the carnage struck terror into the hearts of the settlers. They expected an attack by the Bois-Brûlés at any minute. They mourned the dead and nervously contemplated the horrors that might befall them. Death was bad enough, but what of rape, torture, and mutilation? Very few slept that night, but no attack came.

The next morning, warm sun and a slight breeze presented the illusion of a beautiful day, just like any other. John Pritchard walked across the open prairie of Frog Plain. He walked past the mutilated bodies of his fellow H.B.C. men; some were British soldiers and others were traders and farmers. One body, more than the others, affected him. It was his close friend Duncan MacNaughton. He dropped to his knees and wept. It was emotionally devastating to see MacNaughton's eyes, open yet lifeless, staring skyward. His skin was blue, and his face was bloated, making him almost unrecognizable. At the top of his head, skull bone was exposed where a knife had taken away his scalp. Pritchard rose to his feet and continued toward Fort Douglas. He only made it a couple steps before he stumbled, doubled over, then vomited profusely. Once at the gate, red-eyed and smelling of puke, Pritchard yelled up to the watchtower. Burke, noticing it was Pritchard, quickly ordered the gate open and men ran to meet him.

...

A large group of canoes paddled south on the Red River toward Fort Douglas. In a canoe with Jacob and Chief Peguis was one of the settlers, showing signs of injury from the battle. His shirt was bloody, and his head had been wrapped in a cloth. There were more than twenty Salteaux warriors in the group as they came ashore. As the group of warriors emerged from the grove of trees along the river, gunfire erupted from the watchtower. Jacob and the others dove for cover. The settler removed his white shirt and waved it above his head.

He yelled, "It's me, Michael Kilkenny. Stop shooting, God damn it!"

From inside the fort, a loud voice was heard. "Cease fire! Cease fire! They're friendlies." As the cloud of musket smoke cleared, the man got a good look with the spy glass and continued, "Come to the gate. Watch yourself, the half-breeds are still out there."

John Bourke sat in a chair on the front porch of Governor Semple's residence. "Where's Semple?" asked Chief Peguis.

In a voice devoid of emotion, Bourke answered, "Dead. They're all dead. Pritchard was here this morning. He witnessed the whole thing. He said they killed all the injured and desecrated the bodies."

"Where's Grant and the Bois-Brûlés now?" asked Peguis.

"They're camped up at Frog Plain. They've set up a blockade on the river. Pritchard brought a message from Cuthbert Grant. He said anything short of complete surrender would mean our lives. If we don't give ourselves up before nightfall, they'll starve us out."

Peguis shook his head and said, "Doesn't seem like much of a choice."

Bourke continued, "Afraid you're right, Chief. There were a few of the half-breeds sniffing around after sunup. Drove them away with the cannon, but that's not going to work long term. We have women and children here."

Peguis asked, "Where's Pritchard now?"

Bourke answered, "He left about an hour ago with a message that we would surrender. Pritchard is supposed to come back with instructions."

Peguis said, "A good leader is willing to swallow his pride for the good of others. You've done a good thing."

With a skeptical look on his face, Bourke offered a thought, "I don't know. I hope so. I really don't know if I can trust Cuthbert Grant. Even if I can, I'm not sure he can control his men."

Peguis added, "My warriors can help you protect the women and children. We will stay. Keep the Bois-Brûlés honest."

The heat of the day was rising as Peguis, Jacob, and ten warriors walked toward Seven Oaks. They carried white flags of peace. As they approached the bodies, three men on horseback rode up at high-speed uttering a war-whoop. Peguis raised his hand in peace. The horses stopped.

Peguis, in Ojibwe, said, "What you have done here is not right." The Bois-Brûlés warriors on horseback spoke to each other in French.

One of them, wearing a hat that was clearly Scottish and stolen from one of the H.B.C. dead, kicked the sides of his horse and moved a bit closer. He asked in Ojibwe, "Why are you here? Why shouldn't we cut you down where you stand, the way we did to Semple's men?"

Peguis responded, "My friend, I have no fight with you. Many of you are of my tribe. We are here out of respect for the dead. Let us bury these bodies so their families can have some measure of peace. So the animals don't scatter their bones."

The Bois-Brûlés warrior in the Scottish hat squinted at Peguis with distrust, then said, "Okay, bury the bodies. But then I want you gone. If you linger at the fort and if you're seen bringing them food or water, we will have a problem." The men rode their horses around Peguis' warriors in a menacing manner, raising their weapons high in the air and whooping. As they circled, Jacob noticed three bloody scalps hanging from the musket of one of the men. After a final whoop they rode off to the north.

Many of the bodies lay where the battle first began, but others were scattered about as injured men attempted to escape to the bushes and trees near the river. It took hours to locate and gather them all. Jacob drug the body of what he thought was a young man. It was hard to tell his age as a musket ball had struck him in the head making his face unrecognizable. The man must have been shot from behind while running toward the river. *How tragic*, thought Jacob. Had the man made it another twenty feet into the trees he might still be alive. The pile of gathered bodies was a gruesome sight with corpses in various states of violent injury and mutilation. As Chief Peguis looked over the carnage, tears streamed down his cheeks. Jacob placed an arm over his shoulder.

Peguis said, "You'd think after all the death I've seen it would not hit me so hard. I guess in moments like this the Great Spirit wants you to feel what has been taken and what has been lost. Life is precious, Jacob. It should never be wasted or taken if it can be in any way avoided." Jacob pulled Peguis in tighter. Then, after a moment of silence, Peguis grabbed a shovel and began digging. Jacob and the others followed Peguis' lead and grabbed a shovel. They dug a deep pit, rolled the bodies in, then covered them with dirt. Fittingly, at that moment, the sun also began to sink down into the ground.

Thundering hooves broke the quiet as a group of fifteen Bois-Brûlés warriors approached at full speed. As they neared, arrows could be heard whistling past. One of the arrows found its mark in a Salteaux warrior's chest and he fell backward. Jacob dove for cover behind a dead horse as one of the Salteaux warriors scrambled to a cart that was nearby. The warrior grabbed an armload of muskets then ran through the tall grass. He tossed one of the muskets to Jacob as he passed. Dodging arrows, Jacob popped up from behind the horse. He shot one of the riders, dropping him to the ground. The horses circled continuously, and arrows flew from all directions. Two Bois-Brûlés spotted Jacob and sped toward him. They fired arrows, one after the other, as they rode. Years of buffalo hunting on horseback made the Bois-Brûlés extremely proficient at firing arrows accurately at full speed. Jacob was a sitting duck, so exposed out in the open prairie. He fired a shot and took down another rider, but they kept coming. No time to reload, Jacob pulled a tomahawk from his belt. Jacob threw the tomahawk, and it flew end over end toward the rider but narrowly missed. The rider approached Jacob and jumped down from his horse. The other Salteaux warriors were engaged in battle. The Bois-Brûlés warrior walked toward Jacob, holding a very large skinning knife. Jacob, no longer having a weapon, was defenseless. He tried to run, but the warrior was swift and caught him, tackling him to the ground. The man lunged with the large skinning knife but missed. Jacob grabbed the man's arm with both hands, restricting movement. Now the knife was just inches from Jacob's chest as the two struggled for control. Jacob was not strong enough and the knife inched closer and closer until it finally pushed against his chest, cutting through his shirt and breaking the skin. Jacob thought he was about to breathe his last breath when a shot rang out from the trees, punching a hole in the warrior's forehead and knocking him backward. Jacob rolled over and grabbed the knife, scanning the field for approaching Bois-

Brûlés. The riders who moved back and forth across the open field continued to shoot arrows. Many of the Salteaux warriors lay dead on the ground. One by one, the Bois-Brûlés began to drop from their horses as shots continued to ring out from the trees. Jacob ran back to the dead horse and re-loaded his musket.

Having heard the gunfire, Sheriff McDonnell and five H.B.C. men ran from Fort Douglas toward the battle site at Seven Oaks. A horse belonging to one of the dead Bois-Brûlés warriors wandered over to the trees to get a drink from the river. A man who was hiding in the trees jumped up onto the horse. He rode at full speed toward the remaining Bois-Brûlés warriors firing a shot that killed one of them. Dropping his musket, he now pulled the bow from his shoulder and began firing arrows. His first shot hit a warrior in the mouth and went right through the back of his skull. As the rider neared, Jacob realized it was Thunder Bear. He continued his approach and killed two more Bois-Brûlés warriors with accurately placed arrows. Another shot rang out from the trees, dropping one of the Bois-Brûlés riders. Realizing their peril, the remaining riders turned and rode off in retreat. As the musket smoke cleared, a man emerged from the woods. It was Bottineau. Peguis smiled and laughed, surprised by his good friend's appearance. The battle now won; the Salteaux yelled in a high-pitched war-whoop. Thunder Bear took the scalp of the Bois-Brûlés that tried to stab Jacob. He jumped back on his horse and rode toward Jacob and the Salteaux warriors. Suddenly, the sound of a gunshot startled Jacob. He spun around and saw Sheriff McDonnell in a cloud of smoke, with his rifle pointed in Thunder Bear's direction. Thunder Bear fell from his horse.

"No ... No!" screamed Jacob as he ran toward Thunder Bear. He dropped to his knees and pulled him close.

Peguis yelled to Sherriff McDonnell, "What have you done?" The Sheriff was frozen in shock, stunned at the mistake he had made.

"I'm so sorry. I thought. I just thought ..." stammered Sherriff

McDonnell.

Blood drained from a wound on Thunder Bear's neck, soaking his doeskin shirt. Jacob hung his head and began singing an Ojibwe mourning song. Bottineau ran up, knelt beside Jacob, and began to look over Thunder Bear. He put his ear close to his mouth, inspected the wound, then felt his neck.

His eyes widened and he looked over at Jacob. "There's a heartbeat," said Bottineau. "Jacob, he's alive. We need to get him to the fort, now!"

Jacob jumped onto a horse and Bottineau helped lift Thunder Bear into position. Jacob removed his shirt and pressed it against Thunder Bear's neck, trying to slow the bleeding. The sky was getting dark as they rode back to Fort Douglas.

Chapter 33.
Hanging by a Thread

Inside Governor Semple's residence, Bourke cleared the kitchen table, pushing bowls and flowers onto the floor. Bourke helped Jacob lift Thunder Bear up onto the table. Blood immediately pooled under his neck as Bourke gave Pritchard instructions to fetch Rachel Emmerson. Rachel was Dr. James White's assistant and now the only medical practitioner at Fort Douglas as Dr. White was killed the day prior in the battle.

John Bourke was an experienced military man from Ireland and had seen his share of gunshot wounds. By applying pressure, he was able to slow the bleeding until Rachel Emmerson arrived. Carrying her medical bag, she came running into the house with Pritchard.

"Oh my god. There's so much blood," said Emmerson surveying the situation. Jacob looked at Rachel, his eyes begging.

"You've gotta' help him. Please help," said Jacob with pain registering in his voice.

"Do you know him?" asked Rachel.

Jacob paused for a second, then answered, "He is my brother." This revelation placed a heavy weight on Rachel. She could feel the pressure of the moment intensify.

Rachel yelled, "Get more light in here. The candles aren't enough, we need torches." She leaned in closer and lifted the cloth from Thunder Bear's neck. Blood spurted out of the wound almost immediately as the pressure was removed. Now fully realizing the severity of the injury, Rachel said, "This is surgery. I'm not a surgeon."

Bourke said, "You're the closest thing we got." Rachel groaned a nervous groan, dug into her medical bag, then went to work.

After closer examination, she surmised, "His right internal jugular vein was ruptured by the bullet. Luckily, it wasn't completely severed." She turned to Jacob. "Hand me that needle. I'm going to have to stitch it." Rachel squinted in the dim light, then said, "Hold those torches closer, but not over the wound."

Rachel methodically worked for several minutes, every flicker of torchlight making her job more difficult and more dangerous for Thunder Bear. The time seemed like an eternity for Jacob who looked on nervously. After several failed attempts to stitch the wounded vein, Rachel began to cry.

"If I could just get a stitch in it. Just one stitch. We're running out of time," said Rachel with a throat choked up by tears.

Jacob's shoulders slouched and his head hung forward. He walked away and sat on a kitchen chair. It seemed it was time. Time to accept that now he was going to lose another person that he had grown attached to. Jacob mumbled to himself, "Why is this happening again? My heart can't take it. My love makes people die. Just let him live and I'll stop loving. I promise. I'll stop." He wiped a tear from his cheek, stood up and walked out the door. From inside, frantic yelling could be heard.

Jacob didn't sleep at all that night. He wandered around the fort, threw rocks into the river, and cried until he was out of tears.

Early the next morning, Jacob sat by the Red River watching the current push large tree branches north. Distant footsteps broke his trance. He turned and noticed it was Bourke approaching. This was the moment Jacob had been dreading for hours. As Bourke got closer Jacob examined his face for any clue about what happened to Thunder Bear. There was nothing conclusive. Not a tear that would indicate bad news. Not a smile that would indicate good news.

Certainly, Bourke's stoic expression was bad news. *Could it really be anything else?* Jacob wondered. Now Bourke stood right next to Jacob. He got down on one knee and put a hand on Jacob's shoulder.

"We worked on him all night. Rachel did her best. She really did. No one would have kept at it like she did," said Bourke. Jacob put his face in his hands. Then Bourke grabbed Jacob's face with both hands and said, "He's alive, Jacob,"

Jacob was stunned. He couldn't believe those were the words that came out of Bourke's mouth. "Wait, say that again," begged Jacob.

"He's alive. Jacob, he's alive," confirmed Bourke.

Jacob burst through the door of Semple's residence, ran across the blood-covered kitchen, and into the bedroom. In a bed against the far corner of the room laid Thunder Bear. The entire side of his face was black and blue. His hair was soaked with blood. Cloth was wrapped around his neck. Jacob grabbed Thunder Bear's hand and gave it a squeeze. His eyes fluttered, then opened. The first thing he saw was Jacob's face, still smeared with dried blood. His hair was tangled and muddy.

In a weak, scratchy voice Thunder Bear said, "You look like shit."

Jacob smiled and answered, "You should see the other guy."

Thunder Bear laughed, then winced in pain. "I didn't think I'd wake up again. I remember hearing you and the voice of a woman, then nothing. I figure the woman must've been a spirit or something," pondered Thunder Bear who was a bit disoriented.

"That was Rachel Emmerson. She saved your life," said Jacob as he adjusted Thunder Bear's pillow to help make him more comfortable. Then he continued, "Pritchard came back this morning with demands from Cuthbert Grant. He's saying all H.B.C. men and settlers must leave the fort first thing tomorrow. To refuse would mean death. York boats from Pembina are on the way to transport the settlers to York Factory."

"What about the H.B.C. men? And us?" inquired Thunder Bear.

"They're gonna' take the men who were in the fight to Montreal for trial. I think Peguis can protect us," answered Jacob with uncertainly on clear display in his body language.

"No. 'Think' isn't good enough," challenged Thunder Bear.

"I know," acknowledged Jacob, looking away to hide his concern.

"Jacob, we just killed a bunch of Nor'Westers yesterday. You think they're going to just let us walk out of here? And we can't jeopardize Peguis' trading relationship with the North West Company. His tribe relies on those connections."

"You're right," answered Jacob.

Thunder Bear made eye contact with Jacob and his tone became very serious. "When they discover your ties to the H.B.C., those Nor'Westers will put you on trial for murder. I'm not going to let that happen."

Jacob interrupted, "We can't travel, you've lost too much blood. Rachel said you need rest."

"Get to Peguis. See if he'll give us a horse and a travois. You're gonna' have to drag me back to Lake of the Woods ... and it needs to be tonight," insisted Thunder Bear, clearly leaving no room for discussion.

Jacob nodded, grabbed his musket and powder horn, then left the room. He stopped in the doorway and looked back, noticing Thunder Bear had already fallen asleep from fatigue and weakness. He shook his head then headed off to Chief Peguis' camp.

The grass was still wet with morning dew as a large group of Bois-Brûlés on horseback, led by Cuthbert Grant, trotted across the open prairie toward Fort Douglas. Jacob, Peguis and the Salteaux warriors watched from across the river as the group approached the gate.

Grant barked an order with his very thick French accent. "I want all the weapons collected, placed in carts and wheeled out of the fort. I mean, every weapon."

Scurrying about inside the fort could be heard, and after several minutes the gate slowly opened. Two large carts emerged heaping with muskets, spears, gunpowder, bullets, cannon balls, knives, and anything that might possibly be construed as a weapon. Following the carts, a cannon was wheeled out. The Bois-Brûlés took possession of the carts, wheeled them to the end of a wooden dock that stretched out over the river and dropped all the weapons into the water. The settlers and H.B.C. soldiers were then herded like cattle onto York boats that were waiting at the shore. As the boats floated away, a young Irish boy aboard waved to Peguis who stood across the river. The Chief responded by also holding up his hand. Then the entire group of Salteaux raised their hands. Behind Peguis, Jacob and Thunder Bear blended in so they wouldn't be discovered. Jacob couldn't help but wonder if the Irish boy was now an orphan, just like him.

...

It was dusk when a horse pulling a travois covered with a woolen H.B.C. blanket could be seen crossing the open plain, heading north along the Red River. A group of Nor'Westers camped along the trail took notice.

"It's that Ojibwe warrior and the blond kid," said a Nor'Wester in French. Two of them ran to the edge of the tree line, raised their muskets, and fired. The shots echoed in the trees and the rider fell from the horse to the ground with a thud. The Nor'Westers whooped loudly as they mounted their horses and galloped at full speed toward the horse and travois. A Bois-Brûlés among the group drew his bow and fired several arrows into the blanket covered travois. A Frenchman with a thick mustache jumped down from his horse and approached the fallen body. He grabbed it by the shoulder, turned it over and was shocked to discover that it was the body of one of the Bois-Brûlés that had been killed days earlier. The body had clearly been dressed up in Jacob's recognizable hat and clothing. Now realizing they had been duped, the Frenchman roughly yanked the blanket off the travois. There too was the corpse of one of the fallen Bois-Brûlés, not Thunder Bear. Many of the Bois-Brûlés were distraught by the sight of the dead bodies with their ashen gray and blue faces. These men had been their friends.

Miles away, deep into the Minnesota Territory, an ox cart loaded with pemmican creaked its way east. The cart wobbled from side to side as it navigated in and out of deep wheel ruts in the trail.

"Whoa. Whoa there," Pierre Bottineau yelled as he pulled on the reigns and the large ox slowed to a stop. He jumped from the cart and walked around to the back, on his way grabbing a bottle of whiskey. He pulled the cork and took a big gulp. He kicked twice at the base of the cart. Seconds later a hidden wooden door wiggled, then slid from left to right.

Jacob popped his head out through the opening and said, "This thing rides like shit."

Bottineau laughed then responded in his heavy French accent, "You could always walk. But it's a long way to Lake of the Woods. If you want a ride on the Bottineau Express, you'd best put a button in that lip."

"I guess the ride's okay," retorted Jacob with a chuckle. He emerged from the hidden compartment built into the bottom of the ox cart. He walked around a bit, stretching his legs, then assisted Thunder Bear who struggled to climb through the small opening. Bottineau handed Thunder Bear a chunk of pemmican and said, "Shit, you're as white as your brother. What the hell happened to you back at Fort Douglas?"

Thunder Bear started to laugh but stopped as the laughter caused significant pain. He put a hand on Bottineau's shoulder and said, "Got shot. Lost a lot of blood. Turned white."

"Damn French Indians," snarled Bottineau. He kicked a lump of dirt that sat on the trail, then he went on, "It's gotten to where you can't trust any of these fur trade companies. The Hudson's Bay Company shits all over everybody. The Nor'Westers used to be okay, but now they've lost their minds too. I blame it on the god damned Scottish. I know, without a doubt, they put the Bois-Brûlés up to this. They stirred up all this damned trouble. If you're not with one or the other, you're caught in the middle and the middle is a pile-of-shit mess. Too dangerous." Bottineau spat on the ground, took a large swig of whiskey, then handed the bottle to Thunder Bear who declined and passed it along to Jacob.

Jacob took a drink, then in a flat tone said, "It's a mess. A damned fur war."

Days later, Bottineau's ox cart rolled into the Ojibwe village on Lake of the Woods. Many of the tribe gathered to discover the meaning of this unexpected visitor. Bottineau waved his hand in a gesture of peace, then spoke in Ojibwe, "Boozhoo! I have brought a great gift. A surprise." He then jumped down from the cart as the ever-growing crowd watched closely. He walked to the rear of the cart. Casually he kicked on the wooden panel. When the secret panel wiggled and slid open there were gasps and murmurs among the crowd. Was this magic? Was this a trick? Just as the murmurs subsided, Jacob's head popped out from the opening.

Several in the crowd yelled, "Oza Windib! It's Oza Windib!"

Blue Jay who was near the back of the crowd put her hand to her mouth and began to cry. She pushed her way to the front. Once there she pulled Jacob into her arms tightly. The crowd cheered. They were all very worried since Jacob and Thunder Bear did not return home with the others from the fur trade expedition to the Jack River trading post. Blue Jay kissed Jacob's cheeks over and over, then she looked him in the eye questioningly.

She said just two words, "Thunder Bear?" The sound of a loon singing came from inside the cart. Blue Jay, recognizing this familiar call from her son, turned and began to weep with joy. She yelled, "Thunder Bear!" Jacob and Blue Jay helped Thunder Bear through the opening in the bottom of the cart. He was notably weaker than even the day before. With an arm over each of their shoulders Jacob and Blue Jay helped him to their wigwam. He could barely shuffle his feet enough to make it the small distance. Once inside, they lay him down on a buffalo hide blanket near the fire and pulled a wool blanket up over him. Blue Jay fed him venison and potato soup as she sang an Ojibwe song. It was a song she sang to him often when he was a small boy.

Chapter 34. Moving On

Whistles in the cadence of an Irish jig and a misty cloud of breath escaped Jacob's lips as he trudged his way through knee-deep snow. A strong afternoon wind blew his unruly blond hair. Reaching the edge of a stream, he leaned forward and pulled a heavy metal chain from beneath the icy cold waters. It felt heavier than usual, which prompted him to stop his whistling. With excitement and anticipation, he increased the speed recoiling the chain. There, soaking wet, in the jaws of the trap, was a good-sized beaver. A fine catch indeed. Jacob pushed the trap open and removed his prize. Gutting it on the spot, he then rinsed the beaver clean and tossed it into a large bag. He walked over to his sled, dropped the bag aboard, and stepped up on the back. He yelled a command, and the dogs took off. Working hard, they pulled their way down a snow-covered trail until finally disappearing into the snow blanketed spruce.

Once back at the village, Jacob was greeted by Thunder Bear. Reaching over and wiping frost from Jacob's recently sprouted beard, Thunder Bear joked, "With that scraggly beard, you're starting to look like a real fur trader."

"Yeah, that and a wigwam bursting with furs over there," answered Jacob, tilting his head toward his wigwam and sporting a proud smile. He continued, "I'm taking 'em up to Mackinac Island in the spring. Should be able to get a good price. Enough to set up the tribe for winter. Then I'll use what's left to buy some land of my own; finally free. No one owning me, cheating me out of a fair price for my furs. My H.B.C. contract is done and I'm out."

Thunder Bear scratched the side of his head, eyed Jacob through a rigid squint then asked, "You think they'll let you just quit? Don't think they'll want their furs this year?"

"Those aren't their furs. My contract is up. They've got no claim to what's mine anymore," Jacob answered with piss and vinegar in his tone.

Thunder Bear moved closer, put a hand on Jacob's shoulder and looked in his eyes closely for a moment. "They're not gonna' just let you go. Jacob, they've gotten rich off you." After a long pause, Thunder Bear continued, "This could be dangerous."

Jacob sighed heavily, then went on, "You think I don't know that? But it's time and this isn't just about me, I promised Ed back in London that I'd get what we always dreamed of ... what he'll never have. A place to do what I want. Make a living my way, on my terms. A place to be happy. Freedom."

With a glance through compassionate eyes, Thunder Bear said, "You're going to risk your life for a promise you made to a kid in London you barely knew? And what about the tribe?"

Jacob retorted, "Don't say that. You don't know anything about how close we were."

Thunder Bear interrupted, "I'm sorry, Jacob, I didn't mean it."

Jacob continued, "I have to do this. For me. The tribe means the world to me. Blue Jay has done things for me I can never repay. You're a god to me ..." Jacob pointed to his chest and continued. "...forever in my heart. But it's time for me to go out on my own. Somewhere new. I'm different than everyone here."

Thunder Bear said, "We don't think of you as different, Jacob."

Jacob smiled a bit, then continued, "I know that, but I am. And I always will be."

"Jacob, it's just skin. It's the color of your heart that matters," said Thunder Bear.

Jacob hung his head and said, "Just stop. Please stop or you'll talk me out of this, and I'll never be able to forgive you for that. This is just something I gotta' do. Can you understand?"

Thunder Bear released a sigh and answered, "I can. I just don't want to. Because if I do, that means you won't be there when I wake to the morning sun. That you won't be paddling in the front of my canoe or telling me where all the good deer trails are for hunting. When the sun drops below the spruce you won't be by the fire to laugh at my stupid jokes."

Jacob reached up and wiped a moist drop from his left eye. Fighting the choking feeling in his throat, he said, "This isn't forever. I'll still see you and the tribe as often as I can."

Thunder Bear chuckled a bit, then with a wink, said, "White man promises don't hold up so good."

Jacob answered, "Well, mine do." There was a pause then Jacob asked, "Are you crying?"

"Shut up, I'm not crying," choked Thunder Bear.

"That must be water on your face then? Or maybe your head is leaking?" joked Jacob. Thunder Bear grabbed Jacob by the arm, hoisted him powerfully up onto his shoulder, then tossed him into a deep snowbank. Jacob laughed for a bit, then said, "When I get up, you're getting an ass whipping."

Thunder Bear replied, "There you go. More white man promises." Thunder Bear walked away toward his wigwam and suddenly a snowball hit the back of his head and burst into a cloud of frost. He turned and Jacob took off running. Thunder Bear chased him at full speed into the trees.

That night, as the sun set, a chapter of Jacob's life among the Lake of the Woods Ojibwe came to an end. It was time. Jacob was ready to find his own way in the world. One step closer to keeping the promise to Ed, and more importantly, keeping the promise to himself.

Chapter 35.
Rainy River

It was May 1817. Morning sun glistened off sloshing waves as a paddle broke the surface. The twenty-five-foot birch bark canoe, piled high with furs, creaked and strained its way down the Rainy River in what is today the state of Minnesota. Smoke floated overhead and the sweet aroma of tobacco rose steadily from Jacob's hand-carved ivory pipe. Every stroke brought him closer to Mackinac Island.

The American's gained control of the fort on Mackinac Island in 1815. Diminishing tension with the British in Canada brought an end to Fort Michilimackinac's significance as a military outpost. However, it continued to be an important hub of fur trade activity in the Great Lakes region. The military fort on the island was commanded by Benjamin Kendrick Pierce, the son of the New Hampshire Governor, Benjamin Pierce. Just twenty-six years old, Pierce was a whip-smart officer in the United States Army that had already seen his share of battle in the War of 1812. His intelligence was hobbled by a propensity toward pranks, which had gotten him kicked out of Dartmouth University in 1810.

On Mackinac Island, an American government permit and a bateau full of furs was all it took to put you in the fur trading business. John Jacob Astor's American Fur Company had a dominant presence at the fort, but Nor'Westers mixed openly with H.B.C. traders, independent traders, and Indians from many tribes.

Wintering fur traders came from all directions. The Athabasca region, Sault Ste. Marie, Pembina on the Red River, and the upper Assiniboia. This was the crossroads of cultures, races, and violently adversarial fur companies. Some might call it a tinderbox just waiting to ignite. But all came for a common goal, trade.

On any afternoon, you could hear as many as 5 different European languages and even more native tribe languages. English, French, Scottish Gaelic, Irish, Dutch, Ojibwe, Ottawa, Cree, Iroquois, Assiniboine, Sioux, Potawatomi, and the list goes on. Kin ties and tribal relationships were important in the fur trade, so French and English traders commonly married native women to secure their place.

Back on Rainy River, the sun began to sink in the distant trees. Jacob was exhausted from a full day of paddling. He noticed a clearing on the left bank and paddled over to stop for the night. He grabbed his pack and weapons, three muskets and two tomahawks. His canoe, too heavy with furs to pull ashore, would have to stay. Jacob understood a canoe loaded with furs floating next to shore exposed him to theft and danger, but he had no choice. It was too many furs for one man to move quickly. Jacob just needed three or four hours of sleep. He tied a small piece of fishing line to a bundle of furs then ran the line into the trees tied to three empty sardine cans dangling from a bush. If someone tried to steal the furs or if the canoe came untied and floated away, Jacob would have a warning sound. Near the canoe, Jacob made a campfire and laid out his bedroll. He added enough wood to keep the fire burning for several hours. He lit two more fires a bit deeper into the tree line. This would make it seem to passersby that it was a larger group of voyageurs. Jacob then climbed up a large spruce. About twenty feet up, he found a secure cluster of branches. From these branches he tied a rope and wrapped it with a wool blanket, creating a hammock-style sleeping area. As quickly as he crawled into his hammock, Jacob's eyelids slammed shut and he was off to dreamland.

Sunlight was just beginning to break the horizon with an orange glow when Jacob was awakened by a yell.

"Bonjour!" a deep timbered voice rang out. *"J'ai faim. Avez-vous de la nourriture?"* Jacob leaned over slowly and looked down toward the riverbank. There stood a very large man silhouetted in the darkness of the pre-dawn. The man wore the familiar garments and toque hat of a voyageur, but this was no normal voyageur. He stood well over six feet tall and weighed at least 260 pounds. His shoulders were three feet across. Had Jacob not heard the French words being spoken, he might well have shot the man, mistaking him for a grizzly.

Now switching to English, the man repeated, "Hello. I am hungry. Do you have food?" There was a long pause. "I mean no harm and apologize for the intrusion. I will pay you for any nourishment you can provide." Another long pause. "Look, I have coin," the man added as he held up a bag of silver coins and jingled it.

Jacob yelled out in the most threatening voice he could muster, "We've got you surrounded. Right now, nine muskets are on ya'. You'd do your best to move real slow, stranger."

"Yes, yes," answered the man calmly. "Look, I'm setting down my gun." The man placed his gun on the ground and walked a few steps away from it.

Jacob yelled, "Now throw that hatchet hanging from your hip into the fire." There was a long hesitation and Jacob again yelled, "Now throw that hatchet into the fire! God damn it." Again, a pause.

"But I'm quite attached to this hatchet. *Mon père.* It was my father's." Jacob was able to understand the man's attachment because he felt the same way about the bible his mother had given to him.

Pausing momentarily, Jacob thought it over, then spoke. "Okay, throw the hatchet over by your musket."

The large man laughed and said, "Ah, see! You are a good person. Now you can see I have no weapons and don't want to harm any of your, uh, crew."

Jacob answered, "Okay, keep your hands out in front of you. Don't want to go gettin' shot for nothin', do ya'? I'm going to climb down real slow. If you make any quick moves my crew is gonna' blow your head clean off." Again, there was a long pause. Jacob reaffirmed, "Got it?"

"*Oui*. Yes, yes. I hear you and will not be making any rapid movements that might threaten your safety in any way. I am a gentleman, a man of my word, and you can trust in the strength of my convictions," the man replied very eloquently.

"A simple yes would'a done it," chuckled Jacob as he climbed down the tree. At ground level, the man seemed even larger. Jacob approached with caution. With the sun on the horizon providing just the slightest amount of light Jacob was now able to see the stranger's face. He was a black man with very dark skin. The only time Jacob had encountered black people was in London many years before.

"What's your name?" Jacob asked.

The man quickly answered, "George Bonga."

"Where are you from?"

"I was born on Mackinac Island. Lived in Montreal for a time where I attended the St. Louis Academy School."

"I thought you talked pretty smart, like one of those elite schoolboys," Jacob replied. He took a few steps closer, then questioned, "Where do you live now?"

"I live with my family, south of here. The Leech Lake band of Ojibwe," answered the man.

"You're an Indian?" Jacob blurted out.

The stranger was somewhat upset by Jacob's confusion. "Yes, I am Ojibwe. Do we have a problem?"

Jacob began to laugh. "No, no. It's just funny because I'm Ojibwe too. Lake of the Woods Ojibwe."

The man stood there, just staring at Jacob. He asked, "You're an Indian?"

Jacob explained, "Yeah, we're both Ojibwe, but we don't look the part."

"I guess you're right, but my heart is Ojibwe and will always be," said the towering stranger.

"I understand. Just I've never met another person like me. An Ojibwe that doesn't look like one. I'm just happy to meet you, is all," Jacob replied with a big smile on his face as he reached out to shake the stranger's hand. The stranger tilted his head a bit, puzzled by this blond-haired man's behavior. Then slowly he extended his massive bear claw of a hand. As they shook, Jacob's hand disappeared entirely within the stranger's hand.

Still holding Jacob's hand, the stranger questioned, "Well, don't I have to worry about your crew blowing my head off?"

With a chuckle, Jacob replied, "Heck no. I made all that up. It's just me out here."

"Oh really?" the stranger said sarcastically. "What are you doing out here by yourself? Pretty dangerous to be traveling these waters in a canoe piled high with furs," questioned George.

"I didn't really have a choice. Just finished a contract with the H.B.C. and trying to start out on my own. Had to take on a little risk to get that done."

"Some risk is unwise and could be called foolish," said George.

"Ha! You sound just like my brother. I'm gonna' like you," laughed Jacob, then he continued, "Now let's gather my gear and get you some food." As Jacob collected his weapons and gear, George was impressed by the way everything, guns, provisions, canoe paddles and even a couple packs of furs, were hidden out of sight and in strategic locations. When Jacob cut the trip wire line from his canoe, George really took notice.

He said, "You really are Ojibwe, aren't you."

Jacob answered, "I'm a lot of things my friend. A liar isn't one of them."

"Were you trained by a chief?" asked George.

"No, just my brother."

George rubbed the top of his head and responded, "Well your

brother must be somethin' else."

"He is," Jacob chimed back as he piled a few logs on the fire and began cooking oatmeal. The sun was rising through the spruce trees as they ate and shared stories.

...

Thunder echoed and the clouds flickered with light as two canoes sliced through rough water on a wide stretch of the Rainy River.

George turned back toward Jacob's canoe and said, "Our ancestors are dancing in the clouds."

Jacob asked, "How did you come to be Ojibwe, anyway?"

"Long story," George answered, not even breaking the cadence of his paddling. He was not used to opening up about his personal life.

Jacob, never one to give up easily, chimed back, "It's a long trip."

"Well, you got a point there, kid," George answered then went on, "My grandparents were slaves to a British captain on Mackinac Island at Fort Michilimackinac. He treated 'em pretty good, but before that, they went through hell. They were kidnapped in Africa by slave traders. My grandfather almost died of cholera on the way over to the West Indies. His name was Jean Bonga, a man ... a human being, they treated him like ... well, I'd say they treated him like a dog, but people don't treat animals that way. My grandmother, Marie Jeanne, lost two babies the day they were abducted by the slavers. I'm told, by my father, that he has twin sisters someplace in Africa. He never really knew what happened to them, but he thinks they're still alive ... says he can just feel it. I wonder if it's just wishful thinking on his part?"

"I'm sorry, George," consoled Jacob.

"Sorry for what. I didn't lose babies. It's my grandma that lived her whole life with two chunks of her heart torn out. Taking her freedom wasn't enough, those devils had to go and take those babies too. They say she cried halfway across the ocean. Said the Atlantic rose a couple inches from the tears." George sniffled a bit and wiped snot from his nose with the sleeve of his shirt. "Luckily, my father wasn't born until Mackinac Island. He had a good childhood there. Two parents that loved him, plenty of food, and only occasional bad treatment. The British soldiers and their wives thought black people were beneath them. Not sure if it was because they were slaves, or just because they were different. The fur traders and Indians seemed to not even notice, treated my father just like anyone else. He felt happy around them, so he usually hung out in Frenchtown on the north side of the island. He said that was where he could laugh and play. On that side of the island, he was just like everyone else. Just a kid who wanted to have fun. A kid who wanted to have friends. A kid who wanted to belong somewhere in the world."

"I get that," Jacob said, nodding. After a pause, he continued, "I feel that way a lot. Like I don't belong anywhere."

George responded, "Come on now, you must have parents that care about you?" There was a long pause and George impulsively covered his mouth, realizing he just said something hurtful.

Feeling obliged to tell his story, Jacob answered, "I had parents. They both died when I was little, in Sweden. I don't know why I'm telling you all this. I hardly know you."

"Sometimes people just need someone to talk to," consoled George. Jacob stared blankly for a long time as he continued to paddle in perfect rhythm.

"You said you have a brother," noted George.

"Yeah, but he's not my real brother," said Jacob.

"What do you mean he's not your real brother? Do you care about him? Does he care about you? Would he do anything for you?" George said.

"Yeah. Yes, he would and I'd do the same for him. But he's not my blood," answered Jacob.

"But nothin'!" George growled a bit irritated. "Let me tell you somethin'. If you're lucky enough to have people that care about you in this world, you got somethin'. Don't go discounting that. It's not right. It's shameful to the people who can only wish they had what you have."

"I'm just saying that I don't have a real family," said Jacob.

"Real has nothing to do with anything. You don't even know how damn lucky you are. You have a tribe that took you in. A brother that taught you everything you know. A second mother that loves you. And I'm sure there are a lot of other people that helped you get by out here. That's all family," George said, now pulling his canoe right up alongside Jacob's. He placed his hand on Jacob's shoulder and continued, "You need to let people into your heart Jacob. You've got walls up trying to block out anything that might hurt you. But don't you see you're hurting yourself? You're like a wild animal jumping from one thing to the next, never fully attaching. It's like you have some kind of disease in your heart and you can't tame it. You know what it is? Wilderness of the heart. That's what you got. And no one can cure it but you."

Jacob pondered George's wisdom for a long time as the two men paddled in silence for miles. He thought about all the bad things that had happened to him. But also, the good. The street cleaner in London, the group of street kids, and especially Ed. Jacob thought long and hard about Ed. How his life was cut short by such a cruel world. *Did I show him enough that I cared about him, that I loved him like a brother? wondered Jacob.* Wetness filled the corners of his eyes. He realized that he felt all of these things but really didn't express them as much as he should've ... when he had the chance. Jacob felt regret so heavy in his chest that he could hardly sit up straight. Then he thought about Akami and his canine friend Two-Eye. Jacob knew he never would've survived York Factory without them. Akami's support and mentorship meant so much to Jacob. All the lessons and hours of talking about how to survive in the world and how to be a good person. Did Jacob really thank Akami enough and truly appreciate his kindness and wisdom? Maybe he felt it in his heart, but Jacob knew he never came close to telling Akami how important he was. Jacob wondered where Akami was now. Was he in heaven the way his mother's religion taught? Was he one with the earth the way Akami taught? He wished he could talk to Akami right now. He always had a way of making Jacob think about the world and feel better about his place in it. What a great man. Was Jacob disrespecting him by feeling the way he did about family and being too detached? A warmth came to Jacob's heart as he thought about Blue Jay. She so openly gave him love and acceptance. Jacob always felt a bit guilty for loving Blue Jay too much. He worried it somehow was disrespectful of his biological mother. He knew his mother would've been happy knowing Jacob was cared for and loved. Why didn't he just accept that and push the negative thoughts out of his heart? Why did he tell George that Thunder Bear wasn't his real brother? Jacob did feel truly ashamed that he had betrayed Thunder Bear in this way. He was absolutely the best brother anyone could hope for. Blood, or not. Jacob wondered if he ever told Thunder Bear how important he was. He doubted it. *I think he feels that I love and admire him*, Jacob pondered. *At least I hope he does.*

Maybe George was right, blood has nothing to do with family. These people and Two-Eye were truly all family to Jacob. In his heart, he knew that was the truth. He was determined to show his appreciation more and express his love more openly. But he wasn't certain he'd be capable of it. These thoughts bounced around in Jacob's mind over and over. In fact, it was hours before he spoke a word to George. The two canoes, shadowed by pine trees, disappeared around a bend in the Pigeon River. The only sound was the random chatter of mourning doves and an occasional paddle sloshing the water.

Chapter 36.
Fort Michilimackinac

Long days of paddling along Lake Superior's southern shore brought Jacob and George past Sault Ste. Marie to Lake Huron around Drummond Island. Strong winds and rain forced them ashore before reaching Mackinac Island. With their provisions entirely used up, they were hungry. Rather than setting up camp, they got right to hunting. The rain came down in sheets. Jacob and George were both soaked. They walked about a mile into the woods when Jacob put out his arm, stopping George. He pointed out a deer eating flowers at the base of a large oak tree. Silently, he pulled an arrow from his quiver and took aim. With a whoosh, the arrow cut through the downpour and struck the deer in the neck severing a major artery. It dropped without taking a step. George looked over at Jacob and raised his eyebrows, acknowledging the great shot.

A rear quarter of venison rotated on a tree-branch spit over a flickering campfire. George walked over and cut off a piece of meat. His mouth full, George asked, "Think the canoes are far enough off the water so we won't get noticed?"

"I think we're good. Plus, if anyone comes ashore and gets a look at you, they'll sprint back to the water and start paddling with everything they got," joked Jacob. The two men sat in silence for a few minutes as they enjoyed the crackle of the fire and the sweet smell of venison roasting. Jacob looked up at George. "So how did you become an Indian?"

George answered, "Well, my grandparents were slaves on Mackinac Island. When the English were pushed out after the war, they were pretty much just left there. That's how they got their freedom. They had to find a way to survive, so they opened the first hotel on the island and made quite a good business of it. Enough so that my father Pierre was able to go to Montreal for an education. On the island, my father was surrounded by the fur trade and loved it. He was damned good at it too. Good hunter, trapper, and he learned to speak seven languages. He worked under Alexander Henry, the younger, as an interpreter over at Fort Fond du Lac for the North West Company in the Minnesota Territory. That brought him into frequent contact with the Ojibwe. Didn't take him long to discover that he preferred their company over the traders on the island. He became a part of the tribe, married an Ojibwe woman, and today he's the chief. They treat us like we're one of their own. You'd swear they had really bad eyesight and didn't notice our skin color."

Jacob chuckled a bit, then asked, "So who's us? You got brothers, sisters?"

"Two brothers and a sister," answered George.

"They all giants like you?"

George laughed. "Nah, they're not. My brother is quite a bit smaller, but he can run like the wind and swim like a fish."

Jacob responded, "I look forward to meeting 'em someday."

"Yes, yes, that would be nice. I like you, Jacob Fahlstrom. There's a lot of good in you," said George as he patted Jacob's blond head with his bear-claw sized hand. The two men filled up on venison, watched the fire burn down to embers, and fell soundly asleep.

...

A cool breeze put a damp chill in the air on Mackinac Island. It was evening when they arrived. George and Jacob pushed their way through a crowd of men on the torch lit docks. Each pulled a travois piled high with animal furs. George towered over Jacob, and everyone else they walked past. The French voyageurs, typically men of short stature, seemed even shorter by contrast. They had to tilt their necks skyward to see George's face. To say George was an intimidating presence was an understatement.

Jacob threw a couple pieces of jerky to stray dogs that followed them. They took their place in line as they arrived at the trader's lodge. It was more than an hour before they got their turn in front of the trader.

Both smiling with the ear-to-ear grin one gets with a heaping pocket full of silver, George and Jacob walked into the fort saloon. It's that peaceful moment of comfort when it seems all is good with the world and you can breathe a sigh of relief knowing that, for today at least, you don't have to worry about hunting for your survival.

The bartender tilted her head toward an empty table, inviting them to be seated. Nearby, a table of four British soldiers, all quite drunk, were speaking loudly. One of the men slapped the waitress on the behind as she walked past. They all laughed.

"What are you looking at, Yank," asked one of the British soldiers, speaking to Jacob.

Jacob answered, "I'm not an American."

"Well, what are you then?" the soldier asked.

Jacob answered, "I'm Ojibwe."

The soldier said, "I thought I could smell something strange in here." He sniffed a couple times, then continued. "What is that smell? Swamp mud mixed with deer shit, and campfire smoke?" The man glared at Jacob, then went on, "You're right, you must be a savage."

George began to stand up, but Jacob put a hand on his shoulder urging him to ignore the remark. Jacob boldly blurted, "Wait, wait, I smell something too. Ah yes, a meadow of delicate flowers ... buried in pig shit." The four British soldiers began to rise to their feet when suddenly the saloon owner, a very fat man, almost as wide across as he was tall, walked out from behind the bar. He raised his musket and pulled back the hammer.

"Oh, no. You boys ain't tearin' up my bar this evening." The soldiers raised their hands defensively, then settled back in their chairs as the saloon owner continued, "All of you, out. Now!" He indicated for the soldiers to leave. He then pointed the musket at Jacob and George. He swung the gun in the direction of the door, indicating for them to leave as well. "Go on. Get! Before I make a bloody mess all over the wall," he yelled.

After leaving the saloon, Jacob and George joined a group of Ojibwe and Assiniboine men who had gathered at a roaring fire just outside the fort's gate. They sang, danced, and drummed late into the evening. More than a few jugs of whisky were emptied along the way. They reveled until they just could not revel anymore. Eventually, they all passed out cold in the tall grass under the star-filled Mackinac sky.

Jacob awoke abruptly to loud shouting. As he leaned up on his elbow, he noticed the British soldiers from the saloon struggling to drag George across the long grassy meadow. His hands and feet were bound by rope.

One man was kicking George in the back as Jacob yelled out, "Stop!"

The men turned as Jacob began running up the hill in their direction. Two of the soldiers raised their muskets and pointed them directly at Jacob. A warning shot was fired. Jacob, now about thirty feet from the soldiers, stopped running, and began to speak.

Out of breath, Jacob gasped, "Please stop. My friend, I'm sure, is sorry for whatever he did." The soldiers ignored Jacob, turned, and continued to drag George up the hill. Jacob continued to follow and plead with them.

Finally, the oldest of the soldiers said, "If you keep following us, you'll end up with a beating as well."

Jacob said, "This isn't right. Why are you taking him?"

"He needs to be taught a lesson for disrespecting the Hudson's Bay Company and the British crown," a soldier said.

"We can work this out," Jacob said, now getting desperate as they were nearing the fort gate. He looked around hoping to find help, then an idea struck him. He felt around his pockets and pulled out a bag with one hand while he held up a single silver coin with the other. "Look, it's all I have from my furs. Take it, just let my friend go free," begged Jacob. This caught the attention of the soldiers. In fact, it seemed precisely what they were aiming for.

"Well then, why didn't you make your position clear sooner," said the eldest of the British soldiers. He grabbed the bag and gauged its value by the weight in his hand. "Cut him loose," the man yelled to the others.

"Thank you. Thank you so much," said Jacob as a man cut the ropes, freeing George's hands and feet.

"Now get out of here before I change my mind," said the soldier. He then snatched the single silver coin from Jacob's other hand.

As the soldiers walked away, Jacob wasted no time and helped George to his feet. George was sweating profusely from the struggle and a large gash above his left eye was spilling blood down the side of his face and dripping off his chin.

"Are you okay?" asked Jacob.

"I'm fine. Would take more the four British soldiers to take me down," said George, still trying to catch his breath.

"Looks like they were doing a pretty good job of it," answered Jacob as he used a handkerchief to wipe the blood from George's eye."

"Nah. I was just waiting for my chance to finish 'em off," George laughed as he spoke.

Jacob looked around, nervously surveying, then said, "Let's go. We need to get off the island quick before they change their mind."

George and Jacob ran down to the shore, walked their canoe into the water, jumped in and paddled furiously to put some distance between them and Mackinac Island. They paddled for about five miles before uttering a single word. Then George stopped paddling and hung his head.

"What?" asked Jacob.

George, who was in the front of the canoe, turned back to look at Jacob. He answered, "Why'd you go and do that? Now you have nothing to show for all those furs, Jacob. What about your dreams of freedom ... a place of your own?"

"It's not about silver and riches, George. You're safe and that's what's important. I'm a good hunter. I'll survive just fine," urged Jacob. He then chuckled and continued, "And you might want to get paddling because those British goons aren't gonna' be so happy."

"What do you mean?" asked George.

Jacob said, "They won't be so happy when they find out they traded for a bag full of worthless metal shavings."

George shook his head and smiled a curious smile. "Jacob?"

Jacob laughed a full hearty laugh as he pulled his actual bag of silver coins out of a pocket in the side of his pack. He held it up and gave it a jingle.

George said, "Jacob Fahlstrom, you are a one and only. In all my travels, I've never come across someone quite like you."

"Maybe you just haven't traveled enough," said Jacob.

George scooped up a handful of water and splashed Jacob's face. Now soaked, Jacob laughed, and George joined in. A moose at the shoreline bleated loudly. Ripples on the lake's surface pushed their way to shore as the canoe cut the water.

Chapter 37.
The Cabin

Smoke rose from the river rock chimney of a log cabin. It drifted through the pines past a watchful owl. Below Jacob approached the cabin with a stringer of walleye. He hung the fish from a post, disappeared inside the cabin for a moment, then returned with a filet knife. At a table on the front porch he gutted the fish, placing the prized filets into a bowl of cold water and tossing the guts to a sled dog that sat eagerly at the foot of the porch steps. "Go easy Akami," Jacob suggested to the blue-eyed huskie. An owl squawked loudly, *Hoo ... Hoo.*

Jacob looked up and smiled. He spoke to the owl, "Haven't seen you for a few days. Were you out with your lady friend?"

Hoo...Hoo. the owl seemed to respond.

Jacob paused, as if waiting for more, then continued, "Ah, you never were much for deep conversation." He finished fileting the fish, then walked down the porch steps and over to the fire ring. He sat on a large stump by the circle of stones, pulled out a wooden flute, and began to play an old English tune he remembered from his time in London. After a while, the tune slowed, then came to a stop.

In a whisper to himself, Jacob said, "Ed, I made it. I've got a place. A life of my own." Rising to his feet Jacob pulled a caramel-colored agate stone from his pocket. He held it up to the sunlight and admired its wavy bands, the same way he had done a thousand times over the years. "I've been selfish, old friend. Didn't want to give this up. But ... it's time," Jacob said. Jacob walked over to the supply shed, grabbed a shovel, then walked into the woods. He dug a hole about three feet deep and dropped the agate stone inside. Acting quickly, before he could change his mind, Jacob covered the hole with dirt.

With glossy eyes and a lump in his throat, Jacob said, "Rest peaceful, Ed." As he walked back to the cabin, sunlight blasted through the tall pines and shined brightly on the front porch. The owl departed his perch with a loud flapping of wings and squawked, *Hoo...Hoo*, as he soared through the sunlight. Jacob looked up and smiled. He whispered, "We got our dream."

Jacob opened the door and stepped inside the cabin. At the table sat Thunder Bear and Blue Jay. Thunder Bear, in Ojibwe, said, "If you don't cook that fish, it's gonna' swim away."

Jacob laughed, then said, "Yep. Going to do that now." He turned his glance to Blue Jay and asked, "Can you help me, Mom?"

A tear welled up in Blue Jay's eye and dripped down her cheek.

"What's wrong?"

"You called me Mom," said Blue Jay. "You've never called me that before."

Jacob smiled, shrugged his shoulders, then walked over to Blue Jay and gave her a big hug.

"I'm sorry."

"Don't say that, Jacob. I love you."

"I love you too."

The End

Dear Reader,

For those that love historical fiction laced with adventure and filled with warmth, thank you for choosing *Wilderness of the Heart.* I would love to hear what you think of it! Your honest reviews are not only invaluable to me but also help other readers decide if it's the right book for them. You can do that here. If you've enjoyed *Wilderness of the Heart,* make sure to look out for the next installment in the series due out in 2024!

About the Author

"I write what the ghosts of history whisper into my ear."
-Jason Bergeron

Jason Bergeron has recently burst onto the literary scene with his debut novel, *Wilderness of the Heart.* Born and raised in northern Minnesota, Jason developed a passion for storytelling from an early age, crafting imaginative tales that captured the hearts of friends and family. He found solace in the world of books and was greatly inspired by authors like Ernest Hemingway, Jack London and Jim Harrison. This deep appreciation for literature, a love of history, and a vivid imagination laid the foundation for his journey as a novelist.

Wilderness of the Heart showcases Jason's unique, emotional storytelling voice and marks the beginning of an exciting literary career. This captivating work weaves together historical elements of the fur trade and an orphan's struggle to find his way in the vast wilderness of frontier America, taking readers on an emotional and transformative journey. Jason demonstrates a mastery of character development, creating a relatable and compelling protagonist who faces both external and internal challenges. The novel's richly descriptive settings transport readers to a world that is both awe inspiring and ominous.

When not immersed in the world of writing, Jason can be found exploring nature, savoring a cup of coffee, extra dark, or engaging in thought-provoking conversations with fellow artists.